NECTAR AND AMBROSIA

AN AMARANTHINE INHERITANCE NOVEL

E. M. HAMILL

To Gary,

a source of joy and laughter for more years than I will ever admit to knowing him. (Please burn the negatives now.) We may not be immortal, but our friendship is legendary.

ACKNOWLEDGMENTS

You have no idea how long I've been writing this book.

It started as one of those amazing dreams you have just before you wake up. Florian was in this dream and I was so fascinated by him that I just had to start writing to figure out who he was. He became the main character of a short story that was pretty terrible, but ultimately ended up in much-altered form as chapters two and four.

That was, maybe, ten years ago? Like Florian says, the nights all blur together. But people who read the original first draft of the novel (looking at you, Gary and Gina McNeff) kept saying, "When are you going to publish that mythology one? It's my favorite!"

During the many, many revisions, my long suffering critique partners have prevailed. This book has been around so long that I am certain there are others who read at least parts of it in its early forms, but I can't remember all of them.

Thank you Rev. Kim Dominic, United Methodist Church, my friend and reader, for your early input on this theological mashup.

Thank you Michael Mammay (who reminded me that even a god can't kill a keg in one night), Ashley Miller, Janean Dobos, Jessica Burche, Bev Marsh, Sharon Vann, and Kathy Kubay.

Katharine Henry Alexander of KEHA Studio was also one of those early readers, and she designed my amazing cover. Love you, Clompy.

Thank you, Carly Bornstein-Hayward, the first editor to believe it was worth developing.

Thank you, Taylor Barton, for all your input on one of the final drafts, which helped me finish a better book.

At last, the manuscript received the tender mercies of editor Jami Nord, whose direction speaks to me and whacks me over the head now and then with much needed vigor. Thank you.

Most of all, thanks to my family, who supports my crazy obsession with writing about imaginary friends.

Love to all.

1

ELECTRIC JOLTS BURNED down her spine. The muscles between her shoulder blades contracted with excruciating tension as images seared themselves into her brain.

Blurry views of the glass-fronted arena a couple of blocks over. Skyward facets of mirrored surface. The reflected outline of a dark-winged creature coming for her.

Callie blinked out of the petit mal seizure triggered by the vision's aftermath as pedestrians with wary eyes edged around her. She had no idea how much time had passed while she stood frozen in place on the crowded sidewalk. "Damn it!"

Sweaty strands of russet hair escaped her ponytail and stuck to her face as she shifted the duffel bag back on her shoulder. She wiped them away and scanned the hot, blue-white sky glimpsed between concrete and glass buildings, searching for the airborne threat and listening to her internal early warning system.

It tracked her down again.

Two states' worth of miles between her and that monster still wasn't enough.

The compulsion urging her westward had driven her out of the relative coolness and shelter the Kansas City bus station offered, into busy rush hour streets where she hugged inner edges of sidewalks and hoped the downtown bustle would provide its own sort of cover. She merged in with a stream of liberated workers pouring from an office building.

When that irresistible force abruptly forfeited its tug-of-war with her insides, she was unprepared. Momentum arrested, she stumbled over her own feet. The overloaded duffel bag on her shoulder remained in forward motion and dragged her off balance, wobbling from the curb into the street.

"Shit!" With a backward muppet-flail to the sidewalk, Callie narrowly avoided being splattered across the front of an electric streetcar as it sailed past, a stealthy millipede with a black and white carapace. The frantic beat of her heart slowed as she forced herself to take a couple of deep breaths, the tug inside her replaced by a sense of anticipation. She took in the trendy-looking zone with glass-fronted bistros and drinking establishments.

So, this was the right place. She still didn't know where she was going.

Looking around in bafflement at this hipster-magnet entertainment district, she wondered if this might be the first—and last—time the visions failed her. In a valley banked by high-rise buildings, busy side streets in five o'clock turmoil shimmered with waves of heat. Buses and traffic roared by on main thoroughfares. Although the street corners were crowded with commuters on their way home, she was too exposed. Time to find shelter. She stepped into the intersection with the rest of the herd, but her intuition firmly told her, *No. Turn around, genius.*

That never happened before. When did her inside voice get so snarky?

Callie ignored the dirty looks from other pedestrians and waded back upstream through the press of bodies. She examined the structure behind her with a dubious eye and waited for another clue from her newly sarcastic extrasensory radar.

A three-storied building loomed in pale, faded brick and mortar. With large windows on the ground and two upper floors, the architecture held a turn of the century feel rather than the contemporary establishments all around. It might have been photoshopped into the block, a tintype superimposed against modern business fronts. The plate glass window at street-level gleamed with gold-leaf letters in old-fashioned script:

NECTAR AND AMBROSIA

Bar and Hotel

Florian Pereira, Proprietor

Despite the spotless glass, the place appeared to be abandoned. The street reflected in the window made it difficult to see inside. Cupping her hands around her eyes, she stepped up to the panes.

A wave of dizziness washed over her and she swayed. Odd quiet enveloped her, the noise of the street behind muffled and far away. Callie steadied herself on the window. Cool glass promised air conditioning on the other side, but a weird buzz skittered across her fingertips. She snatched her hand away and backpedaled, the returning blare of horns and exhaust-fume smells of rush hour overwhelming her senses. Bodies shoved and spun her as she stepped back into the path of foot traffic.

"What the..." she muttered.

A small hand lettered sign, faded by sunlight, stood in the corner of the window: HELP WANTED. Smaller writing barely visible underneath drew Callie closer to peer at the notice.

If you can read this, find the door. Immediate employment available. Great wages and unbelievable tips. See Florian, behind the bar.

Where was the door? Right or left, the gold-lettered windows stretched unbroken for the length of the building. Her reflection stared back from the plate glass with uncertain eyes, the ghosts of cars and buses passing behind her.

A banshee scream echoed above the din of traffic and bounced between buildings in a ricochet of nerve-shredding terror. Breath turned to icicles in Callie's lungs. The horrifying cry galvanized a flood of fight-or-flight instinct that scrambled her ability to think.

No one else on the sidewalk even looked up at the skin-crawling sound, oblivious in their after-work trek to cars and bus stops. They wouldn't even see it, she knew.

It wasn't there for them.

She needed to hide, *now.*

Her head whipped side to side to find an escape route from the street. In desperation, she lifted her hand to knock on the window—and the door was there, right in front of her. Brass, wood, and glass gleamed at her in the brutal afternoon sun and she reached for the knob with urgent need, not even thinking to question how it appeared as a shadow grew above her in the glass, like a hawk about to strike.

The door burst open before her hand fully closed on the knob. Momentum took over and Callie lurched across the threshold. A small explosion detonated behind her forehead, not painful, but spreading in waves. She staggered and braced herself for impact with the approaching floor.

Strong arms caught her. A scent like pine and meadow flowers surrounded her and she fell on top of someone in a dizzy, tangled heap of limbs as the unbalanced duffel pulled them down.

"Please, I need to get away from the windows!" Vertigo refused to release its swirling hold on her as she tried to push herself up but only got more helplessly wound in the strap of her bag.

"Let me help." The deep male voice sounded a little breathless. Careful hands freed her from the loop of nylon webbing. A steady arm beneath her shoulders helped her stand. New waves of dizziness scrawled a nauseating spiral inside her head and she closed her eyes. She hoped she wasn't going to puke on this kind person, who assisted her to a cushioned surface that yielded under her.

"Here. Lie back." Her feet were elevated on the traitorous luggage.

The room swung like a pendulum in decreasing arcs. Callie breathed in slow rhythms to ward off the spins as a deliciously cool cloth draped over her forehead. The next attempt to open her eyes proved more successful. The world made smaller revolutions, and the studded leather back of an upholstered bench against a windowless wall swam into focus. A tiled and corniced ceiling provided a level horizon and she lay still until the grid remained stationary.

Indoors, and safe. The tension between her shoulder blades unwound, a welcome sign that let her know the immediate danger had passed. But...Oh, god. Curious stares of undisguised interest flashed her way from the perimeter, where a small after-work crowd gathered. A mixture of expensive business suits and blue jeaned customers leaned at the bar or occupied its shadowed booths. She flushed as she pulled herself upright and her gaze connected with the black, sparkling eyes of a man who leaned out from the murky depths of an alcove across the room.

White teeth gleamed in a leer, bright in his dark, bearded face. Someone at the bar cleared their throat pointedly and the smirking guy vanished behind the high wooden back of the booth. Callie wondered if she was hallucinating. Before he ducked out of sight, she thought she had glimpsed goat-like horns.

"How do you feel?" Callie detected a mild Irish accent in the voice belonging to her rescuer, the tall man busy at the sideboard. He watched her in the mirrored shelves glinting from behind the bar, but faced away from her at the moment. The glare from the windows obscured her view of his face. "Do I need to call an ambulance?"

"No, I don't think so." With an uneasy glance toward the shadowed booth, Callie wiped the cool towel over her forehead and cheeks. "God, how embarrassing." Tackling a complete stranger? So much for the job.

"Bloody hot out there." He continued working on something below her line of vision. "On a day like today, you can get dehydrated and not know it. Drink up. I'll bring you some more water."

"Thank you." On a small table beside the bench, a sparkling glass of ice water waited in a puddle of condensation. She reached for it, and when her internal warnings stayed silent, drank in deep, greedy gulps of water, her parched throat grateful for the cold liquid.

Callie took another gulp and surveyed the layout of her shelter. A solid bar made of maple-stained wood dominated the room, three or four people sitting on its tall stools. Deep booths upholstered in dark green leather lined the walls. A long room to the left of the bar held pool tables and dartboards. Several flat screen TVs occupied walls and corners, out of place and futuristic in an establishment which appeared time-warped from 1900. News channels and talk shows babbled softly below the beat of music.

Tipping the last of the water into her mouth, she pushed sweat-clumped hair away from her face in an attempt to straighten it as the man returned. He carried a pitcher of ice water and a plate with an enormous sandwich. A mortifying roar came from her empty middle and Callie swallowed, her whole being transfixed by the food.

"Are you hungry?"

Eyes only for the sandwich as he set the plate in front of her, she managed to at least pretend a glance at him and murmur her thanks before taking a bite. A blossom of warmth grew in the pit of her stomach, spreading out to her fingers and toes. Pure bliss, the best turkey club sandwich on the face of the planet, and new energy surged up with surprising speed after just a few bites. The man refilled Callie's glass, then pulled up a chair and sat in it backward, his muscular brown arms folded atop the wooden back.

"Thank you so much," she mumbled around a mouthful of turkey, trying not to inhale the sandwich.

"You're welcome. I'm Florian, by the way: Proprietor, bartender, bouncer, and cook."

"I'm Callie Davies." With each bite, she regained strength and clarity. "Oh! The sign said I should ask for you."

"I'm glad you saw the notice. Are you looking for a job?"

"Yes." Callie forced herself to smile as she met her benefactor's eyes. He was younger than she'd expected, perhaps no older than late twenties. A wealth of curly brown hair touched his shoulders, and the warm color of his skin made bright blue eyes all the more intense. The sole giveaway he might be older resided in those eyes. They held weariness and a certain cynicism despite the friendly posture his body advertised, and Callie revised her estimate of his age upward by a couple of years.

She realized she was staring and gave renewed attention to her plate. "I—I'm new to town," she explained around another bite of sandwich.

"Have you worked as a waitress before, or in a pub?"

"Yes, at a restaurant and then a sports bar for the last three years, summers and weekends, until my scholarships ran out." The hurried lie sounded plausible.

"What are you studying?"

"Classical studies and anthropology."

To her surprise, a chuckle rose from one of the patrons in hearing range at the bar, a lawyer-type in an Armani suit. Florian laughed too, and shook his head. The mirth awakened her hesitant smile despite the possibility they mocked her choice in majors.

"It's kind of a family tradition. My parents are both college professors." Callie, perplexed, was compelled to give an explanation. "Why is it funny?"

He stopped chuckling, but an upward tilt lurked at the corners of his full-lipped mouth. "I'm sorry. It's just that those majors may actually be quite useful in this establishment."

"A lot of academic types come in here?"

"Not exactly." He leaned closer and his voice dropped to a conspiratorial near-whisper above the thump of music. "Let's just say my patrons are deeply interested in mythology and legend."

"Wiccans?" She matched his hushed tone. The Armani guy at the bar chatting with the jeans-clad thirty-somethings didn't seem to fit the type, and there weren't enough Guinness signs for that kind of crowd.

"Pagan, definitely."

"My roommate at college was a witch. She and her coven held circles in our apartment sometimes, until..." *Until a winged, screaming thing broke through the window and tried to kill me.* She took another bite before she could accidentally reveal anything that would make her sound crazy. "Well, it was eye-opening, to say the least."

"We attract all kinds in here. It's best to remain non-denominational." Florian's brow creased and he gave a small shrug. "A little tension gets worked up between parties at times, but things always sort themselves out."

Callie finished her sandwich and half of the second glass of water, marveling at how quickly the food replenished her strength. "I feel a hundred percent better already. Thank you. I didn't make a very good impression though, falling through the door." *And on top of you*, she remembered as her cheeks grew red.

"I've done it myself, and with less grace. The first step, as they say, is a doozy." He sat back and regarded her. "As for impressions, you saw the sign, you've got plenty of experience, and that's enough to tell me you're qualified. You're the first one who's seen my advert, and the card's been there a long time. The job's yours. When can you start?"

"Seriously?" Callie cocked her head. "No references? No background checks?"

"No." He considered her with one raised eyebrow. "Is there something about your past you think I need to know?"

I ran out of my seizure meds three weeks ago, and I have visions that stop me in my tracks? "No. It's just different." Callie hesitated and eyed him suspiciously. "You're not owned by the Mafia or anything, are you?"

Again, his face reflected a private amusement she didn't understand.

"No, not the Mafia, nor the Russian Mob, or anyone like that." A deep breath punctuated the pause. "But you have to be able to handle a few shocks."

The leering, bearded guy peeked out of his booth again to stare at her. One black eye glittered in the shadows below the odd shape of his hair—no, it *was* a horn! She shut her eyes for a second, afraid she really was hallucinating in her exhaustion. Florian noted her distraction and turned his head to frown at the customer, who vanished into the shadows again.

"My regulars are a unique group, and they like nothing better than attention." His lips thinned as he turned back to her. "Some of them will do anything to get it. How's your temperament?"

"Pretty even." With a last glance at the dark booth, she focused on Florian and gave it some thought. She amended, "But I'm not afraid to defend myself if that's what you mean. After dealing with drunk frat boys, I'm not going to let anybody grope me and get away with it."

"You shouldn't, and I won't allow it. Tell me if you can't handle them yourself and I'll deal with them. Saturday is the busiest night, so I really need your help then, but you can take any other two nights a week off. The rush starts around seven and we're open until the last one leaves. I can offer you a decent hourly wage plus tips. Believe me, the tips my regulars leave are worth the trouble."

Callie shook her head, dazed. "I can start tonight. I'll need to find a place to stay that will let me float a few days before I can pay them, though. Do you know of any shelters or places I could go?"

"Shelters? No, I'm afraid I don't. You did see the sign out front that this is a hotel as well as a bar, right? There are suites upstairs. My grandmother and I live in the two apartments on the second floor, but I don't have a guest in the top floor now." He grimaced. "I haven't had a guest at all since I took over, if you want the truth. The place is small, but lightly furnished and has access to a roof garden. How about this: You stay here for a month to get on your feet, and then if you like the job, we can talk about rent." He cocked his head and waited for an answer, brows arched with inquisitive patience.

"Why are you doing this?" she burst out. The terms seemed too good to be true. "I know I look awful, and I probably smell worse. You don't even know anything about me except I'm new to town."

Florian looked down, and shrugged as he glanced at her again. "Someone helped me out when I first came here, too. Call it paying a debt forward. I promise there are no strings attached. And to be honest—I am that desperate for someone to work here."

Callie weighed the opportunity with suspicion, listening for any of the internal alarms that so often warned her of something unpleasant. They were silent.

"I think...yes. I'd like to."

"Fantastic!" Florian breathed out and sagged with relief. "I can't tell you how great it will be to have some help around here at last. This is Monday, right? It won't be exceptionally crowded tonight. Tuesday will give you a chance to get used to my regulars. You'll want to have time to rest before you start."

Sweaty and covered in bus funk, it was a miracle he'd hired her. A shower and sleep sounded like Nirvana just now. "I would love that."

Florian went behind the bar and keyed the return on the antique register. The till spit out its gilt-front tray. He lifted up the inside compartment, removed an old-fashioned brass key and held the end out across the bar. The ornate head lay heavy in Callie's palm as she closed her fist around it.

"The stairs are over there." He pointed to the side of the bar closest to the door. "It's unlocked right now but there's a deadbolt inside. Top floor landing, blue door. You can't miss it. Your first shift starts at seven tomorrow night."

"Thank you." Callie hoped nothing would rear its ugly head later to bite her in the ass. The absence of her intuitive alarms unnerved her more than a little, but with her stomach full her mind grew fuzzy with the effects of too many sleepless nights. She hefted her bag and turned toward the stairs but stopped with a frown. "How can you be so certain I'm the right person for the job?"

His expression changed, became more serious. "Nobody else could find the door, Callie. I'll explain later, when you're up to it. For now, rest. Whatever you were running from, you're safe here. I promise."

Increasingly leaden limbs carried her upstairs to the second landing. Odd as it was, this situation felt right: a puzzle piece slipped into place, some of the tight-wound tension easing at last. She was meant to be here.

Not until her hand touched the knob of her door did Florian's last words register in her mind.

How did he know?

Despite his assurances of safety, she locked the deadbolt behind her.

2

Florian watched Callie disappear up the stairs and waited. Once he heard her door shut, he turned back to his patrons.

"Thank you for your discretion," he said at large to the bar. "I didn't want to scare her off with the banshee still outside."

Mutters and acknowledgements of "No problem, Florian," sounded from the depths of the booths. The satyr emerged to stretch, scratched his hairy nethers, and resumed the pool game interrupted by Callie's arrival. His leather-clad opponent gestured at the table. Balls re-racked themselves into a triangular shape on the green felt.

"See, I told you that you wouldn't be sorry. The sign works."

Florian collected specific bottles from the shelf and let one eyebrow arch quizzically as he appraised the dapper figure leaning against the bar. "Define 'works', please." Grey Goose and vermouth comprised the ingredients for Hermes's usual shaken-not-stirred martini. "The sign's been in the windowsill for twenty five years."

"Huh. How time flies." Hermes dismissed the quarter-century with a wave. "And she's majoring in classical studies and anthropology? This will be a huge field trip for her." His wide mouth lifted in a smirk at one corner. "Did you notice she's hot?"

"Close to heat stroke, I think."

Eager, quicksilver eyes followed Florian's movements, observing the construction of his martini as Hermes snorted in derision, "I didn't mean hot, I meant *hot* hot. Don't get me wrong, I prefer tall, dark, and handsome these days. But she's curvy in all the right places."

He understood what he'd meant, but ignored the clarification. Even sweaty and in rumpled travel-worn clothing, auburn-haired Callie was worth a second, and third, glance.

The threshold had prepared itself for a new arrival earlier in the day, but he hadn't expected the strange leap in his heart when Callie hesitated on the sidewalk. Those warm brown eyes sent a ray of sunlight through Florian's chest and thawed something long-frozen in him. Trust in that surprising reaction remained a cynical negative, though, having learned the hard way his ability to judge character was more than flawed.

"Please spread the word everybody needs to be on their best behavior tomorrow night." The shaker parted with a wet pop and he strained the martini into a glass. "I don't want her quitting the first time in."

The shallow, square golden casket under the bar flared hot and cold beneath his hands as he retrieved it. Opening the box, Florian plucked a pinch of softly luminous, cloud-like substance out of the roiling mass inside and rolled it between his fingers. The wisp became an olive. The process repeated three more times, he speared the green globes on plastic swords, dropped them into the drink with a flourish and pushed the glass across to his customer, where it was received with unrestrained anticipation. Hermes retrieved one of the sunken garnish spears with greedy fumbling and shoved the olives into his mouth. A growl of pleasure rose from his throat.

"You don't want to be giving her much of that," Hermes said around chewing, and nodded at the golden casket as it was stowed away again. "The threshold knocked her for a loop, so she's got a hell of a lot of Sight. Too much ambrosia and she wouldn't be in any condition to help you, like sweet Bridget." A jerk of his chin toward the stairwell made Florian glance to be certain his grandmother wasn't standing there.

"Gran understood what she was doing." The pang of guilt that accompanied this admission was nothing new, still sharp in Florian's conscience despite so many years. "I'll be sure she doesn't get too much, but Callie needed the energy this time. I don't think she'd had anything to eat for days." He rinsed out the shaker in the under-bar sink. "Think she's been running for a while?"

Hermes blew a know-it-all *psshht* before he downed more of his drink. "She's got Amaranthine blood, and it's going to attract attention just like yours did. I wonder whose kid she might be." A pensive shadow crossed his angular features for a moment, his eyes far away. He plucked the last olives out of the glass and with relish sucked them off the toothpick, shaking his head appreciatively. "That is a rare talent, Florian. Damn, I wish I could eat the real stuff." He pulled a crisp fifty-dollar bill out of the air and plunked it down on the wooden surface with a papery thud.

His drink polished off in one deep swallow, Hermes rose from the barstool. "I'll send a group text about behavior in my neck of the woods, but I can't speak for anybody else. You know Tuesday is Big Z's bender night."

With a groan, Florian remembered this was indeed the case. "Oh, bloody hell. You'd think I would know by now. The nights all blur together."

"Your new employee may be getting the full treatment after all. Guess we'll find out what she's made of. See you later, my friend." Hermes saluted him and vanished.

He put the fifty in the register and went to check the level on the keg of Guinness, his most important patron's choice of drink-to-oblivion. Almost full. From experience, he knew that even a god couldn't kill a keg in one night. Callie was obviously brave and resourceful, having survived long enough to find the threshold, but Big Z was a sloppy drunk. Florian hoped she could handle it.

3

THE TWO-ROOMED SUITE, though as small as Florian reported, was an absolute jewel. She had helped her parents restore their Victorian-era house, and the apartment reminded her so much of home, comforting with its pale plaster walls and broad wooden casings. A tiny gas stove, sink, and an ancient half-sized refrigerator populated the standing-room-only kitchen, which gave way into a sitting area crowded with an overstuffed armchair and a lamp table.

Six weeks of running had left her exhausted, dirty, and hungry. With her stomach quieted at last, a hot bath in the claw-footed tub now sluiced away the grime and sweat of the last few days. Warmth seeped into her tight shoulders and eased the constant sense of vigilance Callie had been unable to shake on the road. She managed to wash a couple of sets of clothes and hang them over the tub to dry before fatigue hit her without compromise. Sleep came the moment her head hit the pillows.

After eighteen straight hours of unconsciousness she woke refreshed beyond belief, but starving. A homeless shelter in Chicago had provided her last full meal and shower four days ago, before the visions picked up again. The final dregs of cash in her wallet purchased the Greyhound ticket that delivered her into the thick humidity of a midwestern summer. But she needed food.

She worked up the courage to go ask Florian if he would put another sandwich on credit. Upon opening her door, though, she found a basket leaning against the outside. Fragrant blueberry muffins, some fresh fruit and cheese, a loaf of bread, and a jar of homemade jam filled the interior. It was a kind gesture and made her feel even more indebted. Her stomach didn't quibble.

Tension crept back into her shoulders in anticipation of starting the new job. Though Callie hadn't suffered any more visions since the glimpse of the tracking creature, she hoped nothing would hit at work tonight. Her early warning system said something was building, an itchy unrest at the back of her mind.

Previous employers were aware of the seizure disorder, but not the visions that accompanied it. She would have to tell Florian sooner than later. Going cold turkey off her meds proved unavoidable in her hasty exodus, and the frequency of visions increased the longer she went without them.

She clenched her fists, nails making painful crescents in her palms. Deep breaths, she reminded herself. Her adoptive parents were now safe from the thing that stalked her halfway across the country. The vision of their lifeless bodies would never happen—something in her head shifted when she left home, and she just *knew* that it had been the right thing to do. Nothing remained for her back in Vermont without endangering the ones she loved. The fewer traces she left, the better.

It was time to start a new life.

Save for one melancholy figure staring into a glass of Guinness at the far end of the bar, the establishment was echoingly empty when she turned the corner from the stairwell at precisely seven o'clock, determined to make a good impression.

Glancing up from where he chalked the night's specials on a board, Florian greeted her as she rounded the service area.

"Hello, there. Well rested?"

"I am, thank you. Did you leave the basket outside my door?"

"I did. I know you haven't had time to get any groceries."

"Thank you so much." Callie leaned her forearms on the bar, the toe of her sneaker rubbing against the brass foot-rail running parallel to the floor. "I appreciate your generosity. I'll pay you back when I can."

"No, just consider it a neighborly gift from Gran and me. You're welcome." He flashed her a quick smile as he finished his work and propped the blackboard on an easel. "Ready to jump in?"

"You bet."

"Here's an apron for you. Lots of pockets, and you'll need them, though they don't often ask for change." He handed her the black canvas utility smock and she tied it on. "Garnishes are on the sideboard, here." A sectioned bin full of citrus fruit wedges, olives, cherries, and strawberries perfumed the air. "Bottles in the cooler, there. If you don't mind, you can fill those orders yourself and I'll do the mixing. If they want something to eat, tell me. The specials are on the chalkboard, but for the most part, they come to drink. A lot."

A staggering amount and variety of beer in neat rows lined the enormous walk-in refrigerator. A tall wine rack stood beside it. Crowded, mirrored shelves behind the bar held a plethora of liquor bottles, every possible distillation known to Callie, and many others that were a mystery. "Just...wow. This is quite a selection. Do you keep a list of what's available so I'll know when customers ask?"

"They already know what we have, and what I charge. I tried to arrange the cooler in alphabetical order so you can find it easily."

"But what if someone new comes in?"

"I might have mentioned that our clientele is very exclusive. More like a private club." Florian leaned against the counter, considering. "It isn't likely we'll see anyone new, but if we do, they have a patron who's going to be well established."

His voice dropped into a confidential register and he nodded over his shoulder. "The guy at the end of the bar will be here until we close. I'll wait on him, but I'll introduce you now. He's here every Tuesday night."

Callie cast a dubious sideways glance at the customer. A long, gray-streaked mane of hair hung limp around his face. Flannel pajama bottoms and a rumpled gray t-shirt made the man resemble a sleepy, homeless biker. Exactly what kind of exclusive club did Florian run? She followed him to the other side.

"Hey, Z, I'd like you to meet my new waitress. Callie, this is Zeus."

The huge man on the barstool looked up and quirked a bleary half-smile at her. "Pleased ta meetcha." Dark stout stained his silver beard and mustache and he burped with a rumble that might have challenged a walrus. He seemed eerily familiar. Callie couldn't figure out why until a double-take moment of amazement.

"Did anyone ever tell you that you look like..."

Her employer shook his head in quick warning and she trailed off, confused by the deterrent. Zeus chuffed a mournful sigh and wilted.

"Yeah, I used to be somebody. Florian, my glass is empty. Another one, please."

"Coming up, Z." He collected the foam-sticky pint and motioned for Callie to follow him, depositing the glass into the sink.

"Who is that?" she whispered. Her mind already dismissed the theory. The man slumped at the end of the bar only looked like a rock legend, whose recent death was mourned by millions of fans all over the world.

"Who do you think he is?" Florian regarded her mildly as he retrieved a clean glass.

"He looks so much like Harry Mencia that it's scary."

"That's because he used to be Harry Mencia."

"What?" Callie goggled at him in disbelief. "But he's *dead*."

"No, he's sitting at the bar." Florian winked at her. "I said be ready for a few shocks. There's more to come. Keep an open mind, but I think you'll catch on soon."

"Wait a minute." Callie held up her hands, frustrated by his vague answers. "He's not Harry Mencia. Who is he?"

"I told you his name. His real name."

"What?" Suspicion out-flipped the mental gymnastics her brain momentarily considered. "No. No way. You're telling me Harry Mencia is Zeus? As in the king of the gods, Zeus?"

"In the flesh, so to speak." Florian appeared to be dead serious.

"They were gods, once, but nowadays they prefer to call themselves Amaranthine."

The sarcastic bite refused to stay out of her voice. "This is some kind of joke because of what I studied, isn't it?"

"Not at all. Zeus and his pantheon is here more frequently than any of the others, but there are many, many immortals. Most of them frequent my place now, which is why I'm so desperate for help."

"Oh, come on." Did he really expect her to believe this? Hands on hips, she glared at him. "Are you going to continually make fun of my major?"

Straight faced and earnest, Florian shrugged. "It isn't a joke."

She couldn't decide if he was completely insane or just pulling her leg. Dismay grew thorns and blossomed into irritation. How many times had she sat on Dad's lap as a kid and listened to him read the myths they both loved, wishing the gods were real so that she could meet them? Guilt soured the memory, pricking a conscience still raw from abandoning her parents and stoked her anger with Florian for this un-funny jibe at her expense. An adult now, she knew the stories for what they were: make believe, allegorical, a magical understanding of the world primitive cultures could embrace. So what if she still sometimes had dreams about them being real people?

Her warning system usually told her when things were shady. It remained silent in judgment of Florian. She didn't know what to think, her brain overloaded with too much on top of an already unreal situation. Florian had seemed so nice, so generous.

So apparently freaking nuts.

"Huh. I thought you'd think *I'm* crazy," she muttered.

He glanced at her, confusion etched in his forehead. Annoyed, she shook her head.

"It's obvious you need help." *Mental help.*

Then again, who was she to throw shade with visions, and monsters chasing at her heels?

"I promised to try it for a month. I will honor my promise, because I owe you for your kindness."

Florian regarded her a moment, his expression neutral as he pulled a fresh Guinness from the tap. "The rush is starting. You might want to take some orders," he said quietly, as though nothing unusual had been discussed. "Let me know if you have any questions."

"Nobody else is—" Callie turned around to protest and stopped. One of the booths was now occupied. She hadn't thought she was upset enough during their conversation to miss customers walking through the door. Fishing the order pad out of the apron pocket, she walked to the booth and made an effort to put on her cheerful server face.

"Hi, I'm Callie. What can I get for you?"

"Well, hello. Florian's finally got some help, has he?" A battered, lopsided smile graced the huge man's burn-scarred features. "Whiskey. Bring the bottle. Florian knows what I like."

Callie nodded, noting quickly on her pad. "For you, ma'am?"

"Florian's not waiting on us himself?" In contrast to the man seated across the table, his companion was a work of art with luminous skin, alabaster dusted with rose. But the woman sported a major attitude, lush, rouged lips pursed in a sullen pout. Chunky diamonds sparkled from the deep V of breathtaking cleavage as she leaned around the corner of the booth to search for Florian.

"No, I'm sorry. He's working the bar tonight."

"Well." The woman's tilted nose crinkled as she eyed Callie with disdain. "I suppose I'll have a strawberry daiquiri. With whipped cream."

"Coming right up." Callie turned back to the bar, and stopped, her eyes wide. Four patrons sat on stools at the opposite side of the original occupant, as if they wanted to be as far as they could from the inebriated Zeus. No one walked in while she tended those two customers. Impossible. Where were they coming in?

She placed a terse order with Florian. He opened a bottle of Glenlivet 18 and set a tumbler on the cork-lined tray. "It'll take me a minute to mix the daiquiri. The four guys in the back want Coronas and lime, if you'll fill their order first."

More customers now occupied the game room she'd noticed earlier, which ran at a ninety-degree angle to the left of the bar. Callie pulled bottles out of the cooler and popped the caps with the mounted church key, stuffing lime slices into the open necks.

A quartet of enormous, towheaded individuals participated in a loud and boisterous dart game. They cheered when she brought the beer, clapping her on the back with congenial but staggering force. A clump of wadded tens thudded into her tray, her offer of change declined as they waved Callie out of throwing range and resumed play. The darts they heaved looked more like short spears with feathers.

Bemused, she put the money in her apron pocket and went back to the bar. A glass full of sparkling carmine slush garnished with a succulent berry and whipped cream now waited on the tray with the whiskey. Florian talked with his other bar side customers, so Callie just picked up the drinks without speaking, still miffed. She tread careful steps to deliver the most expensive order she'd ever carried and deposited the glass in front of the woman with a paper coaster. The bottle safely on the table, Callie smiled at the scarred man as he handed her two hundred-dollar bills with a wink.

"I'll bring your change."

"Not necessary."

"Are you sure?" She offered the bills back to him. Even with the expensive whiskey, the check couldn't have been more than a hundred and fifty dollars.

"I'm sure. Welcome, Callie." He pressed her fingers around the money, her whole hand enveloped by his massive fist.

"Thank you so much."

"Isn't that a little extravagant, Hef?" the woman asked archly. "All the girl did was fetch and carry."

"It's the custom, dear," the man rumbled in warning. She subsided with a peevish huff.

Hef? Callie thought about Hugh Hefner for half a second, but the scarred, misshapen giant didn't resemble him at all.

"Oh, I get it. You're Hephaestus." she said, grinning.

He grunted in affirmation, his attention on the whiskey. She turned to the woman. "So you must be Aphrodite?"

"Sometimes. I'm Dita Delamour." Sweet poison dripped from her voice as she smiled at Callie. Glittering eyes swept her head to toe and sized her up expectantly as if the woman waited for recognition. The name was vaguely familiar, but when Callie didn't react right away, the woman rolled her eyes with a dramatic sigh.

"My wife is a designer," Hephaestus offered before raising the glass to his lips.

The name registered in a gossip blog kind of way. "Yes, I think I've heard of you."

"She thinks." The woman laughed bitterly. "Twelve new lines in twelve years and they still don't know me. It's not enough. I need to be in New York and Paris more often instead of this backwater bar every Tuesday night!"

"Not now." The huge man never raised his voice, but the woman fluttered and harrumphed and settled back in the booth, arms twisted in a petulant knot over her chest.

Whoever this designer-clad bombshell thought she was, her personality was fingernails down a chalkboard for Callie. If she read the body language correctly between the couple, there was about to be an ugly marital row. It was time to bow out.

"Pleased to meet you both. Let me know if you need anything else." Callie turned away, trying to decide if Florian and all his clientele were delusional or if it was some kind of big role-playing game for rich people. Folks could have a thing about dressing up in furry animal costumes. She supposed they could pretend to be gods and goddesses too. If it was a mythology RPG, they weren't concerned with the classical part, except for the guy she saw yesterday afternoon. She was relieved to have a rational explanation for the horns.

Something moved outside the glass front door. Her heart seized in momentary panic. What if the monster still lurked out there?

Strange, visible turbulence seemed to ripple the panes. Callie squeezed her eyes shut to clear her sight and prayed it wasn't the aura of an oncoming seizure. Cool relief extinguished the rising sparks of panic as her vision focused on the spiky-haired, punk rock kid who stood just inside the door, years too young to be in any bar.

Callie was still forced to squint in order see him as he strode in, the outlines of his form strangely blurred and soft. Sullen teenaged fluidity rolled in every line of his body. He surveyed the bar with narrow, kohl-ringed eyes before they settled on the heavily intoxicated Zeus. A sneer comprised of equal parts contempt and satisfaction flickered over his mouth.

"There he is, the great king of the gods," he muttered. He moved toward the bar, a glare of disdain sweeping over the other patrons. His eyes widened in appreciation as they passed over Callie, a little smirk growing as his gaze lingered too long on the front of her college t-shirt.

Despite her confusion on how he'd arrived, she gave him a thin smile and a cool nod, crossing her arms over her chest. He stopped short, an expression of shock on his face. Then a quick, sunny grin took over. His blurry outlines sharpened as he drew closer and she relaxed her squinted eyes, no longer struggling to focus on him. She decided it was a trick of the neon-tinted lights hanging in garish advertisement on the walls of the bar.

"My, my, my. Who have we here?" His voice, thick with Cockney vowels, dipped to an intimate tone as he approached. His body language changed to something more unsettlingly mature. He was older than he appeared. "Who do you belong to?"

"I'm Callie. I don't belong to anybody, but I work for Florian," she corrected him politely. "Can I get you something?"

"Well, for starters, tequila." He smirked suggestively. "And your undivided attention."

Callie resisted the urge to roll her eyes. No matter where she worked, the pickup lines were the same.

"I'm sorry, I'm busy working. I'll ask Florian for your tequila. On the rocks, or a shot?"

"On the rocks, love."

"I'll need to see some ID first."

"You *are* new here, aren't you?" He flipped two fingers out, a driver's license between them. She took it. No stranger to fake ID's, this one appeared to be real, and passed him as twenty-one. Still...

"John Smith, huh?"

He captured Callie's fingers as she returned the license and kissed the back of her hand in old-fashioned courtliness, sea-colored eyes glinting in mischief. An odd, visceral twinge from her early warning system made her startle as his lips touched her skin. Goose bumps flecked her arms. A totally alien sensation overwhelmed her senses: it was as if something crawled off her skin toward his mouth. She shivered in response and tried to pull her hand away. His grin widened as he tightened his grip, apparently delighted by her discomfiture.

"Oh, ho. That's a lovely surprise. Don't mind me. I'm incorrigible. Call me Puck." He scribed an expansive circular gesture with his free hand. "Welcome to the watering hole of the damned bored."

Callie forced a smile. "Thank you. Now, if you'll let go of my hand, I'll get your drink."

Puck made a mocking bow over her hand and released it, smirking again as he backed away, still admiring her in undisguised interest. Between them, a well-dressed man stepped directly into Callie's path. He swerved with a graceful spin and apologized as Callie's sneakers squeaked to an abrupt halt on the concrete floor.

"Sorry, hon. Good evening, gods and goddesses!"

"Herm!" came a shouted group greeting from the room at large.

"And fairies," the man belatedly added, nodding at the punk rocker.

Puck offered him an extended middle finger and a dangerous smile. Callie's mouth fell open, recognizing the Armani-suited guy from the previous afternoon.

"Jeeze, homophobic much?" she muttered.

"Trust me love, I am all fairy and he is far from homophobic. Sexual orientation has nothing to do with him being a prick." Puck glared at the man's back with undisguised hatred before another lightning-quick mood change and a devilish grin took over. "Make that tequila a double." He winked at her, eyes making another head to toe rake of her body before he disappeared into the clump of huge Scandinavian-looking, Corona-swilling dart players.

Callie's hair still prickled on the back of her neck even after Puck left, and she rubbed it, troubled. She turned back to the room, stopped short, and stared. More customers sat at tables and in the shadows of the booths, each group just a little stranger than the last. None of them used the door.

And the Armani guy—he'd stepped into her path. Right out of the *air*.

Something intensely freaky was happening that she couldn't rationalize away, no matter how hard she tried.

Was Florian telling the truth?

Instead of fear, a deep, visceral excitement flip-flopped in her abdomen, butterflies on steroids.

She never pinpointed exactly when wonder began to crowd out her reservations. Rushing between the cooler and the tables, she caught snatches of conversation and shouted greetings when others appeared. Having to bite back questions when she delivered their beverages replaced the urge to roll her eyes. She fought to keep a professional demeanor rather than fangirl all over herself when Florian introduced the Armani guy to her as Hermes. Hermes! One of her favorite characters in Greek mythology.

Three hours into the shift, she took a quick bathroom break. Her back against the door, Callie put her hands over her mouth and muffled something that sounded suspiciously like a shriek. Whether it was fear or excitement, she couldn't quite say. Her breath came fast and short until she got dizzy. She spun the tap on the sink and the shock of cold water on her face helped bring her back down.

"What the hell, Callie? Are you really going to believe this?" she muttered to herself in the mirror. She grabbed a paper towel to blot the moisture away and waded back out into the crowded bar.

4

"HEY! No touching, you horny goat! The next time I have to tell you, this tray gets smashed over your skull."

Florian's head shot up at the strident note in Callie's voice, his attention broken at a crucial moment during the straining of Hermes's martini. The ice shifted and caused a minor flood over the bar, and he cursed as the messenger of the gods raised his arm just in time to prevent his Armani suit from becoming an expensive towel.

"Sorry." Florian fumbled for a rag tucked in the waistband of his apron and sopped up the mess.

"No problem." Brushing at his immaculate cuff, Hermes advised, "Don't worry about Callie. Seems like she can take care of herself. Pan could use a good thrashing now and again."

"I just don't want her to quit the first night because she's getting groped." Florian reached for the bottle of Grey Goose and constructed a new martini. Unruffled, Hermes downed the portion of the drink that made it into the glass and replaced it on the bar.

"I'll straighten him out or make him leave. Didn't you tell her who she was going to be serving?"

"She didn't believe me. She thought I was mad." The way Callie said, 'It's obvious you need help,' had unmistakably been in reference to psychiatry.

"I'd say you've been vindicated."

After midnight, the clientele got heavy on the less humanoid side of immortality. In their usual perverse way, the Amaranthine seemed to be disinclined to help him break in his new staff despite Hermes's report he had spread the word to go easy tonight.

Florian managed to strain the martini into the glass this time, just as Callie flounced up and slammed her tray down.

"I need six shots of tequila and a blow job," she said darkly.

"Don't we all?" Innocent lechery oozed from Hermes's voice as he collected his drink and slid a crisp bill across the counter. Florian laughed out loud until Callie shot a dirty look at him.

"Okay, not funny," he amended quickly. Hermes grinned and indicated in silent gestures as he walked away that he would talk to Pan. Florian set up six shot glasses and poured tequila. "Are things going well in the back room?" he inquired in a low voice.

"Oh, yes, just fine." With a vengeance, Callie stabbed slices of lime from the sideboard into a tumbler and plopped a shaker of coarse salt on the cork liner of the serving tray. She didn't look at him. "I got felt up by a satyr and propositioned by everything vaguely male in there. Just a typical Tuesday night."

"It took me a while to get used to them." Bailey's and Kahlua filled another shot glass. "And that was when they still pretended to be mostly human."

"How could you mistake anything in the back room tonight as human?" She punctuated her words with clipped consonants. "A talking crocodile wants fish and chips, by the way."

"Oh, Sobek's here? I missed him coming in."

"How could you possibly miss a huge-ass, two legged crocodile?"

"He doesn't always arrive that way," Florian defended himself. "Sometimes he looks like Idris Elba."

"Of course he does." Callie gave a short, hysterical laugh. Florian hastily topped off the last shot glass with a head of whipped cream created from ambrosia earlier in the afternoon. So far, he managed to avoid shaping anything while in her sight, not sure how she might react.

Order in hand, she stormed off toward the back of the game room with fierce, silent determination. Frustrated his reticence to reveal the truth up front might have been in error, Florian slammed the piping bag of cream down on the bar—a mistake that resulted in a shower of sticky-sweet white foam that clung to his cheeks and hair. He closed his eyes and heaved a deep sigh of defeat.

"Oops." The timbre of the amused, sultry voice and a hint of expensive perfume clued him to the speaker's identity before he even turned his head. Aphrodite sat in the seat just vacated by Hermes, a suggestive smile on her lips as she reached out. One scarlet-tipped nail stroked up his cheek, removing a blob of whipped cream. She brought it to her lips and raised her eyes to his in a sensual challenge, tongue darting out to delicately lap the cream from her finger. "If you like, I could help you clean up."

"Thank you for the offer, but no."

"Oh." Disappointment pursed her lips into a plump cupid's bow as he wiped his hair and face with a clean towel. "You're no fun anymore."

"What can I get you? Another strawberry daiquiri?" Not in the right frame of mind for her games tonight, he checked the hint of irritation which escaped through his voice. "Where's Hef?"

"Drinking with the Norse." The goddess stuck out her tongue in disgust. "Barbarians."

"The Aesir declared a holiday, if I'm not mistaken." He busied himself blending her drink. "They said it was Loki's birthday."

Aphrodite snorted. "Like that spawn had a mother." She heaved a dramatic sigh. "I'm so *bored*, Florian. If I can't get out soon I think I'm going to do something desperate. Do you know how long it's been since I had a moment to myself without Hef hovering over me?"

He raised one eyebrow at her in disbelief, and she twitched her bare shoulder in innocence. "Well, I suppose you do, don't you?"

"You know I do." He carefully topped off her glass with the whipped cream and slid in a straw before delivering the drink.

Returning the piping bag to the refrigerator, he straightened and craned his neck in search of Callie as another boisterous toast went up near the pool tables. Why the Aesir had decided to go full Viking tonight for the party, he couldn't say, but it was a change from the usual onslaught of Ikea executives. He found her as she elbowed her way out between a wall of furry backs. Callie was clearly an expert at navigating a rowdy bar atmosphere and he admired her ability to adapt to what must be, for her, an unbelievable turn of events.

He watched a little too long, because the clink of a glass replaced too pointedly on the wooden surface startled him. Aphrodite glared at him, his loss of attention noted. Garnet-stained lips thinned into a hard line, her gaze followed his new employee as she rushed between patrons with her tray. The goddess's expression changed and she looked down at her drink with a flounce.

"Your new waitress is very pretty. Pan seems to be enamored."

A dangerous mix of jealousy, petulance, and false insecurity played in her voice. She fished for a compliment, her insatiable self-absorption at odds with the idea anyone could be more interesting than she.

"Pan needs to keep his hands off my brand new employee." He heaved a mental sigh and played the game. "Is that a new scent you're wearing tonight?"

"Florian, I'm so pleased you noticed," she purred, preening. "Yes, it's part of my new line for summer. It's called Tryst." Her expression deflated when he didn't react to the name and she looked away in moody resignation. "Hef's corporations are expanding and he won't take me to the trade shows. I've had to rely on my assistants for all of the marketing. My newest fashion empire is suffering and he doesn't even care. Sales are abysmal. Nobody knows who I am anymore! I'm starving."

"I can make you something to eat."

"Not that kind of starving." A hungry look flitted through her eyes. "Although a little attention from certain individuals could do wonders right now."

"Florian." Zeus slurred from the end of the counter, where he had moved on from pints to liter mugs. "My glass is empty again."

"On my way." Relieved to have a reason to abandon this dangerous conversation, he excused himself and pulled another liter for Zeus. "That makes eighteen, Z. Maybe you should slow down a little."

"Don't lecture me, youngster. You're not my wife, and you can't tell me what to do." The stout drained with one long pull, Zeus let out a burp that shook the room. Several of the bar-side patrons looked up in disgust and Aphrodite waved a delicate hand in front of her wrinkled nose, but none of them said anything to the offending party. They knew who was in charge, drunk or not. Florian would be surprised if any of them dared to say something cheeky.

"I love her, Florian. My wife is my world, and I'm gonna make her proud of me again." Big Z pushed the empty mug at him, and he turned back to the tap with a shrug for Aphrodite, who gestured with sharp, slicing motions and wide eyes.

"I used to be somebody," the giant man muttered again, staring with pickled morosity into the refilled vessel. "I can be somebody again, just like the old days. Watch me, Florian. I'm gonna do it." Florian murmured placations and edged away.

"Why can't you cut him off?" Aphrodite's theatrical whisper wasn't meant to be private. "I tried to talk to him earlier and he can't even focus. You remember what happened the last time he got this drunk."

"I'm not going to be the one to tell him no."

"Scaredy-cat."

"You tell him, then."

"No, I don't think so." She shuddered. "Hera dearest is going to be livid. Thunderstorms. Count on it."

"As long as they're outside my establishment this time, I can handle it." Broken chairs and tables were still piled in the cellar, charred by the melee.

"Damn it. I really needed to talk to him, but I can't even with the breath tonight." She heaved another theatrical sigh and leaned over the bar. "Can you keep a secret?"

Florian kept several—one in particular from Aphrodite. "Of course."

"I'm trying to get my restrictions lifted."

"Oh?" A dull flare of hope sputtered and died before it took hold. Despite intertwined offenses, his own sentence was a separate entity even if hers ended. She was thrilled about the prospect, but he knew well enough she didn't register his own parole as a factor.

"Yes. I'm sure my idea will help both Zeus and me get out of this slump. I'm working a new angle." Her eyes glittered with excitement, rivaling the flash and fire of the stones around her throat. "Don't say anything about it yet, though. Not to anyone. Promise?"

"Not a word." It was much safer to keep an Amaranthine secret than to risk the lightning.

He created the fish and chips order, working fast with Callie out of sight. Chips he had down to a science now, drawing out in rapid succession long strands of the vaporous element between his fingers. Each one took on a golden brown crispness as the ambrosia cured and hit the plate with a *plink*. Aphrodite observed the process for a moment but lost interest when he continued to ignore her. Bored, she disappeared into the crowd in search of an ally.

Florian watched Zeus's upper body slump and melt into a drunken puddle atop the bar, snoring with a rumble like far-off thunder. He moved the liter aside before it could spill and sighed.

Just another typical Tuesday night.

At the first sound of shattering plastic, his head shot up. He craned his neck to see a flushed and angry Callie walking away from Pan while the rest of the bar erupted into cheers.

Maybe not so typical now.

5

BY THE FIFTH time she was propositioned ("Hey, beautiful, would you like me to Mount your Olympus?"), Callie found herself rather disappointed that many of the so-called gods behaved no better than the annoying frat boys she served back home.

It was the freak with the horns she could learn to hate.

Ridiculous pickup lines she shut down with acid scorn, or no reaction at all. Slinging drinks at the crowded sports bar during tournament season taught her how to handle that kind of attention. Tonight, she was too busy to linger in one place for long. Suggestive comments fell flat when she turned her back and walked away. It took a lot to piss her off.

But the fucking goat guy wouldn't give up.

All hairy-legged, slit-eyed and curly horned, the satyr leered at her as she delivered the sixth round of Coronas to the furry warrior group. "Hey, baby. When are you going to show me those tits?"

Callie ignored him. She waited while the Aesir argued about whose turn it was to buy the round and pulled more sweaty money out of their pockets. The bills shoved in her apron, she gathered empty bottles and lime rinds from the table. These guys were huge, loud, and gregarious. Bruises were forming on her shoulders from their friendly pats, but they didn't aim their huge paws directly at her ass, like some of the other jerks back there.

Speaking of whom…the hand that slipped between her legs could only belong to the freak.

Edges of the tray gripped in white-knuckled fury, Callie took a deep breath and whirled. She brought the plastic down with a resounding crack and bludgeoned the satyr with three vicious swipes. The broken tray she left impaled at a jaunty angle on one of his horns like a beer-scented, cork-lined fascinator as he blinked in shock. The Norse roared in laughter and created more bruises on her back with approving slaps as she walked away.

After that, nobody touched her.

On the strange side, Callie's early warning system wasn't bothered by any of them, even the groper. Those special senses were unusually silent save for her earlier reaction to Puck, who haunted a dark booth in the back room.

The clientele showered cash on drinks and tips like worthless paper. Not sure how or where they got it, the currency was real enough in Callie's bulging apron pockets. The Amaranthine drank amazing amounts of alcohol that would have been fatal at any frat party. Some ordered food, which Florian unfailingly delivered in a diverse array that went far beyond usual bar fare.

She grabbed a few plump strawberries from the sideboard when her stomach roared a reminder that the muffins were hours ago. They were so delicious she reached for the bin a second time, but restrained herself from eating more than four of the fragrant berries. To her surprise, the fruit energized her the way a full meal did, and she didn't want any more.

Things tapered to quiet after three AM. A whiskey-mellowed Hephaestus collected the wayward Aphrodite from the bar stool where Callie had seen her attached most of the night, taking numerous duck-faced selfies and flirting with Florian in an unrequited way. Others winked out in groups as they'd arrived, without fanfare. Puck, the only one to at least pretend to use the door, blew Callie a kiss on his way out. At last, no one but Florian, Hermes, and

Callie remained in the empty front room with the inebriated Zeus, who roused enough to order another Guinness.

While Florian tended to Big Z, Callie interrogated Hermes in search of validation for her burgeoning acceptance. They sat together in one of the booths out front and the former messenger, who claimed to now be a lawyer for the gods, indulgently fielded her rapid-fire questions as he ate the remainder of the olives from Florian's garnish tray. His funnel-shaped glass overflowed with green spheres and a token amount of alcohol.

"You might try a drink with your olives, sometime. That's a pretty serious habit you have there," Callie noted.

"Silence, mortal scholar. I'm allowed my vices. I don't have many others." He popped more into his mouth. "So what other burning questions do you have?"

"So, why would gods bother taking on a human form at all, or an animal one? I always wondered about that."

He shrugged. "In our native form you'd be unable to perceive us as anything but bright lights or energy. We take on whatever appearance will get us where we need to go, or in Zeus's case, incognito to avoid pissing off Hera."

The last part of the sentence emerged *sotto voce*, and Hermes looked over his shoulder as if expecting Hera to appear. She giggled, glancing with cautious guilt at Zeus's back.

"Interacting with humans is more practical in a corporeal body. We can be male or female—or both, depending on the situation. It makes it easier for you to relate to us, and there are distinct advantages in the field of biology." He waggled his eyebrows suggestively, and Callie snorted, amused.

"Yes. Rather prolific advantages, as I remember."

"Not so much, anymore." He shifted, and became serious. When he spoke again, his voice held gravity. "There are rules in place now that make it less practical to procreate with humans. We can't intervene in our children's lives in any way that would alter their destiny so the decision should be given more consideration than it gets. Conception happens without fail unless we take some pretty drastic precautions. In most cases, it's a temporary decision and a temporary body, but we become governed by emotions that aren't the norm for our kind when we take on a permanent human form. We're not big on humility or love or being good parents unless we're constrained by the human condition."

Hermes went silent for a moment, an odd, wistful expression on his face as he regarded her. "Every now and then, we decide to live out a human lifespan just for kicks. But biology can't be cheated. When we truly become human in this world, eventually that persona is going to die of old age or as a result of abuse to which the body is subjected. Like that one did." He jerked his chin at the drunken Zeus, still disguised as a now-dead rock star. "Losing this identity has been exceptionally hard. Nobody's ever seen him like this. He didn't even mourn losing Henry the Eighth this badly."

"So, the cult of celebrity has become the new worship?"

Hermes looked impressed. "Score one for the lady. You worked it out in no time at all."

"Not that hard to see. Some of those celebrities are too perfect, or too weird to be human. Tom Cruise?"

"Trust me, not one of ours. The celebrity or rock star status works for some of us. Me? I prefer to be the normal everyday Joe with power, money, and good taste that everyone else wants to be." He saluted her with his martini. "Envy and imitation work almost as well as fame, without the paparazzi. They suck."

"So how many are professional athletes?"

"Not as many as you might think. There are a lot more porn stars."

"Eww." Callie wrinkled her nose.

"We take attention where we can get it."

"Don't take this the wrong way then, but Hermes was always one of my favorites." Her face heated up and she covered her eyes, confused at her own reaction. "Oh my God, I sound like I'm fangirling."

Hermes laughed. "Thanks, but I have a boyfriend. I'm flattered. Don't worry, your admiration is appreciated for what it is."

"When I was little I loved the story about stealing Apollo's cows.

Dad read it every time I asked, even though he must have been sick of it. I know it's probably allegorical."

"Oh, no, that one's relatively accurate. It didn't take much to impress people back then, but making cows walk backward isn't as easy as it sounds."

"Apollo was my favorite." Callie sat back. She traced a pale glass-ring in the tabletop with one fingertip and struggled to maintain an academic distance. There was too much to assimilate and pretending it was some kind of immersive game remained easier than admitting it might be real. "Does he come here too?"

"Err, no." Hermes ran a hand over his chin and avoided her gaze. "He's not as charming as he used to be, and out of favor at the moment. He and Zeus had a major difference of opinion about a lot of things, but primarily Mrs. Zeus. Speaking of whom—" He upended his glass, consuming the last olives at the bottom with an expression of pure pleasure. "I should make sure he gets home before Hera comes looking. You don't want to meet her that way."

He left a pile of bills on the table as he bid Callie good night. Walking around the side of the bar to exchange a brotherly handshake with Florian, Hermes put his arm over Zeus's shoulder and they disappeared in a rush of wind. A paper coaster fluttered to the floor, tracing a cyclonic pattern in the empty air.

The sound of techno music from the digital jukebox thumped against sudden stillness left in the wake of their departure. Florian hit a switch on the back wall behind the counter, and quiet descended, a welcome change after the last noisy, incredible, unreal eight and a half hours. Callie continued her busy work, feeling a little guilty as Florian made his way down the bar top with a cloth and soapy water, scouring away the last of the sticky spilled drinks. Out of the corner of her eye, she saw him glance her way several times as she loaded the last of the glassware into the industrial washer. Finally, she shut the stainless steel door and rounded on him at the same moment he turned to her.

"Florian—"

"Callie," he said in tandem, and they both stopped. "You first," he invited meekly. He straightened in preparation for an onslaught.

"I'm sorry for being such a bitch earlier." Callie twisted her hands together in a plea for clemency.

"I'm the one who should be sorry," he countered, his tall frame relieved of its expectant stiffness by her words. "It was unfair not to warn you right up front, and I deserved it."

"No, you were right, I wouldn't have believed you. I would have walked right out the front door, and I think it would have been the biggest mistake of my life. Did I really serve a talking crocodile?"

"Yes." Florian's mouth tugged upward in a half-smile.

"So, if that's true, I might have to believe the rest of it. That I actually met gods tonight."

"Ex-gods. But yes."

She put her head down on the bar and giggled, hilarity tinged with hysteria. The giggles changed abruptly, and through mortified tears she realized she was sobbing instead of laughing.

The past few weeks at last demanded their emotional toll. She had severed all ties to her loving parents, who would never understand why she abandoned them. A creature with wings and talons dogged her heels halfway across the country. The visions were more numerous and full of nightmare images the longer she was off her meds, and mere luck ensured none hit her tonight during work hours. Now, to learn the myths and legends she loved might be real...

Dimly, she became aware of Florian beside her, close enough to touch, but all he did was lean on the bar next to her. When she straightened up, he offered her a clean towel with an understanding half-smile.

"Thank you." She wiped her eyes with the towel, and took a deep, shaky breath. "That had to be unattractive, and slightly psychotic. I'm sorry."

"No need to apologize. They've had the same effect on me once or twice." A hint of bitterness lent sharp edges to his voice. He continued with better cheer, "However, there are some perks to this as I may have mentioned. This is yours." He scooted a rubber-band bound stack of bills across the wooden expanse. "Your share of the tips tonight."

Blinking, Callie picked up the pile of money. Her jaw dropped in disbelief as she flipped through the bills. "This is almost five hundred dollars!"

"A little high for a Tuesday night. We're not usually this busy, but the Norse were having a party. I think they were glad to .see a new face."

"Other parts of my anatomy too, I guess."

Florian cleared his throat. "About that. Is this a habit of yours, breaking trays over the skulls of anyone who gets out of line?"

"I told you I wouldn't let anyone get away with it. I'll pay for it." She peeled off a twenty from the clump of cash.

"No, don't worry about it. I just want to say that I'll order more trays." A slow smile spread across his face. "That was the most satis-fying crack I've ever heard."

The genuine grin was a breathtaking sunrise, blue eyes bright with laughter. Her insides fluttered a bit. He was unreasonably attractive, something to which she considered herself immune, but she couldn't help smiling in return. It changed her awareness of how close they stood together, leaning against the bar. As if coming to the realization at the same time, they both moved in opposite directions, Callie to straighten and stuff the bills into her jeans pocket and Florian to punch the start button on the dishwasher. She changed the subject.

"They sure drink a lot of Coronas. Only one case is left in the cooler."

"I'll have to call my supplier later. Wednesday is Sidhe night. With one or two exceptions, they prefer hard liquor so we won't be short even if Pete can't deliver until Thursday." He counted whiskey, bour-bon, tequila and vodka bottles on the shelf. "We should be all right for this evening. Pete delivers our grocery orders as well. If you want some things to keep upstairs in your apartment, leave a list by the register and I'll add it to the order."

"I am starving again," Callie admitted. "I ate a few of the strawber-ries from the garnish bin."

Florian's face stiffened into a mask of dismay. "Callie, you don't want to eat those very often." He ran a hand through his hair. "There's so much more I need to explain, but it might have to wait until later."

"What's wrong with now?" Racking up questions on her own, she wanted a few answers. At that moment a woman's voice called Florian's name from the stairway.

"Yes, they're gone, Gran!" he called back, and returned his attention to Callie. "Gran comes down and we make breakfast every morning after closing time. She's looking forward to meeting you. She's...a little eccentric."

A tiny, elderly woman wrapped in a thick shawl emerged from the stairway. "I thought the old sot would never leave," she grumbled, and hefted a basket onto the bar beside the drop leaf. Her voice quaked with age and carried more of the lilt of Ireland than her grandson's, but her bright blue eyes were very much like Florian's as she smiled at Callie. Unlike her grandson though, she possessed fair, papery skin dotted with faded freckles, white hair caught up in a thick braid encircling the back of her head.

"Good morning, dear," she greeted Callie. "We knew you were coming, so I got the bed all made up yesterday. It's so very nice to see you again."

"Gran, this is Callie, my new waitress," Florian corrected gently. "You haven't met her yet."

"Oh, yes, of course. I'm Bridget Callahan Pereira." The lady nodded in absent agreement. Her gaze moved between Callie and Florian, then back again. "Lovely to meet you. I brought the breakfast, Florian, but I seem to have forgotten how to cook."

"That's all right, Gran, we'll do it down here just like we always do." Florian soothed her and picked up the basket. It contained eggs, bread, butter, and a rasher of bacon. "Callie, will you join us for breakfast? We have more than enough here."

A renewed howl in her neglected stomach made the decision easy. She accepted the invitation with thanks. From a cabinet, Florian produced a hot plate and a battered iron skillet, which he proceeded to set up on the bar. She wondered why he didn't just cook in back, but figured the as yet unseen kitchen was already clean.

The fantastic smell of frying bacon permeated the air as Callie did a quick run with the push broom around the pool tables and dartboards. The worst behavior had been confined to the back room, which she found inexplicably clean of lime rinds or spilled food. Only faint white streaks remained, random smears against the tiled floor that seemed to evaporate before the broom reached them.

"How do you like your eggs?" Florian called.

"Scrambled, please." The push broom tucked away in its closet, Callie found the light switch to the back room and shrouded the pool tables in shadow. Around front, Bridget perched on one of the high-backed barstools near the stairs. At first, Callie thought she was engrossed in watching Florian cook, but the elderly woman's expression proved vacant and dreamy as she mumbled to herself. Easing in beside her, she picked out a few words.

"So much fire. We must stop them, must stop them, but how do you stop angels from fighting?"

Bridget swiveled toward her in a sudden movement. The blue gaze sharpened, fixed and unblinking on Callie's face with unnerving clarity.

"You." The single word dropped between them. "You're the key."

There was no aura, no warning other than the stretching, telescoping sensation that accompanied her worst seizures and the most terrifying visions.

"No, not now!" Panicky, she fought to stay in the moment but her sight dimmed and the images crushed her with merciless detail:

Fire rains from the heavens. Soot and ash coats everything in sight. People run, screaming. Some lay dead in the streets. Buildings burn. A winged being with gleaming armor soars through the smoke and sparks and grapples with a red-caped figure on the ground. Someone laughs: high, maniacal, and full of absolute glee.

It was the worst one yet. An anguished sound born of horror and helplessness rose in her throat and spilled over into reality.

"Callie?" Florian's voice came from far away and shook her out of the vision as it ended. She slumped forward, exhausted in the seizure's aftermath. He caught and eased her into a seat on one of the stools. Again, that heady scent of pine and meadow surrounded her. It was his cologne, perhaps, and she breathed it in like a calming drug. Cartwheeling, dizzy swoops of vertigo slowed as her forehead rested against his chest. Her arms crept around him, seeking warmth and comfort.

The embrace became something more intimate than support as they both leaned into it. A sense of safety flooded through her, and an awakening warmth deep inside. His heartbeat sped up against her ear. Neither pulled away until the awkward realization she was hugging her new boss clamored in her newly coherent thoughts. She lifted her head and disengaged as soon as she was able. They stared at each other for the span of several breaths. Florian appeared a little stunned.

"Are you all right?" he asked with concern. Humiliated, Callie nodded. She had to tell him about the seizures now.

"After a vision that strong, eating is the best thing for you, I've found," Bridget pronounced.

Callie's head rose in shock and she stared at the older woman, who already gazed elsewhere, eyes focused on something only she could see.

Florian portioned out a serving of bacon and eggs, bread and butter for Callie. He repeated the process for his grandmother. As he set the plate before her, Bridget shook herself, gave him a brilliant smile and a kiss on the cheek.

"It looks delicious, dear. Thank you."

"You're welcome, Gran." He fished out a set of salt and pepper shakers and silverware from beneath the counter and joined them on the other side, nodding to Callie in encouragement. "Gran's right. You need to eat."

Callie, still lethargic with the postictal effects of the seizure, fumbled for a fork and took a bite. Her interest sharpened as the food hit her still-neglected stomach. Beside her, Bridget tucked in with a hearty appetite. They ate in silence for a few minutes.

"So, Callie, tell us a little more about yourself," Florian requested quietly. "Why did you come to Kansas City?"

"I'm not sure how to explain that."

Bridget waved her bread. "It's clear as water. You left home because of the banshee. You were led here by your blood."

Callie went cold. "What did you say?" she whispered. Her heart dropped into her stomach as she stared at those eerie, knowing blue eyes.

"Gran didn't mean anything by it," Florian interjected quietly, and Callie cut him off.

"No, she's right." She searched the woman's face. "How do you know that? How can you know any of that?"

"I saw the banshee when I was out in the garden. There it was, circling above. A nasty thing, and in broad daylight too. But it can't see you here." Bridget went back to eating her breakfast and left Callie speechless.

"They don't come out often in the day unless they're tracking. How long has it been after you?" Florian asked interestedly, and Callie dropped her fork with a clatter.

"Who are you people?" she demanded. "What's happening here? None of this is normal!"

"No, of course it isn't." Florian put down his own fork. "Callie, do you remember I said I knew you were the right person for the job because you saw the sign? That no one else could have found the door?

"Only people who have Amaranthine blood can find my establishment. It means somewhere in your recent ancestry, you are the descendant of one of the immortals, like Gran and me."

"Wait, what?" Callie shut her eyes for a moment and tried to process this information. "You're telling me that one of them is my father?" She had enough memories to recall her biological mother definitely had not been immortal: just a young, frightened woman.

"Or a grandfather. Just like in mythology, their descendants retain some of their attributes. It makes us sensitive to the thresholds and lets us find them." He gestured around him. "Nectar and Ambrosia was built around a threshold, the only one in North America."

"A what?"

"A threshold is a doorway where the Amaranthine can cross directly from their world to ours. There are two other places where that can happen: Athens and Rome, but there are hundreds of smaller doorways they can access from any of the three thresholds to travel all over the world. Each threshold has a Doorkeeper, like me. We offer shelter to anyone with Amaranthine blood. There aren't many people like us left. You're the first to arrive since I took over this establishment."

Callie digested that information a moment. "Why aren't many left? Hermes made it sound like they still have no qualms about procreating with us."

"Mostly because of the hunters. You're well acquainted with one kind."

Horror dawned. "You mean the banshee."

"The old stories about how they only wail for certain bloodlines is true. They wiped out entire families with any hint of Amaranthine ancestry. Adulthood brings full manifestation of any gifts we might have inherited, and marks a transition where those creatures become aware of us.

"With rare exceptions, not many of us live to see old age." His voice held a note of regret. He nodded at Bridget, a fond smile softening his expression. The elderly woman's gaze rested on the unseen landscape in her own mind, unaware Florian spoke of her. "Gran's family learned all the tricks to evade them and passed them down through the generations. Our survival rate is higher than most, but everyone makes a sacrifice of some kind."

The metallic taste of fear coated the back of her tongue. His words triggered a memory of her own, far too close to what he described to be coincidental. Callie wanted to ask another question but the cold shudder rattled the words back into her throat.

Florian straightened and collected the breakfast plates. "It's been a long night. Why don't you get some sleep?"

"We can't just leave it there," she protested. Her mind kept lurching in clumsy circles around Florian's story and his declaration they were both children or grandchildren of a former god. In spite of her protests, the mention of sleep proved irresistible and a jaw-popping yawn overruled her objection.

"I promise to answer any more questions you might think of when you come downstairs later. I'm not going anywhere." His mouth twisted in an ironic half-grin that his eyes did not reflect. "I'll take Gran back to her room and then finish clearing up."

Callie mumbled a distracted goodnight, which he echoed but Bridget did not. She climbed the steps with automatic movements. The soft murmur of Florian's voice followed her up the stairwell as he cajoled Bridget into action.

Once inside her apartment, the old fashioned, bolstered bed pulled her across the room with irresistible magnetism. She flopped down on the mattress, sorting through the wild assertions made that night. Florian's story about the hunters fit more jagged puzzle pieces into the gaps in her life, and answers to questions she would rather not have confirmed. Answers about her childhood and her biological mother, images carried more in her heart than in her memories.

Is this really happening?

As a teenager, she once asked Richard Davies if the gods were real, and received a curiously noncommittal answer from the anthropology professor. "All stories begin somewhere," he'd said. "From the beginning of history, human beings have been convinced of the existence of something more gifted or more devious than ourselves. I tend to hold there's truth in that—but just maybe not what we think it will be."

"Oh, Dad, what would you think of this?" she whispered to the darkness. "Should I believe it?"

Tears burned in her eyes. Missing Richard and Caroline burned with a fierce, knotted pain inside and forced its way out in a gulping sob. Florian spoke quietly to Bridget on the landing below and she pulled the pillow over her head to muffle her tears so they would not hear, until weariness allowed sleep to intervene.

7

CALLIE WOKE in the same position she'd flung herself into bed: face down, head buried under the pillow. She brushed disheveled bedhead hair out of her eyes and blinked in sleepy denial against the bright wedge of light coming through the edge of the blackout curtain. Her wristwatch said it was only two in the afternoon.

An attempt to reclaim sleep soon proved futile. She got up, showered, and put on her last clean shirt and jeans, making a mental note to ask Florian if a washing machine existed on the premises.

One large window in the front room looked out on the cityscape. She edged away from the panes with wary caution. The memory of her shattered apartment window and a nightmare creature clawing for her through the narrow frame was still too close. The French doors in the bedroom, as Florian had mentioned, gave access to the terrace of a roof garden but Callie had barely glanced through the lace curtains the previous afternoon when she pulled the blackout drape over them. She still could not bring herself to go outside where she might be exposed.

She pulled her hair back in a loose braid and caught the end with an elastic band as she stepped out to the landing. The doors of both apartments on the second floor remained closed while she descended and she wondered if Florian would even be up yet.

The murmur of the flat screen televisions reached her at the foot of the stairs. He was already in position behind the bar. An ancient golden box, ornate and beautiful, lay open before him. Whatever was inside sent spatters of reflected light dancing over his face and hands as he worked something in his fingers.

He didn't see her at first, his attention on one of the television screens, and she took the opportunity to study him for a moment. Florian's perfect profile was something seen only on marble sculptures in the museum, his full lips slightly parted as he looked down to regard his work. The man was stunning but seemed impervious to the flirtations of the immortal beauties in the bar, male or female. He treated everyone with the same casual, professional courtesy, including Callie. Only when he spoke with his grandmother did that cool exterior begin to show warmth.

Or during the few moments he'd held her in the aftermath of the vision, unexpectedly tender and arousing.

Callie shook herself out of that train of thought when he reached for something within the toolbox-sized casket and withdrew a cloud-like wisp of luminous stuff. Drawn through his fingers, it took on a more solid form and Florian shaped it into a crescent. The sharp scent of lime reached her nose as the material flushed with a pale green cast in the wake of his touch. Callie caught her breath as the perfect lime wedge, formed from nothing more than a glowing pinch of vapor, landed among the already half-full bin of green, yellow and orange citrus wedges at the sideboard.

Hearing her stifled gasp, Florian turned. "Good morning."

She walked up to the other side of the bar and sat on the stool in front of the box, transfixed by the swirling gleam of the stuff inside.

"What is that?"

"Ambrosia, the food of the gods." He gave a dramatic flourish worthy of a Shakespearean actor. "Hence comes the name of my establishment."

"Where does it come from?"

"It is a naturally occurring energy that just floats loose in the atmosphere. The Amaranthine are able to distill it into something more pliable. Hermes refills the casket for me once a month, but a little ambrosia goes a very long way."

"What about the nectar?" Callie, fascinated, stared as he formed olives with deft movements and tossed them into another section of the bin.

"You didn't guess?" He raised an eyebrow. "Alcohol *is* nectar, and the only thing the Amaranthine can consume in its man-made form. It has something to do with the vapors. Burnt offerings and alcohol were traditional offerings to the gods because it used to be the only way they could taste real food."

"How did you learn to do this?"

"It's my gift, such as it is. I can manipulate ambrosia into any food they want as long as I've tasted it myself. Ambrosia gives them energy and nourishment, but in its raw form tastes a little like lightning must: sharp and metallic, with a hint of black pepper." He took another pinch of the stuff and formed a perfect strawberry, the sweet scent reaching her as the fruit took on a crimson blush.

Callie clapped her hand over her mouth in realization. "But I ate those strawberries last night!"

"Because of our ancestry, we can consume and benefit from the energy the ambrosia gives. In moderation, it can keep us from getting ill, energize us better than caffeine, and even prolong our lives." He paused in his work and looked down, then met her gaze, his expression apologetic. "Part of the sandwich you ate Monday was ambrosia. I shouldn't have given you any without your permission, but you were dehydrated and malnourished. I'm sorry. One small meal every couple of days won't hurt you, but anything more could be dangerous."

"How dangerous?" Callie stiffened.

"We can't consume too much. The energy stokes those special gifts we inherited like a coal furnace. If we consume more than this over the course of a day—" he lifted a cupped handful of mist out of the box. Trailing vapor leaked over the sides of his hand in a hazy waterfall. "It can be fatal. At the very least, crippling." He let the ambrosia flow back into the casket. "It's your choice whether you want to eat any at all. We don't need ambrosia to survive the way the Amaranthine do."

"Can I touch it?" Callie asked in a small voice. Florian took a pinch of the stuff and held it out to her. She picked it up gingerly between her thumb and forefinger. A strange sensation brushed her skin as the ambrosia ruffled against invisible air currents: icy cold and hot at the same time, slippery and soft, malleable but formless.

This is real. The food of the gods. This is real. A soft laugh of wonder escaped her lips.

She tried to shape the ambrosia into something simple like a marshmallow, but it stubbornly remained a wisp. She poured the vapor back into Florian's palm. He effortlessly drew it out into a celery stick and tossed the garnish into the bin.

"Don't feel too bad about not being able to shape it." He quirked a grin at her. "This seems to be a rare gift. The last person to wield this particular talent was Stefanio Pereira, a Portuguese immigrant."

"Your grandfather?"

"Not by blood." Florian paused as if choosing his words with care, and fashioned another piece of fruit. "He and Gran first met on a ship bound for Ellis Island. They married not long after. Later, when I emigrated, he took me in and gave me a job. But he died after a very long life. I took his name when I took over the establishment, in honor of his memory." His voice became softer. "He was the closest thing to a father I ever knew."

"How long have you been in charge?"

He jerked his head behind him and to the right. "There is real fruit over there, and some yogurt in the refrigerator under the bar if you're hungry. Help yourself to anything you like." He fashioned another slice of lemon, tossed it into the pile of garnishes and never answered her question even though she waited politely.

Not rude, exactly, but weird.

Callie retrieved a banana and a container of yogurt and came back to sit across from Florian while he continued to work. He said nothing else, but behind the spoken words Callie had sensed the deep affection and gratitude Florian held for Stefanio Pereira. It touched her, and perhaps inevitably her thoughts turned to the couple that had taken her in and raised her as their own child. Her eyes stung with the threat of guilty tears. The hasty note left on the mantel, vague and pathetically inadequate in expressing her love and gratitude, still shamed her: *Dear Mom and Dad, I'm sorry. I can't tell you where I'm going. Please know how much I love you.* She had to turn down a new avenue of thought or risk another unattractive meltdown.

With Florian silent in his own thoughts and overly attentive to the creation of garnishes, she turned her own focus on breakfast and the televisions around the bar. On the largest screen, a horde of screaming, excited women danced and clapped as the host made her way down the aisle, waving and blowing kisses.

Her voice was silky, hot chocolate and brandy. "Welcome to Christmas in June, everybody! You're all going home with a brand new car!"

A fresh wave of screams and adulation swept the audience, the camera lingering on several women who wept with joy. Callie couldn't help but smile. "You really watch the Sarah Freewin Show?" she asked Florian with a curious chuckle, trying to break the melancholy mood they'd developed.

"Oh, yeah. Any time the Amaranthine launch a new celebrity face, they're on the couch. Sarah is Hera."

"No. No way!" Callie stared in disbelief at the screen. Hera's current identity embodied one of the most powerful multi-media icons in history. Her influence was widespread and benevolent, with large operations in literature, clothing, television, and film. She admired the host for her efforts to empower and educate women in third world countries and her effortless, sisterly connection to her guests—to some of whom Callie served drinks last night. By the time the fifth A-list celebrity showed up in the bar, she was disillusioned enough by their bad behavior to no longer be impressed.

She sat back on the bar stool and digested this information with an increasingly jaundiced eye toward the entertainment industry. "Is anybody in Hollywood not an immortal?" she asked Florian as she finished her yogurt. "How can you tell if they're Amaranthine?"

"Oh, easy. They don't get plastic surgery," he replied. "That doesn't mean they don't lie about it in interviews, though."

"They lie about many things." The voice startled them both, and Callie jumped with a squeak.

Sitting beside her on the next barstool was an angel.

8

Florian experienced a moment of sheer disbelief. The existence of this particular pantheon was well known to the Roman Doorkeepers, but angels never visited the North American doorway before, not even when staunchly Catholic Stefanio Pereira was in charge. He schooled his features and glanced at Callie, closing the golden casket in front of him and stowing it beneath the counter. Callie edged off her seat warily and stood at the side of the bar.

"Welcome. What can we get for you?" Florian inquired.

The stranger at the corner seat raised his head. His smooth, unlined face suffused with unearthly radiance, he smiled gently, eyes reflecting the golden glory of the afternoon sun streaming through the front window.

"I'm not sure," he admitted, flexing his white-feathered wings in a shrug. "I'm not much of a drinker, save for the odd glass of wine. What do you suggest?"

"I can make you a soft drink or some orange juice," Florian offered, but the customer shook his head, his lips curving in a hesitant twist.

"No. I haven't tried anything new in a long time. But do choose something mild for me, if you please."

Florian raised an eyebrow, considering. Beside him, Callie had tied on her apron and was all business, remarkably resilient.

"There's still some Angry Orchard in the walk-in," she ventured tentatively.

"Excellent idea. Hard cider it is, then." He nodded at Callie, who retrieved a bottle from the cooler. Florian popped the cap with the mounted church key beneath the bar and set the bottle in front of their customer. "Give this a try, and see what you think."

He couldn't help but stare a little as the stranger took a cautious sip, and then smiled at Florian in pleased surprise. "An interesting choice. Apple juice with a kick, eh?"

"Something like that." Florian grinned. "Do you want a glass?"

"Please."

Florian ventured as the stranger poured the foaming liquid into the glass, "I'm the Doorkeeper here."

"Yes, I know. Florian, isn't it?" The winged individual extended a hand, warm and strangely smooth as Florian shook it.

"And this is Callie." She came forward. The angel nodded at her, his eyes narrowed thoughtfully, but he didn't extend his hand.

"Yes. Hello, Callie." Florian noticed Callie shiver as she returned the nod.

"What brings you to the threshold, sir?" He collected the empty bottle.

"I'm meeting someone. Please call me Gabriel."

Callie did a double take. "I'm sorry. You're *the* Gabriel?"

"Yes."

"So you're an—"

"An Archangel." The feathered wings spread in demonstration, twelve feet of snow-white, glistening pinions gleaming in the afternoon sunlight as Gabriel smiled indulgently.

"Pleased to meet you," Callie said faintly.

"Likewise." The wings folded away. "They keep you busy, I hear."

"Most nights we're full," Florian acknowledged.

"Do you ever wonder what they do during the day?" Gabriel asked. Florian exchanged a glance with Callie, baffled by the question.

"I know what some of them do." He nodded at the television, where Hera interviewed an Amaranthine celebrity. "They don't particularly keep a low profile."

"They aren't the ones I'm concerned about," the angel declared. "What do the others do—the ones who don't currently play out false lives in front of the public?"

"No idea. I can't say I ever thought about it."

"Charitable works? Gardening? Or do they get blind drunk every Tuesday night?" Gabriel widened his shining eyes meaningfully. "They're seldom idle, the old gods, and when it appears they have nothing to do, they're at their most treacherous."

"Now, Gabe, is that any way to talk about me behind my back?" a familiar voice interjected.

Hermes flashed a crooked grin at the archangel, who rose and greeted him with the warmth of an old friend.

"Hermes. It's been far too long."

"A little less than two thousand years, if I remember correctly." Hermes gripped the archangel's hand and clapped him on the shoulder.

"So even though he has nothing better to do at the moment, he declined the invitation," Gabriel stated matter-of-factly, and Hermes gave him a shrug.

"Did you really expect Big Z would stoop to meeting with the messenger, however exalted you might be?" he asked with a wink. "He sent me, brother."

Hermes took a seat beside the archangel at the bar, greeting Florian and the bewildered Callie. "Hey, kids. I'll drink what he's drinking. It must be a red letter day when one of the Most High's most high wants a beer."

"Cider," Florian corrected automatically.

"Whatever. Just keep 'em coming."

Callie scrambled to set a bottle before Hermes, who tipped half the liquid into his glass and raised a toast to Gabriel. "Here's to the messengers."

"To successful negotiations." Gabriel met Hermes's glass with his own, taking another cautious sip. Hermes took a healthy gulp and turned his attention to Florian.

"Can we have a little space? I think Gabe's got something he wants to discuss with me."

Florian nodded and motioned to Callie, and they both went to the other end of the bar. He opened the dishwasher and they quietly stacked away the clean glasses. From that vantage point they could still listen, and not be intrusive.

Hermes downed a goodly part of his drink and smacked his lips in appreciation. "So, what's the scoop from on High?"

"He wants to know if Zeus is serious about this." Gabriel's radiant face creased with concern.

Frowning, Hermes stiffened, and then sighed. "Is Zeus serious," he repeated, his voice rising on the last word as if in question. "Of course he is."

"If he's asking permission to violate the contract, he isn't going to receive it," the archangel said in a clipped tone.

"He isn't asking for permission." Hermes's expression hardened a bit. "He doesn't have to. Call this notification of intent. He's the King of the Gods, for God's sake." He put out a calming hand as the archangel's wings ruffled in irritation. "Sorry."

"King of the old gods," Gabriel corrected. "Hermes, the contract is inviolate. Even our side can't, and won't, negate it on matter of principle."

"Our side?" Hermes quirked a grin, but his eyes didn't reflect humor. "So we're choosing sides, now. Man, does that sound friendly."

"Did you think it could end any differently?" Gabriel countered.

"I suppose not." Hermes downed the rest of his drink and signaled to Florian, still listening as unobtrusively as he could without appearing to eavesdrop. He placed another opened bottle on the bar in front of Hermes and rejoined Callie as the god continued, "I was hoping it wouldn't come to this."

"So was God." Gabriel took another tiny sip of the golden liquid in his own glass, and smiled thinly. "Michael's spoiling for a fight, though."

"Yeah, well, so is Ares. We need to keep an eye on them." Hermes shook his head. "Big Z just wants his due. The rise in practitioners of the old ways proves that humans want something real and tangible in terms of gods. They want proof positive we exist, like in the old days, and Zeus feels we should give them another chance."

"And he's going to do that here?"

"Right here in the heart of America, in the giant, sparkly buckle of the Bible Belt?" Hermes tipped his glass. "Nah. He's not that kind of confrontational at the moment. His plans are more subtle."

"The words *subtle* and *Zeus* are never used in conjunction. The contract expressly forbids divine intervention and material apparition." Gabriel glowered fiercely beneath his radiant brow. Hermes snorted.

"Funny, since the Jesus situation provoked the whole contract issue in the first place. He gave them proof in living flesh that He exists."

"And they killed him. His mortal body, at least," Gabriel reminded Hermes. "Zeus would do well to remember it. They may want proof, but when it appears they don't accept it."

"He reckons he can handle any negative flak." Hermes's voice took on a cowboy drawl.

"But can the humans?" Gabriel tapped on the bar with one finger to mark the point. "This isn't a game, my old friend. Casualties will be astronomical, mark my words. They already fight amongst themselves over the names of God and which is the True Faith. Can you imagine what might happen if mythology is suddenly proven to be true? The potential for bloodshed is staggering."

"Not if Zeus intervenes."

"But if Zeus intervenes in material form, by default God would seem the new mythology. He is not happy about those implications, believe me." Gabriel took a healthier swig of the cider, and coughed. "He truly is a jealous God, Hermes. He won't stand idly by if Zeus makes a bid for supremacy. And if we in the heavens go to war the debris will rain on Earth."

"And He won't intervene?"

"No." Gabriel's mouth became a grim line. "These humans choose their own path. He won't violate the contract on Earth, but He will take it out of Zeus's hide if he tries to change the balance."

Hermes downed the remains of his second drink. "Then we have a problem."

"You always did have a gift for understatement." Gabriel sounded resigned. "Will you give him this, then?" A sealed scroll appeared in the archangel's hand, drawn from nowhere.

"What, no burning bushes? No pillars of fire?" Hermes took the scroll. "What is it?"

"A declaration of war." Gabriel stood and nodded to Florian and Callie, both of whom had ceased pretending not to listen and now stared in alarm at the archangel. "This place will be neutral territory if any further negotiations are necessary. But the terms are clear enough."

"It doesn't have to be this way." Hermes rose also, facing the archangel squarely.

"Yes, it does." Gabriel smiled sadly. He extended his right hand. "Goodbye, my friend. I hope when next we meet, it is not on the battlefield."

"Me too, Gabe. Me too." Hermes took his offered hand, and placed the other on the archangel's shoulder. Gabriel returned the gesture, his expression full of regret before he blinked out of sight. The messenger of the old gods watched him disappear, and then swiveled back to where Florian and Callie stood gaping behind the bar.

"You look like you could use a drink, kids." Hermes slid Gabriel's abandoned glass of cider, nearly full, toward Callie. "Go ahead. You can't get germs from an angel."

Florian couldn't process the conversation he just heard. "Did he say war?"

"Yeah." Hermes looked grimly at the scroll and tucked it into the inner breast pocket of his suit jacket.

"Then Zeus was serious last night about making a comeback?" Florian blurted in disbelief.

"Why does everybody keep asking me if Zeus is serious?" Hermes growled in irritation. "He's bored." His eyes narrowed. "But what I want to know is this: who told Gabriel? Zeus isn't ready to make his move yet. We're weeks away from opening night. So how did they find out?"

"He said people are going to get killed." Callie, pale and stricken, rounded the bar.

"Not by us, if we can help it. Zeus is betting God can't keep His hand out of it if things really get shaking. It won't be like last time."

"Last time?" A rising note of alarm sharpened her voice.

"Mmm-hmm." Hermes downed the last of Gabriel's drink when it became apparent she wasn't interested in it. "Hey, did he stiff you for the beer? That's rich." He pulled a fifty out of the air and put it on the bar. "Thanks. I'll be seeing you soon."

"Wait a minute!" Florian stammered, both curious and afraid to know what happened 'last time.' Hermes raised an eyebrow and regarded them both, leaning conspiratorially on the bar.

"The less you know the better. Trust me on this. Otherwise, your mind will be running off on tangents every time you see a disaster on the TV. Shit happens all the time and we're not—well, we're *usually* not responsible. When Z makes his move, you'll know."

"But can't you talk to Zeus?" Callie came around the bar to plead with him.

Hermes snorted. "Like he listens to me. I warned him about Atlantis, but did Zeus listen? No. The whole continent sank." He paused as he took in Callie's distress. "Maybe that isn't such a good example at the moment. Don't sweat it. It will all work out. Trust me."

Hermes disappeared, leaving them in the deserted bar, the blended murmur of the televisions the only sound except for Callie's rapid breathing. She put her hands over her mouth and made a small, strangled sound.

"Callie, these little squabbles between pantheons happen more often than you think. You just didn't know about them before." Florian came through the drop leaf. He left out the fact that to his knowledge, God and His angels had never taken part before. It unnerved him a bit more, but he kept that opinion in his own thoughts. "Hermes is right, it will work itself out."

"No!" Callie shook her head vehemently. "Your grandmother, that's what she was talking about last night. About the angels fighting."

"Callie, Gran is—" he searched for the right words. "You can't always take what she says to heart. She's not right in her mind."

"But this is what I've been seeing in my visions!" Callie grasped the edge of the bar, trembling. "Angels fighting in armor. There was fire and ash, and people dead everywhere. It will happen if I don't stop it somehow."

Confused, he shook his head slowly. "Why do you have to stop it?"

"Bridget said I was the key. That I had to find a way."

"Her visions have never been reliable, even before she..." he stopped himself, not certain he wanted that particular story in the open just yet.

"Maybe not, but mine have been." She paced restlessly, one knuckle pressed against her teeth. "All my warnings or visions have come true. I have put up with this thing, this gift, since I was thirteen. I took medicine and the seizures got better. The visions got less frequent but never went away, but they have never been so clear or as detailed as the one I had last night."

He knew why. Florian cursed silently before he spoke. "It was the ambrosia. I told you it makes those gifts we have more powerful."

"I almost saw them. Someone is watching, and laughing." Callie, wide-eyed, covered her mouth with her hand. "I think it might the person who told Gabriel about Zeus's plans. They want this war to start!"

9

DESPITE HERMES'S attempt to reassure them, Florian was glad to have something to occupy his mind and his hands. He spent most of Wednesday afternoon creating fruits and vegetables from ambrosia, not only garnishes but more salad-bar fare and whole oranges which he would juice once his customers arrived.

"You sure about these being safe?" Callie looked up from her task. He had set her to polishing fragile crystal bowls, an attempt to take her mind from the frightening vision and unsettling information they'd learned. "They look way too delicate to hold up to a crowd like last night's."

"They'll be fine. It's Sidhe night." He pulled another puff of ambrosia out of the casket in preparation to make pastry.

Callie set the bowl down with care and eyed him dubiously. "Sidhe night. You mean, like...fairies. I thought Hermes meant Puck was gay."

"Puck doesn't prefer one gender over another. Most Sidhe don't." Neither did Florian, and he wondered briefly what she might think of that. "But it's odd he was here. They don't usually mix with the Amaranthine—Puck, in particular. I didn't expect him to be here last night."

"Why not?"

"Tension between the Sidhe and the Amaranthine has gone on forever, and I do mean, forever. I don't know why."

"So are they huge party animals like last night, or what?"

"Well, they will drink anyone under the table regardless of size, and a couple of them are sugar junkies." He grinned at her from the sideboard where he began to craft a layered torte. "But they're much better behaved, for the most part. Stefanio granted the fairies access when he first took over the threshold because he insisted America is the land of equal opportunity. It caused a lot of grumbling, but he stayed adamant. All immortals are welcome here, no matter what pantheon or origin."

Callie blew fragments of dust from the last piece of faceted crystal and gently attacked it with a soft cloth. "Stefanio sounds as if he liked to shake up the status quo."

"You have no idea. That was just the first time he stood up to the Amaranthine. " Florian swallowed against the sudden, bittersweet taste of nostalgia in the back of his throat. He missed Stefanio and his endless patience, kindness, and mentorship. "He was never afraid to stand his ground when he believed they were wrong. They can be a bit self-absorbed, in case you didn't notice."

"Really? What else did he do?" Callie set the last bowl down and leaned forward, ready to listen.

"Saved my life." He hesitated, surprised he'd blurted it out like that. He teetered on the edge of confession, but at the last second backed away from it. He was not ashamed of who he was, but couldn't say the same about how he'd behaved. Before she could ask anything more, he quickly changed the subject. "There's a cabinet in the back room. If you open it, you'll find some drapes for the pool table. Would you cover them, please?"

"Sure." He chided himself for his cowardice as questions created a furrow between Callie's lovely brown eyes, soft eyes that made his breath catch every time she turned her gaze on him. She slid from the stool and did as he asked while he pretended great industry over the next layer of torte and cursed at himself under his breath. He was out of practice talking to people. What did one say to start a friendship these days?

He heard her exclaim in triumph as she opened the louvered cabinet in the back room. "Ah, sweet! You do have a washer and dryer. Am I allowed to use them for laundry?"

"Yeah, of course. The detergent is on the shelf. The drapes are on the other side."

She came back out with an armful of beautiful velvet covers, decorated with satin fringes and intricate Celtic embroidery. "You mean these?"

"Yes. Just cover the tables with them. The Sidhe don't play pool. They're more the dancing type."

He quickly finished the torte as she worked. Drizzles of moon-pale ambrosia eclipsed to dark, velvety chocolate in mid-drop from his fingertips and sketched ganache lace atop the dessert. He set it aside on a cake pedestal and stole another glance at Callie. This gravitational pull toward another human being was understandable, given the circumstances, but it went beyond a passing interest. As Doorkeeper, he was bound by tradition to offer a safe haven, and Stefanio had cautioned him not to take liberties with those he sheltered.

She caught him watching her as she smoothed the first of the velvet covers over a table. His mouth opened, but nothing came out. Embarrassed, he quickly glanced away and shut the lid of the ambrosia casket.

"Every time it seems like you might want to say something, you take two steps back," Callie said lightly. "I'm sorry I was such a jerk yesterday. If there's something you need to say about work, I promise I won't bite."

"It's nothing, really." He busied himself brushing non-existent crumbs from his workspace. "And you weren't a jerk, just caught off guard. You're handling this very well. I know it must all seem completely mad."

She straightened. "How did you handle it, when you found out?"

The soft huff of self-deprecation accompanied his crooked grin. "Not as well as you. I got monumentally drunk afterwards."

"No." She cocked her head. "Really? I can't see that. You seem to be kind of detached from the crazy, even last night when things were wild."

"I've had a lot of time to get used to things."

"How long?" The question was innocent, but Florian sidestepped it clumsily.

"You'll get used to them, too. I need to go up and check on Gran. Would you fold the bar towels in the dryer when you're finished there, please? Then we're done until seven or so."

"Yes, boss." A bemused smile played on her lips as she spread the second cover, and he ducked around the bar in hasty retreat. While he ascended the stairs, he wondered if it were possible to kick himself in the ass.

"You shouldn't be afraid," his grandmother said.

Florian glanced up from chopping vegetables for the late night meal they would prepare after closing. Seated across the kitchen island in his apartment, Bridget had spoken as she stared into her mug, both hands wrapped around the warm porcelain. It was an old, comfortable habit for them to have afternoon tea together before the evening rush.

"Afraid of what, Gran?" he prompted.

"To talk to her. She's a good girl. Not like them."

"You mean Callie?" His knife dissected yellow squash into neat slices.

"Do you have any other girls hidden about the place?" His grandmother looked up at him impudently and sipped her milky tea. He gave her a half grin and scraped the squash into a bowl.

"I'm not afraid to talk to her, Gran. I've done nothing but talk like a blithering idiot since she got here." He started in on the zucchini.

"I don't mean that. You must start somewhere if you're going to love her."

Florian fumbled the knife in surprise, barely missing his fingers. "Are you matchmaking?"

"You're beside her all the while, until the very last," she mumbled.

He put down the knife and wiped his hands on a towel, coming around to kneel in front of her chair. If Bridget entered one of her rare lucid moments, he didn't want to waste any time. "What do you mean? Did you see something?"

"I saw the way you held her after the vision."

Florian cleared his throat. The remembered feel of Callie in his arms created an unexpectedly poignant longing. "I like her, but I don't want to take advantage of her, Gran."

"Nonsense. Your paths are intertwined. But I can't see how it ends. I never can." The mug in her hands drooped and threatened to spill. He gently took the tea from her and put it on the counter, and as he rose Bridget urgently seized his wrists to draw him back down. He noted the coolness of her fingers, despite their having been wrapped around the hot mug, and enveloped them in his own to warm them as she searched his eyes and said with fervent, pressured speech,

"Don't be afraid. She needs you. You understand what she's up against, and your heart is too lovely not to leave it open for others to share. When I am gone, I don't want you to be alone." Her eyes were losing their focus as her sight turned inward again. "He walks among the other angels and whispers, but they can't see him."

"Who?"

Already lost to whatever landscape she viewed in her mind, her lips moved in nonsensical mutters. Florian held her hands a few minutes longer, but they never truly warmed.

To Callie's relief, Wednesday night's crowd turned out to be an entirely different scene than the previous high-testosterone, frat party vibe which pervaded the bar's back room on Tuesday. For one thing, the Sidhe actually entered through the door—or at least, phased through the glass instead of just popping into the room.

Diminutive, winged fairies fluttered about and used the wooden surface itself as a seating area. Florian moved carefully among them and filled the crystal bowls with fruity drinks that they consumed in a communal fashion, slurping in a disconcertingly uncouth manner for such ethereal little creatures. More human-sized fair folk occupied the booths and reminded Callie of new-age bookstore clientele in their tie-dyed, free-flowing clothes, gauzy scarves and glittery jewelry. Ambient trance music played on the digital system, and the boho-chic fairies spun and swayed dreamily in the empty spaces between the tables.

It was a much more relaxed atmosphere. Callie didn't have to rush back and forth dodging gropes although some of the brownies were pinchers. For the most part, if someone wanted service, their body emitted a silvery glow. It was a relief after being hailed with *Hey, babe!* every thirty seconds during her previous shift.

Just as Florian said she could expect, the covered pool tables went unused for gaming. They became a kind of lounging area full of pillows and wildflowers, which appeared out of nowhere. A male and a female, both of them beautiful and ageless, occupied the two tables closest to the front. Smaller fairies clustered adoringly around them and nestled into the cushions.

"Who are they?" They made Callie think of the elf queen and king from the *Lord of the Rings* movies, but only if it were remade as an artsy porn film. The couple emitted a decidedly sexual aura, each gesture a study in sensuality.

"That's Ron and Sunshine. You probably know them as Oberon and Titania."

"As in, Shakespeare?" Callie bounced gleefully. "So, *A Midsummer Night's Dream* is a historical play and not just a comedy?"

"No, not exactly. They'll tell you that the whole play is a lie, and that they never invited Shakespeare to any of their parties because he was a frightful bore."

"So, what about *The Tempest*? Was Prospero an Amaranthine? Was there really an Ariel and a Caliban?"

"I never asked." Florian grinned at her. "You look like you're in a candy store."

"Are you kidding? This is what I used to dream about when I was seven! I still can't believe fairies are real, too. Next you'll be telling me hobbits exist."

He gave her a sidelong, meaningful look, and her jaw dropped. For a split second she believed him, and then noted the twinkle in his eyes. A definite smirk pulled at his lips.

"You have a mean streak, don't you?" she accused.

"It was just too easy." That smile was back and he laughed, a deep, infectious sound that made her grin. A few of the little fairies hovering around the bar stopped and stared as if they'd never heard laughter before, and tittered among themselves.

A rippling luminescence, like silver light reflected off water, called her to the back room. Still grinning, Callie went to ask what the royal couple required. The scent of flowers and essential oils forced her to stifle a sneeze, and she choked it back.

"Good evening. I'm Callie. What can I get for you?"

"Ah, new blood!" Oberon rose up on one elbow amidst the pile of satiny cushions and nudged smaller fairies out of the way. He wore a pirate sleeved silk shirt, his silver-blond hair caught in a loose pony-tail. His features were delicate but with an unmistakably masculine beauty. He extended his hand palm up, and Callie realized belatedly that he wanted her to take it. She hesitated but at last put her hand in his.

Oberon brought it to his face, softly rubbing his nose and lips against her palm. It reminded her of the way a cat marked people, but with calculated suggestion of unspoken pleasures. He grinned up at her and one eyebrow rose as he inhaled her scent. The sensation of something invisible moving against her skin toward his open mouth made her muscles tighten but she didn't pull away. It was less discon-certing than the crawly sensation she experienced with Puck, more sensual, and heat rose to her cheeks.

"Hmm. Sunshine, this one is delicious."

Titania extended her hand languidly from the other table. For a moment Callie juggled her order pad indecisively, for Oberon still hadn't let go. She stuffed the pad into the apron pocket and hastily gave Titania her other hand, which the queen of the fairies examined in the same manner as her consort: feline and erotic, no less arousing. In fact, caught between the two of them it was damned sexy. Heat blossomed in places that made Callie's knees go rubbery. She with-drew her hands politely but firmly, uncertain whether she should be creeped out or flattered. Her warning system gave no twinges either way.

Titania exchanged a glance with Oberon from beneath raven curls, mischief in her eyes.

"This one's not for play, darling. She has a destiny."

"Oh." Oberon pouted in disappointment.

"Can I bring you something? Food, drinks?" Callie suppressed an urge to fan herself with the order pad.

"Absinthe, if you please." As Titania stretched and displaced some of the cushions, her long hair fell away from her body and warmth rushed back to Callie's face. Naked, Titania's lush figure was adorned with nothing but a rope of pearls and some strategically placed body glitter. The little sprites snuggled against her lovingly and tucked themselves into intimate areas. Callie cleared her throat, turning to Oberon.

"And for you, sir?"

"Find out what Florian has in the way of sweets tonight, my pet. I'm in the mood for sugar."

Scribbling on her order pad, Callie escaped the heated, carnal atmosphere that bathed the royal couple. She was no prude, but the way Titania and Oberon regarded her was almost as if she were on the menu as well as the house special.

Halfway through the night, Puck reappeared. He wore a black trench coat and eyeliner, more emo than his punk incarnation. She also noted he looked older tonight, closer to her own age. A cloaked figure walked with him, veiled in shadow. Try as she might Callie could not quite focus on his companion.

"Who is that?" she whispered to the busy Florian as he fashioned a chocolate torte for Oberon.

"Who?" he glanced up quickly.

"With Puck."

He craned his head, looking. "I don't see him. I'm sorry."

Puck and his shadowy cohort slid into the booth farthest from the king and queen, a dark and intimate corner. He caught Callie watching him and frowned for a second, then blew her a kiss as he slid into the shadows. When she approached to take his order after delivering the torte to Oberon, Puck sat on one side of the table, his phantasmal companion on the other side. He waved her away with a troubled expression.

Later, Puck finally came and leaned on the bar beside her as Callie waited for Florian to fill an order of tofu and sprouts. The soy paste seemed easy enough to shape, but the sprouts finicky, and he was preoccupied at the sideboard with the meal preparation. Her early warning system manifested itself as goose bumps, and she didn't give Puck a chance to touch her. She greeted him with courtesy and kept an arm's length away.

"Well, aren't you a sight for sore eyes, love," he said. "Tequila straight with lime, when you have a moment."

"No salt?" Callie asked innocently, and Puck recoiled with a dramatic hiss. On the counter, several of the little winged creatures froze in midair and stared at her balefully. Callie eyed them with trepidation until they dived face first back into the bowl of vodka and orange juice and slurped noisily.

"New girl, Florian's not teaching you what you need to know," Puck proclaimed. "We fae can't abide salt. Magic lore 101, love. Get your facts straight before you cause an unfortunate accident."

"Pan used half a shaker last night," Callie remarked, puzzled, and Puck sneered.

"Goat men aren't Sidhe." His expression darkened. "We're different from those Amaranthine barbarians. We're much, much older, and more powerful. We never bothered with temples and virgins. Never had any use for virgins, myself. Zeus and his lot had nothing better to do than pose for statues, blunder around destroying things, and listen to their sheep make up stories about their fucking greatness."

Not sure how to respond to his unexpected vitriol, she stayed silent. Puck noted her discomfiture and shook himself. His features softened back to a mischievous mien.

"Anyway, back to tequila. Care to join me for a shot?"

"I'm sorry, I'm working." Her stock answer was received with a skeptical raised eyebrow, and she nodded toward his shadowy booth. "Besides, don't you have a guest?"

"No, I think not." His answer was short as he ran a hand through his spiky hair, his gaze darting to the corner. She followed his attention and saw a group of brownies piling into the now-empty booth.

When he spoke again his voice was gentle and husky, taking her by surprise with its sensuality. "Whenever you're not working, I would be honored to share a drink with you, Callie."

"I'm sorry, are you flirting with me?" Callie asked incredulously.

"Why are you surprised?" Puck's smile was slow and seductive. "You're a beautiful woman. And full of many talents, I suspect." His lips, full and inviting, entranced her and Callie forced herself to look up and meet his eyes. They were blue-green, shimmering like sun on the water, and they mesmerized her.

"I..." Callie was flustered, her early warning system shrieking a faint and frantic alarm behind the warm, sticky sweetness beguiling her mind. "I really have to go back to work."

"Yes, she does, I'm afraid." Florian's voice cut sharply through the tangle of confusion and startled her back into clarity. "Here's the order you've been waiting on." He set the plate of tofu and sprouts in front of her on a tray.

"Thanks," she managed. She shook her head to clear it. Something had almost happened, but it was fading in her consciousness. Florian looked angry, and she didn't remember why. Puck leaned beside her, smiling and smug. "I'm sorry. I'll take this out right away."

She picked up the tray and hurried toward the waiting customers, the incident already forgotten.

PUCK'S EYES lingered on Callie's behind as she walked away. "Quite interesting, indeed."

"I'll thank you not to use glamour on my wait staff." Florian's voice was low and dangerous.

"Oh, lighten up, mate. I don't plan on hurting her. I have something much more pleasant in mind."

"Leave her alone." Florian said it a bit more loudly than he intended. Puck stared him down, and a couple of the fluttering fairies nearby looked up and giggled.

"OOOOooooh," they said in chorus, as if marveling at Florian's bravado, and giggled some more.

"Oh, I get it." Puck grinned broadly. "You're starting to fancy her, aren't you?"

"I—" it was Florian's turn to be flustered. He turned away and seized a bottle of tequila and a shot glass. Puck watched him pour the amber liquid with a knowing smirk. Florian stabbed a lime crescent with a toothpick a little more violently than was necessary, and held it out.

The fairy plucked the lime slice from the skewer and met Florian's eyes in a defiant manner. "I think there might be more to lovely Callie than meets the eye, hmm?"

"She doesn't know how to defend herself against your kind yet."

"Oh, but she did, nonetheless." Puck muttered. He threw the shot back and shredded the lime with his teeth, sucking the juice with relish. He flicked the spent rind at Florian. It hit his chest and dissolved into a faint white wisp that floated down to cling like fog on the front of Florian's black t-shirt.

Puck lowered his voice as Callie came closer. "I don't peg her as the type that goes for older men."

Florian stilled, and Puck crowed delightedly.

"Oh, you haven't told her any of that yet!" He leaned in to whisper loudly, "Cradle robber. When are you up for parole, anyway?"

Florian motioned him to keep it down. "There has been no time or opportunity to explain."

"Time is something you have in spades, isn't it?" Puck narrowed his eyes. "Well, get a move on. I don't wait. She's caught my eye. But a little glamour goes a very long way. If you're lucky you can still take a ride on my coattails tonight, so to speak." They exchanged a lingering glance: Puck's of challenge, Florian's of anger. Puck finally walked away, chuckling as he made his way slowly to the back room.

Florian scowled and swept away the white vapor from the front of his shirt, then tossed the shot glass carelessly into the suds-filled sink below the bar. The two tiny, winged fairies serving as spectators to his altercation with Puck giggled again. He glared at them. It only increased their giggles even more.

"What's so funny?" Callie inquired, returning with a fistful of cash for the register.

"Nothing," Florian assured, with a warning glance at the two fairies. Gleefully, they zoomed in circles around Callie's head, and she ducked, laughing nervously. Little white flowers drifted down in their wake and formed a delicate wreath that landed atop Callie's auburn hair, the scent of lily-of-the-valley strong and sweet. *She is so beautiful,* he thought helplessly as she laughed in delight and examined her bottle-framed reflection in the mirrored shelf.

Infuriating though he may be, Puck hit a nerve. Bridget's heartfelt admonition forced him to admit it.

Florian was lonely.

The wall he'd built around himself was a reminder not to mistake the Amaranthine's interest as anything but self-serving. He had played with fire and it nearly cost him his life. The cautious friendship with Hermes, different from any other, was still at a distance as he went through the motions of his indentured service. Florian's devotion to Bridget was both a penance and an honor, returning what she'd given him without reservation and which he could never repay in full.

Then Callie stumbled across the threshold with her persistent efforts to engage him. He was alive again where he had been all but dead in name and prospect. The wall tumbled down, never meant to stand against an avalanche of hope.

How he came to be Doorkeeper could change Callie's perception of him forever, but he would have to tell her the truth.

12

THE SIDHE DIDN'T LINGER, and the bar emptied at midnight. The fairy Court paraded out through the glass front of the establishment, cushions and pillows disappearing in increments and leaving the faint scent of flowers and patchouli in their wake. On his way out the door, Puck stopped where Callie wiped down the tables. Before she could find a way to prevent it he claimed and kissed her hand.

"Good night, lovely Callie," he said in farewell. Instead of the sensation of something flowing toward him, Puck breathed out against her skin. Warmth spread across the back of her hand and into her veins. Inexplicably she found herself blushing, a little breathless and pleasantly aware of the soft and sensual touch of his lips against her skin. A strange, disconnected arousal threatened to override her warning system's urges to retreat, but she pulled away weakly. He smirked as he released her hand. Callie opened her mouth to protest but stopped. He hadn't done anything but say goodbye...had he? The odd feeling something should concern her didn't stay in her mind for more than a few seconds after he let her go. She stood there, blinking, uncertain what just happened.

Puck strode away, catlike, with a raised eyebrow and a finger pointed at Florian. As he winked out across the threshold, his trench coat swirling around him, Florian glowered at Puck's back until he noticed Callie watching. He quickly checked his expression.

The tips were slightly less generous than Tuesday's haul, but still more than she ever made in one night's time waiting the college bars. While they were cleaning, Bridget wandered down again with a basket of ingredients Florian had assembled before coming to work. He prepared the quick, light meal of chicken and vegetables, and while he was busy the elderly woman's unnervingly direct gaze fixed on Callie. It made her shiver as she hung up her apron, returning her regard with a wary eye. Bridget's attentiveness did not seem malevolent, but more as if she expected something. Callie took the seat next to her and smiled cautiously.

"Hi, Bridget."

"You look like a bride." Bridget raised a frail hand to Callie's hair and touched the flowers entwined there. A lovely smile lit her face before she withdrew into herself again, her eyes taking on that unfocused gaze. Callie listened to Bridget's breathy mutterings with dread, waiting for her to say something about the war and Callie's role in preventing it. She didn't.

Bridget took her plate upstairs, favoring them with a beatific smile that made Florian grin and shake his head. Callie wondered what *that* was about. They were alone in the deserted bar, and he took their plates to one of the empty tables rather than sitting at the counter.

Callie savored the first bite of chicken and its rich, buttery pan sauce with a happy sigh. "This is amazing."

"Thank you. I like having someone besides Gran and me to really cook for. Ambrosia doesn't require the same sort of preparation."

"Did you study?"

"I did, a bit. I was a commis chef. I worked in hotel kitchens all over Europe—even India and China for a few months. It expanded my experience with different cuisines and that helps with the ambrosia when they order something unusual. But I never stayed long enough in one place to really master anything. Some creature would catch up with me, and I'd be off again."

"How did you keep escaping from them?"

A long pause. Callie waited for the door to slam in her face again. To her surprise, he took a breath and answered as he stabbed at a piece of chicken on his plate.

"For a while, one of the Amaranthine kept me safely hidden until I was able to find a new place."

"Do they do that often?" Callie could not help but wonder how things might have been different, if someone had protected her mother.

"Only when they want something from you." He pushed his food around with the fork before he looked up and met her eyes.

"If one of them starts paying you undue attention, it isn't necessarily a good thing," he stated quietly. His voice rang with regret. "It's flattering. They can make you think taking notice of you is the most incredible thing in the world. The power, the beauty: everything's intoxicating at first. But that's all a lie. They aren't human and never will be despite their occasional dabbling with a mortal life. Most of them do it only because of the rush of energy they get from our attention. They don't care how they hurt us, or what it costs us."

"What did it cost you?" The question left her lips before she could stop it.

Florian hesitated. "Ask me again sometime. Just don't make the same mistake I did, Callie." He cleared his throat and shifted in his chair. "Enough about me. All I know about you is that you majored in the classics."

"Well, I'm from Vermont. A little college town where both my parents are tenured professors."

"Ah, that family tradition you mentioned."

"Yes." Surprised, it warmed her he remembered that.

"So, which one of them has Amaranthine blood?"

"Neither, I guess. I'm adopted." She pushed her food around her plate. "I was old enough though that I remember my real mom. She was very young."

"What happened to her?" His voice became softer. She loved the way Florian listened to her with his full attention, his head cocked to the side.

"Since you told me about the hunters last night, I've been thinking it must have been something like the banshee." Callie swallowed, her throat dry. "I remember sleeping in strange places and more than once waking up in the middle of the night to leave really fast. One night we were sleeping in her car because we ran out of gas, and there was this weird howl that woke us up. She kissed me and covered me up with a blanket. She told me not to move, to be a big girl and not to cry, and she'd be back for me as soon as the sun came up. She never came back. I think that she must have led it away from me."

She shivered, remembering. "I got scared, so sometime after dawn I got out of the car even though she had told me to stay. I wandered around crying and calling for her and ended up downtown near the campus. The sun was really bright and reflecting off a plate glass window in front of me. This security guard just appeared out of nowhere as if he walked out of the light, like a picture of Apollo in the book I had as a kid." She laughed softly. "Funny how you remember stuff that way when you're little. To me it was magic. He picked me up and told me not to worry, that he would take care of me. The couple that adopted me were already foster parents in the system and he took me to their house."

"I'm sorry." His eyes were sympathetic. It occurred to her this was almost more like a date than two co-workers talking. She loved the way he gave her his full attention, his head cocked to the side as he listened.

"Thank you." She shrugged. "Richard and Caroline Davies are the best parents anyone could ask for. I couldn't have chosen better myself."

"Do they know about your visions?"

"They were more worried about the seizures. The doctors said I have audiovisual hallucinations brought on by my disorder, but Mom saw some of the things I said coming out of seizures actually got reported on World News Tonight." Callie pushed a piece of squash around her plate. "My meds made the seizures a lot less frequent but I ran out of them after I left home. Ever since the banshee, the visions got more intense. I feel like I need to warn people about what I see coming but it all sounds crazy." She swallowed heavily. "And if I don't warn them, it will be my fault if they die."

"That's too a heavy burden to place on yourself," Florian shifted uncomfortably in his chair. "There's no guarantee they would believe you if you did. Why should it be your fault?"

"I know it's not rational. But it's how I feel. There has to be some kind of meaning to it. I hope I don't have visions just to make my life suck."

They talked long after they finished eating, mostly about less consequential things like music, books, and movies. Florian seemed to have read every book and seen every movie there was, except for the most current films. When Callie remarked on that, he responded wryly that by necessity he didn't get out much. His deep laughter came more often and made her smile but he always managed to deflect conversation back to her when she would ask questions.

Finally, their plates loaded into the dishwasher, Florian turned out the lights. They climbed the stairs together and her arm touched his as she turned the corner at the landing, an innocent brush of skin on skin that made her shiver deliciously. He stopped, one hand on the newel post, and Callie paused on the second step, his face just a few inches below hers. She watched his expressive mouth and wondered what it would be like to feel those lips on hers, to pull him against her and—

She mentally shook herself. What was wrong with her? She never thought these things!

He had been smiling, but his expression changed as his eyes moved to her mouth: a spark of desire, its heat as it grew to flame drawing her closer. That hungry blossom of fire made the butterflies in her stomach dance.

"Good night, then." The rough edge of need in his voice destroyed any reservations she may have had. He began to move away, but before she could stop herself she leaned over the rail to kiss him.

His surprised intake of breath lasted only a second before he responded. His lips moved against hers with maddening softness; one hand reached up and traced her jawline with gentle fingers. She was filled with a sense of rightness, of safety, and growing arousal. It was exciting, but Florian seemed to be holding back. She pulled away slowly.

"I'm sorry," she faltered, but the longing and cautious hope in his expression stunned her.

"Oh, please don't be sorry." His voice husky, he drew her back to him. Master of this kiss, the tip of his tongue teased the edges of her mouth. A hungry electric current passed through them. Callie's arms went around him, the bannister an unwelcome obstacle between their bodies. His fingers threaded through her hair, dislodging the sweet white flowers that still crowned her, devouring her lips with a fire she answered in kind until he pulled away abruptly. Trembling, his breathing as quick and ragged as her own, he cupped her face with his hands as if holding a fragile, precious thing.

"Callie, you don't know anything about me yet," he managed to say, his forehead against hers.

"I don't care." She sought his lips again. He groaned like a broken man and kissed her for a brief, heated moment before he closed his hands gently upon her shoulders and moved back.

"You have no idea how much I want this...want you, Callie...but Puck used a glamour on you tonight. It's a bit like being drunk, and this may not be entirely your choice. It should wear off by morning. If you still feel the same way, we have time." A stilted laugh escaped him. "There is so much time." He fumbled for the doorknob to his apartment, stumbling backward over the threshold with endearing clumsiness. "Good night."

His door closed. Callie lingered in confusion on the steps for a moment until hot embarrassment prompted her retreat. She took the stairs two at a time and shut the door, leaning against it. Her defeated libido still reeled in a steaming, fantasy-laden muddle from that kiss.

Fairy magic?

It might explain the odd, visceral twinges her warning system gave whenever Puck touched her, not to mention the strange, arousing encounter with Titania and Oberon. Her abruptly misplaced inhibitions concerning Florian were not solely due to glamour, though. Her attraction to him was clear—something of a novelty for her, but not unheard of.

Irrationally peeved at him for turning down her advances, part of her still recognized he was being honorable. She stalked off to her bedroom and flung herself down on the bed but found it difficult to sulk with the memory of that hungry, desperate kiss. She touched her lips and smiled, a silly, giddy bubble bursting in her chest.

The last of the fairy-gifted flowers in her hair tumbled to the quilt when she rose at last, and she picked one up, lifting the waxy white bells on their slender stalk and inhaling the perfume.

The next breath came in a convulsive gasp as a vision gripped her in paralysis, her muscles screaming.

An explosion erupts in the air. Windows shatter into deadly needles of glass. Cries of terror and the sound of running feet. Bodies lay in the streets. Blood pools black in the darkness. Toppled columns, like a library leveled by a bomb. Shapes grapple in the smoke and red light, wings and spears and armor. The unseen person beside her laughs, a sound filled with cackling glee and malice. A solitary figure of a woman stands silhouetted against a burning sky.

A strangled cry, extruded from her painful exhalation, rang in her ears when she came back to awareness. Driven to her knees beside the bed, she buried her head in her arms and sobbed against the quilt, shattered by the vision.

War was coming.

Callie had no idea how she could be the one to stop the carnage.

13

Sun streamed through a gap between the blackout curtains. Her wristwatch read early afternoon, so Callie lay for a few moments and absorbed the warmth of the narrow beam until its heat against her cheek became too much.

She stretched, yawned, and froze as she remembered her uncharacteristically forward behavior with Florian. The glamour had worn off, and with it, most of her confidence.

Groaning, she punched the pillow. Romantic relationships had never before held an allure for her. Consequentially, they weren't a strong point.

During the time other girls her age were testing the waters of boy-girl parties and holding hands, she spent countless afternoons in the waiting rooms of clinics for tests and diagnosis of her petit mal disorder. The seizures got worse with puberty and at thirteen, visions were thrown into the mix. If she hadn't been a social pariah before, emerging from staring silence with a shriek or incoherent babbling clinched the title.

New medication during her junior year of high school greatly diminished the seizures, but she remained comfortably disengaged from her peers' preoccupation with sex and dating. It just didn't interest her. College started with a whole new group of classmates who didn't remember her awkward phase. Callie still preferred the company of her books but gained a small group of friends and an off-campus roommate.

She'd seldom dated anyone. Just once. A friendship with an art major who worked beside her in her first job at a trendy restaurant started to turn into something more. It was going somewhere until a frightening and inconvenient moment. Nothing quite like teetering on the edge of losing her virginity and going catatonic with a vision of her almost-lover's future career in house painting. Coming to her senses naked and vulnerable, she dressed and fled. He didn't call after. She quit the restaurant and took another job.

The ability to read people with uncanny accuracy blunted her desire to socialize. Answers eluded her to the profound mystery of how other women navigated the terrifying roulette game of dating. Callie learned to trust her early warning system and had accidentally 'spilled' drinks more than once at the sports bar to prevent unsuspecting women from being drugged.

But Florian already knew about her visions, even accepted them. He'd behaved like a gentleman when it counted and was seemingly unaware of his own beauty. Neither of them could ignore that kiss or its potential.

If it didn't work out, the apocalypse was coming, anyway.

She showered and dressed quickly. The options of clothing, limited to jeans and mostly t-shirts, were now at least clean after her discovery of the laundry room. The most attractive top in the pile, a layered cami t-shirt, possessed a deeper neckline. Silencing the practical voices in her conscience, she put it on.

Outside her door Callie turned to descend the stairs and found Bridget standing at the bottom step. The elderly woman held a kettle in her hand and looked lost.

"Bridget, can I help you with something?" she called softly, not wanting to frighten her.

Bridget blinked twice as if coming back from a dream or a vision and turned her eyes to Callie as she reached the landing.

"Oh, hello, dear. I'm looking for Florian but I can't find him. The well isn't where it used to be and I wanted to make some tea."

"I'm happy to help make tea if you want me to," Callie offered, and the woman agreed with relieved eagerness.

Callie followed her through the door opposite Florian's. Twice the size of Callie's, but much different in decor, the apartment gave off the atmosphere of nothing less than an Irish cottage. A comfortable parlor with an unlit fireplace invited someone to sit down for tea at the linen-covered table. Callie filled the kettle with water from an old-fashioned, pump style tap and lit the stove as Bridget took delicate Belleek china cups and a teapot out of the cabinet.

Tenderly stroking the edge of one of the cups, she announced, "These came on the boat with me from Ireland, packed in my underclothes."

This was one of the first coherent things Bridget had said to her. The older woman giggled at Callie's surprise.

"Oh, I have washed them many times since out of necessity," she said with a mischievous glint. "The tea cups *and* my underclothes. Will you join me?"

"I'd like that."

The kettle whistled its steam song. Bridget got out a plate and some bread and butter, a jar of strawberry jam, cream, and sugar. While they waited for the brew to steep, they sat together at the table in the parlor and ate. Bridget appeared unusually lucid this morning, and Callie decided to take advantage of it.

"Can I ask you something about your visions, Bridget? How old were you when they started?"

"Thirteen, it was. I remember well because I was kissing Michael Flaherty behind the convent wall." She favored Callie with an impish smile as she poured the steaming liquid. "I had a vision showing Michael was the one responsible for the death of my cat a few nights before. I gave him a black eye to wear in my moggie's memory and ran, but later I learned he was a brute to women as well as animals."

"You have visions of the past. Do they always prove to be true?" Callie sipped her tea thoughtfully.

"Oh yes, like flipping back the pages of a book. The story never changes."

"Can you see things that haven't happened yet, too?"

"Never so clearly. The Sight points me in the right direction, but the branches twist and turn so, I never seem to take the right turn at the fork in the road. When all is done, I know the path that should have been taken. My gift is the past." The woman's shoulders drooped. "If my visions of the future were clearer, I might have saved them."

"Who, Bridget?" Callie sat forward, listening.

"My husband, my daughter, and all the other poor souls who went down on that ship." Bridget closed her eyes. "Kevin and Maire went ahead to make a safe place for us, and Florian and I stayed behind. He wasn't a year old yet."

"Oh, Bridget, I'm so sorry."

"All I saw was the ice, and I feared Florian would become ill on the crossing. He often got sick as a baby. I didn't even stop to consider it would sink that enormous ship."

The story sounded suspiciously familiar. Callie cocked her head, unable to connect it as Bridget continued, "I made the journey much later. Stefanio and I met on that boat, so it was the will of...of ..." A crisp flap of her hand imparted frustration at her inability to finish the thought. "Well, someone's will, I suppose. Florian was being a naughty boy by then, just twenty, and we parted ways when I emigrated. I was furious with him."

"Oh?" Eager to hear stories of a young, rebellious Florian, Callie sat forward. "What did he do?"

Bridget glanced at her sideways. "Boys will be boys, and some that are beautiful are wicked. Handsome men and wicked women. But all so long ago. He's a good young man and he will make you a fine husband." As Callie blinked, confused into speechlessness, Bridget poured more tea in her cup although she had not sipped any at all. The tea overflowed on the table and created a dribbling cataract to the floor. "Oh, dear. There seems to be a flood." Her forehead creased. "A flood..."

"I'll get a towel." Callie rose to her feet to go to the kitchen, but

Bridget seized her wrist with bruising force. The teapot fell from the woman's other hand, knocked over the cup and sent tea everywhere, the sound of shattering china harsh in Callie's ears.

"The flood! Oh, the water is taking everything!"

The vision filled Callie's sight, her hearing drowned with a rushing noise, like a violent wind.

An immense wall of water pushes inland like a tsunami. Cars, houses, and people churn through a city in its inexorable wake. The heavens on fire. Earth shakes and splits open.

Beside her once more: laughter, maniacal giggling. A woman stands in front of the burning hilltops, faceless and shadowed.

Her wrist wrenched free of the elderly woman's forceful grip as her knees buckled, and she caught the edge of the couch with her hip.

Dazed and reeling with the strength of the vision, she realized it was not the same one that blindsided her last night. The city she saw was familiar to her from a scholarly summer vacation with her parents.

Rome. A city much too far off the coast to be at risk from a tidal wave.

More terrible things loomed in the near future. Without any knowledge of how to prevent them, Callie could only stand by in impotent horror as they approached. She rubbed her bruised arm where Bridget's fingers had encircled it and stopped, suddenly staring at the mumbling woman beside her.

Not only had she and Bridget shared the identical vision, it hadn't triggered a seizure.

14

"WHAT JUST HAPPENED?" Callie murmured, not expecting an answer.

Bridget whispered, "Three to share the burden, three to clarify the Sight, always three: past, present, and future."

"What do you mean?"

The elderly woman retreated into muttering confusion once more, the lucidity of the morning shattered like the teacup and saucer. Callie waited in hope she might say more, but the words remained unintelligible. She mopped up the spilled tea with a towel and cleaned up the broken service, placing the delicate china pieces in a box she found on top of a wardrobe in hope they were reparable. Bridget never moved from her place on the sofa, lost in her own mind. Callie waited a moment to be certain she was safe to leave alone.

As she closed the door of Bridget's apartment, she nearly ran headlong into a shirtless, sweaty Florian. Hands brimming with scarlet tomatoes and other vegetables, some of his burden went tumbling. She caught a falling tomato, still warm from the sun, before it hit the floor and they stared at each other for a moment in awkward silence.

"Bridget invited me in for tea," Callie said at last. Florian smiled.

"Did she bring out the Belleek?"

Callie explained in shorthand what happened. The part about the shared vision she left out until she could puzzle out on her own what happened.

Florian sighed and his gaze flickered to Bridget's door. "Gran has spells like that sometimes. She'll be all right. I'll check on her in a little while and repair the china if I can." He gestured with his full hands. "I brought you these, from the garden."

Callie took the offered bounty and tried not to stare. Florian's physique was well defined: not in a gym-rat kind of way, but a hard-working-man kind of way. He was lean and broad-shouldered, with even, tawny-brown skin disappearing under the waist of battered denim jeans. Even covered in perspiration, his scent reminded her of forest and green, growing things. Yep, no question: Florian needed no glamour to attract her. He did perfectly well on his own.

"Pete will be here with the delivery soon." He shifted on his feet. "I wondered if you might let him in while I take a shower. You're safe from the hunters as long as you don't step off the loading dock. The threshold extends partway into the alley."

"Yes, I'll let him in," she blurted. "Thank you for the vegetables."

"Have you been out in the garden yet? The threshold protects it too, so you're safe to go out through your apartment. I think you'll be surprised by it." He lingered a few seconds more, on the cusp of saying something else, then turned with reluctance to his door. She put a foot on the first step to her landing.

"Callie, can we talk about last night?"

She blushed and faced him. The memory of their heated kiss made her pulse trip with a quicker rhythm.

"I understand if you want to keep the relationship between us strictly professional. I meant it when I said there were no strings attached."

"Oh." Dismay and embarrassment deepened the blush. Her heart sank. That kiss...she had been certain it didn't fit the bill of polite reci-procation.

With a rush, he continued, "But if you do think we might...I don't want to have any secrets from you, Callie. You need to know some things about me and how I came to be here. Then, if the glamour isn't the only reason you—" He was adorable, uncertain, and definitely blushing.

"No, not only the glamour." Quick to reassure him, she still found it difficult to meet his eyes directly. A stupid grin tugged at the corners of her mouth and she fought it without success.

"I'm glad." Relief lit up his features. "Then we'll talk later?"

"Yes. I would like that." Before she could embarrass herself any more, she turned and ran up the stairs, hoping she looked graceful doing it. Callie fumbled for the key, juggling tomatoes, and then remembered she left the door unlocked. She hoped he wasn't still watching, but as the knob turned, the click of his door made it clear his exit was delayed.

The back-door bell buzzed like a large, annoying metal wasp by the time she came back out. Callie flew downstairs past Florian's apartment, trying not to envision him in the shower. She pushed open the swinging door to the back room and skirted unopened beer kegs waiting to supply the taps behind the bar. The long, narrow storage area ran the length of the building, parallel to the game room. At the far end, a steel double door loomed.

Shoving the bolts aside, she blinked against the brightness and heat of the summer day as the heavy door swung open. Two men worked inside a delivery truck parked in the alley, backed up to the loading dock. The older of the two, gray haired and with a lined face Callie judged was nearing seventy, looked up and grinned at her.

"You must be Callie. Florian told me on the phone he hired some help. I'm Pete Mackey. Pleased to meet you."

"Good to meet you too, Pete." She found the latch on the other door and swung it open. "I don't know where everything goes yet, but you probably do."

"Been delivering here for around fifty years," Pete agreed as he made a tally mark on his clipboard, "and running errands for Florian ever since he took over. If you'll sign here, I'll start bringing stuff in. That's my grandson. Gary." He nodded toward the younger man in the back of the truck and lowered his voice. "Gary unloads the stuff off the truck, but he can't see through the threshold."

"You can, I take it?" Callie whispered.

"It's a little blurry. I can still cross, but my kids and grandkids can't. My family had a gifted ancestor four or five generations back. The soup's pretty thin now."

"You don't have to worry about the hunters?"

"Not tasty enough, I guess. Doesn't keep me from running away if I see one though."

Callie signed the delivery confirmation. He took the clipboard back and thanked her, hanging it on a hook inside the truck. Gary pushed a two-wheeled dolly laden with cases of beer just up to the loading dock, and Pete took it the rest of the way inside as Gary heaved boxes on another two-wheeler in the back of the trailer.

Callie scanned the alleyway and the slice of sky above before taking a few tentative steps out to the edge of the dock. "Can I help you?"

Gary startled. "Wow! You're not Florian." He laughed at her. "I never get used to that."

"Get used to what?" she smiled back.

"The way you appeared out of thin air, like he does." He shook his head and peered toward the doorway. "I can't see anything but a brick wall."

"Really?" To Callie, the doorway was there in plain sight, just as she'd seen the windows out front. She spotted Pete inside, unloading cases of beer. Gary shrugged.

"I've been coming on runs with Gramps since I was a kid. I never know where he goes with the deliveries."

"I only started working here myself," Callie admitted. "Things are just a little strange."

"Strange is right." He secured the load on the dolly just as Pete came back with the empty two-wheeler, and traded it out for the loaded one.

"Less talk, more work, Gary," he quipped, rolling it away.

"Yeah, Gramps," Gary hefted more cases of beer. "Florian's one of our biggest customers. He's a nice guy. It's weird how he never changes, though."

"How so?" Callie cocked her head sharply.

"Well, it's like he never ages, I mean. I've known him since I was a kid, and he always looks exactly the same." He started loading cases in earnest. "The grocery boxes are over there. They aren't too heavy if you want to take them one at a time."

Callie thanked him faintly and picked up one of the cartons. Surely Gary didn't mean what she thought he did.

She moved all the groceries inside by the time Florian arrived downstairs, his hair still wet from the shower. He greeted Pete with long-time familiarity and Callie watched out of the corner of her eye as she sorted through the boxes of beer. They treated each other like old friends, and Pete asked after Bridget in hushed tones. But Pete could have done business with Stefanio Pereira and perhaps continued the friendship with his successor.

That didn't ring true in her gut instinct. Callie juggled paradoxes to see where they fell. Given the strangeness of the entire situation and the oddly familiar story Bridget told her that morning, all evidence suggested Florian was decades older than he appeared.

15

WHILE PETE and Florian sorted out the coming week's order, Callie put away cases of beer on the shelves of the massive refrigerated unit in the back room. The same cooler opened into the bar, and the glass-fronted doors provided an abbreviated view of the room on the other side. Through condensation forming on the panes she glimpsed the angels' return.

One moment they weren't there and the next, wings everywhere.

Gabriel stood with a second angel who cast baleful glances around the empty room. She looked over her shoulder. Florian was still outside the back door with Pete after unloading the last cartons of liquor from his two-wheeler. Deeply involved in paperwork, he wasn't aware that customers waited inside. She decided she could handle this on her own for the moment.

Shutting the steel doors on the backside of the cooler, she went into the service area. Gabriel smiled at her, his eyes cool but kind, while the other one continued to scowl with thinly veiled impatience.

"Welcome back, Gabriel."

"Good morning, Callie." A sweep of his hand encompassed his companion. "This is Michael."

The other angel nodded curtly. Like Gabriel on their initial meeting, Michael seemed to be taking measure of her with narrowed eyes, and Callie swallowed, studying him as well. His angular wings resembled those of a bird of prey rather than Gabriel's more dove-like ones. A jolting pause rocked her when she noted he wore armor: a gleaming breastplate, and wrist to elbow vambraces which clanked as he crossed his forearms over his chest and stared at her. The danger was now more tangible, unable to be dismissed.

It was the armor from her visions.

"Is there a large table on the premises?" Gabriel inquired. "We have called a council."

"They're late." Michael's voice rumbled with inconvenience.

"Yes, back here." Beckoning them to follow her, Callie showed them the spacious, twelve-seat table occupying the front of the game room, with benches that would accommodate their wings more easily than chairs.

Michael raised his head and sniffed. "Smells like fairies." A sneer concluded his derisive observation.

A lingering scent of flowers remained in the air even hours after Oberon and Titania vanished. "The Court was here last night," Callie informed him.

"They weren't invited, were they?" a bristling Michael asked Gabriel. Archangel or not, he was a jerk. The other angel shook his head in dismissal.

"No reason to include them. The Sidhe were never part of the contract and would be no asset to our cause. Besides, our territory encompasses theirs."

Callie turned the corner to flick on the lights and stopped short, her eyes peering through the gloom. For a moment she thought she saw a figure lurking in the shadows of the dark game room, a pale crescent of face and a swirl of a coat or cape. She snapped the switch quickly but the room was empty. A shiver left the hair on her arms standing at attention, and she rubbed them, uneasy. The angels walked past her without indication they saw anything amiss.

"This will be adequate. Thank you."

"How many will be joining you?" Callie inquired, and the white-winged messenger made an indecisive gesture.

"The major pantheons were alerted out of courtesy, but I suspect few will take note. Perhaps six, or as many as eight."

The angels took up the position facing the front of the room: the seats of power and control. Callie hurried back to the bar with the intent to call Florian, but a flutter of air made her look up. She skidded to a stop before she ran into the individual who materialized there. Dark haired, with a definite sapphire tint to his skin, eagle's wings folded away as she watched him manifest. A glimpse of a sharp, curved beak transforming into a more human aspect of nose and mouth caught her off guard. Golden eyes turned in her direction.

"*Namaskar.*" He bowed, palms together before his chest, and beamed at her. "I hope I am in the right place." His rich, Oxford-English accent rippled with the fluid modulations of India.

After a second's shocked pause, Callie bowed back. "Are you here for the council?"

"Yes I am, but I haven't been to this threshold before and I fear I somehow became lost. I'm late."

"Everyone else is running late too," Callie confided. "They are over there in the back room. Can I get you something to drink?"

"Not to drink, thank you. But I've heard Florian makes food we can actually eat." A wistful note graced his voice. "I would give the talons on my right foot to try a dish of curry. Is he here?"

"Yes, he is," Callie assured him. "I'll place your order with him. Please forgive me if I'm wrong, but are you Garuda?"

"Indeed, I am." He bowed again. "Messenger of Vishnu, at your service."

"And I'm Callie. Let me know if you need anything else."

Callie stole a surreptitious glance at his feet as he rounded the corner. He did have the talons of an eagle, claws clacking on the smooth floor. Murmured greetings came from the back room as he disappeared. Another figure misted into being and glided into the bar, an Asian woman with gentle eyes and glossy blue-black hair.

"Good morning," she said softly. "Has the council already begun?"

"In the back room," Callie directed. "May I get you something?"

"I always wanted to eat a peach," she said after a moment's thought.

"We will bring it to you shortly," Callie promised. As the woman joined the rest of the council, Callie turned to call Florian, but the prickling on the back of her neck was insistent. She shuddered, looking around the deserted front area of the bar. In the dust motes that sparkled with slanted early morning sunbeams through the glass, there was definitely a humanoid shape.

"Hello? Are you here for the council?" Only silence responded to her query and the dust dissipated into random patterns, but Callie couldn't shake the feeling that she was under surveillance. She turned and hurried through the swinging door. Florian and Pete still talked as Gary waited patiently in the driver's seat of the truck. She pitched her voice to carry only the length of the room.

"Florian! We have customers and food orders, and possibly...a war council."

16

THE SCENT of curry hung in the air as Florian willed heat into the manipulated ambrosia, stirring with one finger. Thick golden sauce sent up webs of steam in curling threads, the temperature just skin-tingling hot.

A melange of coriander, cumin, and red pepper spread in delicious warmth over his tongue as he brought the finger to his mouth to test the curry and be sure it was satisfactory. The small blossoming wave of energy that always accompanied ambrosia ingestion in even the tiniest amounts followed the path of that heat down into his core. He placed the bowl on a tray with the stack of naan created a few minutes earlier. The tray also held a knife and a tiny plate presenting the single, fragrant peach fashioned for Kwan-yin.

At the back table, four beings stood uncomfortably together—at least, the angels looked uncomfortable. Garuda and Kwan-yin chatted amiably while Michael knotted his arms over his breastplate and scowled, and Gabriel impatiently tapped his fingers on the drink-ringed tabletop.

The tension of the pending war council seemed to give density to the air, and neither he nor Callie spoke. She took the tray to the table, where Kwan-yin received the peach with cries of delight.

Garuda eagerly took the bowl and ate with relish, tearing the naan into pieces to shovel curry into his mouth, eyes rolled skyward in bliss.

Florian smiled to himself despite the gravity of this gathering. A sense of pride and satisfaction came when someone complimented his culinary skills, even non-verbally. Though it was ambrosia, it was his manipulation of the raw material which imbued its special properties and infused subtle levels of taste, texture, and scent.

Stefanio had only been able to make basic things like bread and cheese and some meat, but never consumed ambrosia himself on a regular basis. Small, regular infusions of energy since coming to the threshold allowed Florian's gifts to strengthen and develop to this level. They were built upon existing worldly skills honed by study, apprenticeship, and practice during his nomadic existence.

Before his mistakes stripped away his freedom.

He pushed those thoughts aside and offered a smile of reassurance when Callie returned to the bar. She lifted her empty hands in a silent, urgent question, and Florian knew she was thinking the same thing: Where in the bloody hell was Hermes?

They didn't have to wait much longer. Hermes breezed in on a sudden wind, followed by a second, grinning being who turned his dark gaze on Florian as he manifested. The grin faded.

Despite the seven-plus decades since Ares had set foot in the bar, Florian's heart still thumped in an erratic rhythm. An unexpected memory of mutual laughter brought nostalgia into the mix of potent anger and resentment which swept through him, but that flared and died quickly, a sputtering match head against the violence of their last acrimonious meeting. The loss of his freedom had smashed any fragile remnant of a complicated relationship.

Arranging his expression into careful neutrality, Florian dipped his chin. "Welcome back, Ares."

"Not my choice of location," the other responded. Ares appraised him then offered a nod of his own.

"The usual, my friend." Hermes winked at Florian in reassurance. "It's five o'clock somewhere, right?"

"Can I get you something, Ares?" He fell into the role of Door-keeper and affected an air of distant courtesy.

The former god of war stared him down for a moment. There was heat behind the gaze, but his face hardened as he glanced into the back room. A lopsided smirk grew on those chiseled features as he registered Michael, armored and ready for a fight.

"See, Herm, all the other kids got to wear their armor." His clothing, rather mundane jeans and a fitted t-shirt that showed off his impressive physique, morphed into a Spartan breastplate and a scarlet cape. Hermes rolled his eyes and shook his head minutely as Ares narrowed his eyes at Florian.

"You still have my bottle?"

Florian nodded once.

"Bring shot glasses." Grimly cheerful, Ares spun away in an eddy of red fabric, like a flame.

Beside him, Callie's breath caught and she stared after Ares with an expression Florian could not name. A small shudder vibrated her shoulders.

"Are you all right?" he whispered.

She glanced in Florian's direction, her eyes troubled. "Something from a vision. It's nothing important. What about you? Are you okay?"

"Fine. Yes." The tension between him and Ares was visible and it bothered him she might have noticed before he could explain. She set up the tray and glasses without further comment as he mixed Hermes's martini with the mandatory olives, then retrieved the requested bottle from a murky cabinet beneath the bar. It was ancient and dusty, the label faded almost into illegibility, a little less than half full of dark, amber liquid.

He followed Callie as she delivered the tray to the waiting group, who stood in a tense clump around the table. Ares and Michael still stared at each other as greetings wound down.

"Late as always." Michael shifted, his hands clenched at his sides.

"Sorry folks. There seem to be some commuter problems this morning. Did anyone else experience issues with their doorways?" Hermes asked.

Garuda and Kwan-Yin exchanged glances and nodded, but Gabriel indicated the negative. Hermes shrugged.

"Ah well. I'm sure it's a transient bug in the network." He motioned to Florian, who stepped forward. "For those who are meeting him for the first time, this is Florian, our host. I know I speak for him when I say that any and all combatants must take it outside the bar if blows are struck. I'm looking at you, Ares and Michael."

"That won't be a problem for me, old friend." Garuda, unruffled, lifted empty hands. "I didn't come to fight, only to respond with our position."

"As did I," Kwan-yin agreed.

"This is neutral territory," Michael grudgingly conceded, his wings and arms tense and quivering. "I will not be the first to break tradition."

"Me either." Ares grinned. He uncorked the aged bottle Callie set before him and filled the shot glasses. "Will you join me, Michael? Another custom not to be broken: I always drink with a worthy opponent."

Michael stiffened and clearly intended to refuse, but Ares offered the shot glass with a challenge in his eyes. The angel took it clumsily and watched the war god throw back his own shot without a flinch. He mimicked the movement, gasped and coughed as the liquid hit the back of his throat, and glared when Ares smirked at him.

"If we're done posturing we will get down to business." Gabriel seated himself and motioned for Hermes to take the seat opposite. Michael and Ares faced each other. Garuda and Kwan-yin took up the positions on either end of the table.

Ignored, Florian and Callie ducked into seats in one of the nearby booths, huddled together like children. The steady tremble of Callie's ponytail betrayed her anxiety and his hand sought hers in the shadows under the table. She entwined her fingers with his and flashed a grateful wisp of a smile. He held her hand between his own and masked the concern that created an uncomfortable thickness in his throat. Ares' presence here could mean only one thing. As far as he knew, this gathering was unprecedented.

"Has anyone heard from the Prophet?" Gabriel asked.

Garuda shook his head. "Not coming. But I have a message from him."

"What is it?"

"The same tidings as I bring from my lord Vishnu. If you are bent on this path, you will avoid the areas where he holds sway. We will not take part in this."

"It doesn't matter to you that Zeus is breaking the contract to which we all agreed?" Gabriel frowned.

Kwan-yin spoke up. "It is of little significance to us. What the humans choose to believe or not was never our focus. We also require you do not initiate battles over those territories where we are dominant."

"Which leaves North and South America, Europe, and the inner chunk of the Asian continent," Hermes nodded at Gabriel. "Your real estate will be taking one hell of a beating, brother. Are you certain it's worth the loss of thousands, maybe millions of that precious flock of His if this becomes all-out war? Zeus isn't asking for the whole adoration pie, so to speak. Just a slice."

"Belief in Him is strengthened in times of tribulation," Gabriel responded. "Zeus can always change his mind and abandon these plans. It is too powerful a medium in this day and age to use in this manner."

"Your disciples use it," Ares accused.

"But not God Himself," Michael shot back. "That is the crucial difference."

"May I ask a question, old friend?" Garuda interjected gently to Hermes, who gestured in encouragement.

"Why now? Zeus found contentment all these years in the guise of kings, conquerors, and celebrities. What happened that he once more wishes to be divine?"

A transitory shadow eclipsed Hermes's cool exterior, almost too subtle for Florian to recognize, and the messenger downed the majority of his drink before he spoke. "I don't know the answer," he admitted. "It's a question I have asked him, and he has chosen not to enlighten me. Like the rest of you I am merely doing my lord's bidding."

"It's been millennia since we walked among the humans in our true forms. I'm kind of looking forward to it." Ares placed another filled shot glass in front of Michael and raised his own in salute. Michael hesitated before lifting the bourbon and knocked it back, only coughing a little bit. Ares slammed down his empty shot and refilled the glasses.

"We will not allow his plans to go forward." The armored angel's wings ruffled threateningly.

"What will this accomplish?" Kwan-yin questioned in her gentle voice. "You cannot kill each other. You can only inflict untold damage on the human world and its people, and their adoration, even in the smallest part, is what allows us to remain immortal. Why would you do anything to depreciate their regard?"

"All Zeus needs to do is call off this ill-conceived plan for material apparition and direct intervention, and the world will turn as always: without our help, and without them knowing for certain we exist. When they know, they fear." Michael tossed back a third shot without prompting from Ares. "They become disobedient, disrespectful and ungrateful."

"Oh, but that's when the fun starts." Ares bared his teeth in a smile.

Hermes tapped his fingers on the table, as if in thought. "I don't believe this is going to be as big a deal as you're making out," he said after a moment of silence. "This medium, as you say, is a potent tool, but we've been using it for decades in our human guises. It's a fickle audience and most of them receive the input with a healthy dose of skepticism. Reality is just as much a perception as anything else, and in this situation I think it will be perceived as entertainment."

"Until the miracles start," Gabriel interjected. Hermes shrugged.

"Even then I think people will dismiss it a publicity stunt, a setup to generate a buzz. These folks are a lot more jaded than they used to be. It takes something huge to impress them."

"I don't know if it requires as much as you think," Garuda snorted, mopping up the last remnants of curry with a chunk of naan. "I've seen some of these things. The allure escapes my comprehension, but the power is undeniable."

"What are they talking about?" Callie whispered under her breath. Florian shook his head, puzzled.

"This is our final warning." Gabriel stood. "It is our understanding the first event will occur tonight."

Hermes narrowed his eyes suspiciously. "You certainly are well informed."

"It isn't too late to cease this folly. If this goes on as planned, we will retaliate immediately," Michael growled. He reached for a fourth shot, slammed it, and ignored the warning glare of his white-winged companion. "I think we're done here." Rising to his feet, he staggered, hawk-sharp wings spreading reflexively to counterbalance, and saluted Ares with unsteady martial gravity.

"By the sword, then."

"I'll be there, Mike," Ares nodded, obscenely cheerful.

Gabriel and Hermes exchanged looks, Gabriel's pleading for capitulation, Hermes's communicating resignation. He shook his head with regret. The archangel sighed.

"*Fiat*," Gabriel murmured. "The rules of engagement have been determined. No strikes will be allowed over the territories where we are not dominant."

"This is acceptable." Kwan-yin inclined her lovely head. "I will continue to hope for a peaceful alternative."

"Agreed." Garuda rose to his birdlike feet and beamed at Florian and Callie. "I shall be back for more of that excellent curry, you can be sure."

In a heartbeat's time, only two Amaranthine were left in the silent bar. Hermes's jaw set in a tight line, eyes dark and angry, body rigid. Florian knew him well enough to read his dismay and fear.

A glance at the other, whom he'd also once thought he knew well enough to read, showed that Ares could barely contain himself. He downed the last shot in front of him and grinned.

"Damn, but that's fine." He corked the bottle. "Too good to waste on anything less than war. Make sure you hide it again, Florian."

Florian said nothing as he slid from the booth, his thoughts in too much turmoil to ask about what they'd witnessed. Callie, however, scrambled off the bench to stand at the end of the table.

"You're really going to do this?" she accused.

"Doesn't look like we get a choice anymore." Hermes glanced at his unfinished drink, sighed, and slid the glass away with uncharacteristic temperance. "Even if I don't like it, I'm not the boss."

"Ah, don't be such a pussy, Herm. It'll be fun, like the old days." Ares crowed and drummed his fists on the table in violent enthusiasm. "I've been waiting a long time for this." The scarlet cape swirled about him like blood in water as he jumped to his feet. "There are plans to draw up and troops to gather. You know where to find me."

His gaze found Florian once more. Sparks snapped in the depths of his irises. Florian did not look away and returned the stare with dispassionate calm.

The air collapsed in a whip-crack sound from the space Ares had occupied and left them alone with Hermes. The messenger closed his eyes and breathed out a sigh. His shoulders sagged into weary, downward angles.

"Can't you do anything to convince Zeus not to go ahead with whatever these plans are?" Callie pleaded.

"Believe me, I tried. I have certain interests, shall we say, which I'm personally invested in protecting. I don't want to lose them." His eyebrows drew together in consternation. "But it seems we have a—what's the animal that tunnels? A meerkat in our organization, who's giving Gabriel information."

"You mean a mole," Callie corrected automatically.

"Yeah, yeah. It's a rodent."

"What exactly is Zeus planning to do? This medium he wants to use sounds terrifying."

The godly messenger snorted. "Oh, it can be. Especially when Kardashians are involved."

Callie stopped, her mouth open.

"Err, what?" Florian asked, confused. "You mean Zeus is going to..."

"That's right, kids." Hermes finally reached for the martini glass, and drained it. "Our timetable got moved up dramatically when Big Z found out they already knew. His first episode airs live tonight, exclusively on the new Olympus Channel."

"Episode of—no. You're freaking kidding me." Callie's voice dropped into a growl of disbelief. "You're going to war because Zeus is making a reality TV show?"

17

"THE GOSSIP BLOGS even picked up on it. All the cable companies are trying to figure out who hacked them and how." Callie surfed the Internet, her battered laptop open on the bar. "I guess they don't like it when digital channels appear out of thin air."

Florian had confessed that while his Wi-Fi and satellite were technically pirated, the threshold's barrier posed no interruption to service. They'd already found it on one of the TVs: a seemingly live shot projected without voiceover or music of a misty mountain peak with a blue lightning-bolt station identifier in the bottom right corner. In the broadcast cable guide, the channel was listed as "OTV" and showed a beginning airtime of 9 PM Thursday night for a program designated *Next Top God*.

"He could come up with a better name," she muttered to herself.

"What, you mean like *The Real Housewives of Olympus*?" Florian quipped in an attempt to add some levity. His crooked smile invited her to join in, and made Callie laugh.

"It may as well be *Live from the Apocalypse*." She sobered and shut the computer. An ache grew in her chest as she thought of her parents, and hoped they would be out of harm's way.

"I suspect we might attract a larger crowd than usual tonight,"

Florian allowed, tossing a last lime wedge into a bin near to overflow-
ing. "Neutral territory means we won't need to worry about any
battles nearby. Anyone looking for a safe place to watch will undoubtedly show up here." He moved to close the glowing box and hesitated.
"No ambrosia consumption since your first night, right? Any more
visions?"

"No." She didn't understand why she chose to lie to him, and guilt
lashed her conscience. Ares' swirling red cape and Michael's armor
were far too close to the images of war in her mind's eye to be coincidental.

"A small amount should be all right. I can make you something, if
you like. Again, your choice."

Callie thought a moment, and said hopefully, "Mint chocolate chip
ice cream?"

"I can do that." He washed his hands in the under-bar sink, fetched a
glass goblet from the rack and placed it on the bar. A pinch of ambrosia
from the box was cupped for a moment between both hands as if molding
a snowball. His brow furrowed in concentration. When he opened his
hands, a pale green sphere flecked with dark brown lay between his
palms. He transferred it to the glass, and the concoction took on the
creamy-looking texture of her favorite comfort food. She caught the
faintest scent of mint and sharp cocoa. Florian fashioned a mint leaf from
a second tiny wisp and placed the garnish atop the scoop of ice cream.

"Tell me how it is," he requested, and handed her a spoon.

Callie took a bite. The dessert spread across her tongue in an
explosion of cool mint and bittersweet chocolate, and she closed her
eyes in delight. "Wonderful."

"Not too much mint?"

"No, perfect. Fantastic." She took another bite. Icy cold, but not
enough to numb her tongue, the flavors were blended to perfection.
Instead of the sensation of cold ice cream sliding down her throat, the
warmth of ambrosial energy spread out from her core. Nothing
remained in the glass but a faint white vapor when she spooned the
last of the deliciousness out of the bottom.

"Easy cleanup," she remarked.

"Ambrosia doesn't melt. I can't figure out how to replicate that part yet," Florian confessed. He leaned on the bar in front of her with a grin. If anything had come of last night's kiss it was that he had warmed up to her, and that smile was amazing, sparking one of her own. It made him look younger and reminded Callie that she had no idea of his true age. Her smile faded a little around the edges. He looked at her quizzically.

"What is it?"

"You told me ambrosia prolongs our lives." Callie decided to ask outright. "How long have you been here, Florian?"

He stiffened, the smile waning, and she placed her hand quickly over his where it rested on the wooden surface of the bar. "It's all right."

"How did you guess?" he asked in a low voice.

She shrugged. "I think Bridget told me this morning that your mother and grandfather were lost at sea on the *Titanic* when you were a baby. When Gary mentioned you don't seem to age in all the time he's known you, I put things together."

He laughed shakily. "I wanted to tell you but I couldn't decide how."

"Just tell me." Callie reassured him with a squeeze of her hand, and Florian blew out a nervous breath, shifting.

"I emigrated in 1935, when I was twenty-five years old." He searched her face in expectation, and when she didn't react negatively, he continued. "I came to America looking for Gran, to beg her forgiveness. We parted badly."

"She told me you were a naughty boy," Callie said, with a fond imitation of Bridget's Irish lilt that made him chuckle self-consciously.

"That would be right," he confessed. "I was twenty when we got chased all the way across Ireland, the Irish Channel, and half of England by a harpy Gran and I had managed to dodge for some time. We split up to confuse it. I stumbled through a doorway in London and literally into the arms of one of the Amaranthine—a bit like you did here. And that's when I first met them."

Florian ran both hands through his hair, embarrassed. "It was an instant, mutual attraction. A wildfire, really. It turned into an offer of a clandestine affair in return for protection. When we reunited, Gran and I argued rather bitterly about it. She told me who they were and not to trust them, but I was an idiot. I got stinking drunk and refused to emigrate with her to America. I left England and my lover protected me from the hunters and taught me new ways to avoid them."

"I guess that's what Ares was unhappy about? I mean, Aphrodite hiding you."

His body stilled. Quietly, Florian said, "Callie, it wasn't Aphrodite who hid me. Not the first time, at least. It was Ares."

Her mouth opened in a silent O. She snapped her jaw shut quickly when she saw how the blood rose in his cheeks. "I'm sorry. I've made a lot of assumptions."

Florian's gaze was steady. "I said there were things you should know. I have always been attracted to men and women. I realize that must shock you."

She snorted. "Oh please. I went to a liberal arts college." At his look of confusion, she waved dismissively. "A lot of time has passed since you were outside. Being bisexual is not something that scares anybody who matters anymore." She softened her voice. "I'm glad you told me."

"Really?" Taken aback, Florian blinked at her. "You seemed so surprised just now."

"Not because of that. It's just the mythology I learned portrays Ares as this hyper-masculine guy who only had female lovers. He seri-ously does not seem like a warm, fuzzy type in any case. He protected you? Tell me the rest. Please."

"Well, then." His mouth curved upwards and tested a relieved smile as he cleared his throat. "For three years, I traveled all over Europe and Asia with him and worked in some of the best kitchens on the continent. I had freedom like I'd never known before, without the threat of hunters, because of his protection. I could go out, walk down the street, have a drink in a café." Longing rang in his voice. "A normal life. It was grand.

"During that time I saw a side of him I think only Aphrodite knows as well. He's very private about his liaisons. Capable of great tenderness, if you can believe it, or she would have cut ties with him eons ago. For those three years he came to me whenever he could, a regular assignation. And then—" he spread his hands. "There was no goodbye or confrontation. It was simply over. He left a letter for me that said as much. My freedom was gone. I took to drowning my sorrows while I hid in the Paris doorway. That's where I met her.

"I knew who Aphrodite was of course, but Ares had taken great care not to let her find out about me. She was despondent at his lack of attention. Things were heating up in Abyssinia and Italy and he could smell another world war coming. He loves battle more than anything else. More than her. We commiserated as jilted and neglected parties without me revealing we lamented the same person. Commiseration turned into drunken stupidity on my part. I told myself it served Ares right. I asked her for protection, and from that night on she held my leash."

Florian gave a short, uneven laugh. "We met for almost a year. Seldom talked, just fell into bed. One night she told me Ares discovered she was keeping a human lover hidden from him, that he was in a jealous rage. It thrilled her to be the center of his attention again. That was it. She took away her protection and disappeared."

He snapped his fingers. "Just like that, a harpy found me. I managed to dodge the thing until I reached a port town and signed on as a cook on the first ship I could find to cross the Atlantic. When I made it to Kansas City Stefanio took me in and gave me a job, as I told you. Ares came to this threshold often during the civil war, but when I arrived he was embroiled in early World War II in Europe. I didn't expect to see him here. I still don't know how he found out I was the one she'd hidden, but I suspect she told him. Hef was here when Ares all but killed me. He stopped him. But it was Stefanio who stepped between us."

He shifted to stand straighter, his gaze on a memory. "He invoked his right as Doorkeeper to ensure my safety within the threshold and called for Hermes to intervene. The position of Doorkeeper is highly honored by the Amaranthine. It holds authority over them in certain circumstances even though we're mortal. The tradition in Europe is to pass the responsibility to another member of the family. Stefanio had four brothers who were technically in line to take over the establishment, but simply for the love of Bridget Callahan, he told Ares that he had chosen me to succeed him."

"He stood up to Ares?" Callie shook her head in wonder. "I can't think of anything braver. But what about Hephaestus? He still comes here even though he knows?"

"He doesn't even hold a grudge." His eyes downcast, Florian managed a brief smile. "Ares told Zeus I coerced Aphrodite to keep me hidden from the hunters, never admitting he did it first. I think Hef appreciated the irony that she kept me hidden from Ares, too."

He stopped speaking. His eyes widened as if he'd discovered something.

"What is it?" Callie inquired.

"Well, now that I know about the contract, I just realized: Ares unwittingly condemned her for interfering in a human's destiny, but both of them clearly violated it."

"Did she ever find out about you and Ares?"

Florian shook his head vehemently. "Oh, no. I won't be telling her, and she's never said anything to lead me to believe Ares has, either. Zeus punished her, and not for the first time, it seems. She isn't allowed in the human world any more unless Hephaestus goes with her."

"She and Ares have no opportunities to fool around like they used to." Callie fought an uncharitable sense of smugness, but decided they deserved what they'd gotten. Sucked for them. "So he insisted you be punished too, didn't he?"

"Hermes and Stefanio negotiated with Zeus on my behalf. They came up with a compromise that satisfied Ares and kept him from killing me. Because Aphrodite violated the contract at my request, I was restricted to the threshold for one hundred years in service to the Amaranthine. To ensure I live that long, I had to—become immortal. Temporarily, at least."

Immortal, yet imprisoned in the threshold. His freedom, the very thing which had so beguiled him, was now forfeit. It was a brutal, personalized sentence against someone who had merely asked for protection. Callie let the cruelty of his punishment sink in a moment before she asked another question. "But isn't that forbidden? I mean, the gods interfering with a human destiny bit. Making you live forever is definitely meddling."

"Ah, but it wasn't the Amaranthine who did it." Florian heaved a sigh. "My body's normal aging processes are suspended within the threshold by fairy magic."

Callie shook her head. "I don't understand. Why is that different?"

"They were never gods. They aren't bound by the same rules. Stefanio made a deal with Titania and Oberon, and that's how Wednesday's exclusive Sidhe night came about." Florian's voice was dispassionate, but he picked up her ice cream glass and dumped it none too gently into the under-bar sink. "As long as I don't step outside the barriers, I won't die. That's considered a prison break. Until the spell is taken off, age will catch up with me in seconds if I cross the threshold. If that doesn't kill me, Ares probably will. He wouldn't risk the same punishment Aphrodite received, and I'm the only one who knows he's as guilty as she is."

"Now I know too." Fire built in Callie's chest. "What an asshole! What happens when your sentence is up?"

"I'm not sure. But I have responsibilities now. I'm Doorkeeper. I won't be going anywhere else." He shrugged and turned on the water in the sink. "Hermes hopes Ares will cool down by that time, but as you see he still hasn't forgotten." His voice grew soft. "I know I only have twenty-four years of my sentence left, but it doesn't feel like it's been that long. I've seen three quarters of a century pass by that window, but it's all blurred together. I'm not even sure I'd know what to say to people if I were able to walk down the street again."

A stab went through her as she realized how little human contact he'd had since his sentencing.

She studied him as he rinsed the glass. There wasn't any sign of age in his smooth, permanently tanned skin or full-lipped mouth. Only his expressive eyes, now hooded and cautious, gave hint that he'd seen much more than a quarter-century of life. "Does time move differently here?"

"Not time, but space is—complicated. Why do you ask?" Florian put the glass in the dishwasher.

"Your grandmother obviously isn't aging at a normal pace, either."

His expression regained some of that guarded look. "No, but for a different reason. Do you remember what else I told you ambrosia does for those of us with Amaranthine blood?"

"Gives us energy, and something about our gifts." Her voice died as she remembered what he'd said. "It makes them more powerful," Callie breathed.

He affirmed her statement with a solemn nod.

A surge of excitement bubbled in her voice. "Then the ambrosia might make them helpful for once!"

"No!" Florian's denial was too sharp, his answer a little too quick. His mouth pressed in a thin line as she stared, puzzled by his outburst. He wilted. "It's too dangerous. The last thing I want is for you to suffer the same fate as Gran."

A chill walked up her spine. "What happened, Florian?"

He regarded the golden box and then met Callie's gaze again. "Before I arrived, Gran had a vision about me being in danger. Stefanio told me she was frantic, desperate to learn what had happened to me. She knew it wasn't safe but she decided to try to use ambrosia to provoke a clearer vision of my fate. He didn't know she was doing it or he would have stopped her. She saw that I was safe, but at a terrible price. I suppose you could say she overdosed. She nearly died. Gran's mind was...altered."

Florian shut the lid of the golden casket and stowed it under the counter. "She lives in a constant vision-state now. She has moments of total lucidity like this morning. Most of the time she's as you've seen her, confused and distracted. She's lived much longer than we expected given that kind of damage, but Hermes thinks it is because of the ambrosia. Stefanio was one hundred and thirty when he died. Gran's well over one hundred and forty-five now."

Almost a century and a half, her brain babbled. And Florian was over one hundred years old? Callie pressed her hands together in front of her mouth, trying to absorb this information.

"I'm not proud, knowing my selfishness drove her to this." The break in Florian's voice betrayed his pain. "She raised me and protected me at her own peril when I was a child, and I abandoned her. When I came back to tell her I was sorry, I don't even know if she truly understood."

"Oh, Florian, I'm sure she does." Callie recognized the indelible guilt of deserting loved ones, hers born amid the scrawl of a hasty letter to her parents. "People make mistakes. It's part of being human. It's how we learn from them that matters. One of the things she told me today was that you are a good man. Stefanio chose you to be his successor. He must have seen it too."

"I'm not certain about that. I'm under house arrest largely because I couldn't keep my trousers on, and I run a pub catering to bored immortals. I'm supposed to offer safety and shelter to anyone with Amaranthine blood. I still have yet to experience that aspect of being Doorkeeper." Florian grabbed a rag and polish and wiped the expanse of maple-varnished bar top in restless, automatic movements. Callie snagged a towel and moved to help. "The Pereira family has kept the doorway in Portugal for almost two hundred years, and maybe a dozen people lived there at any given time. Here in America our kind aren't living long enough once they reach adulthood to find the doorways."

"Because of the hunters," Callie guessed with grim certainty. "They found my mother and me."

"And me. And Gran, and Stefanio…everyone else I ever met with strong Amaranthine blood. They're deadly trackers." He paused in his work. "How long people survive seems to be directly connected with their proximity to the doorways. There are fewer on this continent than in Europe and Asia and they are much farther apart. The major thresholds in Rome and Athens are easy to find for obvious reasons."

The conversation had taken an entirely too serious turn, and Callie decided to lighten the mood. "But I'll bet they can't say their threshold is the most popular nightspot in the cosmos."

"No, you're right. They can't." Florian straightened and a slow grin lit his features. "Although more people like us live there. You are the first to find this doorway since Stefanio died, but even before I took over only five people found their way here over the years. Gran and I are two of them."

"Well, a dozen people here might be a little crowded." Callie shrugged. "You only have three apartments and mine is definitely a single occupancy."

"This is a threshold. There's always room for more." He noted her puzzled expression. "Remember, I said space is complicated here." Florian threw down his towel and walked around to the outside of the serving area. "You still haven't been out in the garden, have you? Come with me. You have to see this."

18

He held out his hand. Callie left her polishing rag on the bar and entwined her fingers with his as Florian led her upstairs and unlatched the door of his own apartment.

An airy kitchen took up the bulk of the room. A low, comfortably overstuffed sofa in the living area crouched beside a floor-to-ceiling shelf which overflowed with books. Another rack full of DVDs and VHS tapes crowded an entertainment center and a desk lay littered with maps, a laptop computer barely visible in the debris.

She got a tantalizing glimpse of his bedroom on the opposite side through another door. Rumpled quilts and mounded pillows lay in disarray on a large, sleigh-style bed.

"So you do sleep," she noted more to herself than him, and Florian squeezed her hand.

"I don't need much. The ambrosia helps, but my sentence doesn't seem to take sleep into account."

French doors similar to those in her apartment graced the back wall. He unlatched and held one wide for her. She walked through and emerged onto a stone-paved patio, expecting the same blast of heat encountered earlier when opening the back door for deliveries but surprised to discover the temperature unusually mild. Florian's vegetable garden just outside the patio overflowed its raised brick bed. Herbs in fragrant abundance dispersed their spicy aroma on a cool breeze. Leaves rustled on trees far larger than logic told her the roof of a turn-of-the-century building should support. She soon realized it was not the only incredible thing.

As she stepped off the paving stones, the garden expanded. Terraced lawns stretched impossibly far in every direction, a heavy carpet of soft grass underfoot. Where the opposite ledge of the building would normally be, a panorama of lavender, snow-capped mountains rose in the distance. A valley spread out below them, sparkling rivers glinting in the sunlight. The sky was a brilliant palette of sapphire and violet, stars visible even though the sun was shining.

"What is this?" She spun about in delighted disbelief.

"Welcome to the threshold," Florian told her, smiling.

"This. This is incredible!" She took a few more tentative steps into the garden and twirled again with giddy laughter. "How far can we go?"

"Not as far as it seems on either side, I'm afraid." He beckoned her to follow him to the edge of a knee-high brick wall and held her by the waist. "Look down."

Callie bent cautiously over the wall and gulped as she experienced the swirl of vertigo. Her vision seemed to pass through a fuzzy barrier. Suddenly she was peering over the side of the building into the alley beneath, the sun's heat intense and the humidity palpably thicker. She looked up to glimpse buildings and city skyline. Dizzy, she pulled back as Florian's arm tightened around her waist to support her.

"There are infinite rooms in the hotel. I have no idea how many, because the number changes. One appears for each person who arrives looking for shelter, and every suite has a door that leads to this garden. The Amaranthine don't stay here often, but if they actually use the front door the threshold scans them and rooms are tailored to what they like. The same thing happens with us because of our ancestry, even if it wasn't built for our convenience."

"Scans us. You mean our brains? Our memories? That sounds less like magic and more like technology."

"Hermes says it is. To us it might appear magical, just like the gods did to our early ancestors."

"My dad should be in on this conversation. He would love this. He always told me the truth wouldn't necessarily be what we expected." She took in the vista below the garden wall. "What about that? Is it real?"

"Another dimensional window, but this one we can't cross. The middle peak?" He pointed. "That's Olympus."

"That's not anywhere on Earth?" The mountains looked like any other terrestrial formation, save for the color of the ambient light.

"If you tried to go straight on toward the mountains, you'd never reach them, no matter how far you walk. But when you turn around, you're still standing right in front of the garden. I tried." He sounded wistful as he gazed on the far-away crests. "Beautiful, isn't it?"

"Amazing." She looked up into the cobalt sky and discovered phantom images of clouds and jet contrails above in the their own world. His hands still at her waist, she found their bodies had moved together in unconscious intimacy. They fit nicely.

"So you're only temporarily immortal."

"Yes."

"You had an affair with a god *and* a goddess. You can't leave the threshold for another twenty-four years without turning into a mummy or something." She ticked the list off on her fingers. "Anything else I need to know about you?"

His voice vibrated against her back. "I think that covers the most sordid parts of my past."

She turned in the circle of his arms and placed her palms against his chest, looking up at him. His personal scent, meadow and pine and growing things, now made sense. It was the telltale scent of the fairy magic which kept him from aging. But she was certain now there was no glamour stimulating her interest. "I know I like you, Florian. I'm attracted to you in a huge way. For me, that's scary as it gets. I've never...well. I've never, if you understand what I'm saying."

"You haven't?" It startled him. She ignored the blush that flamed in her cheeks.

"The only other time I got close enough to feel this kind of attraction, I panicked and ran. The Amaranthine don't have a monopoly on dumping people without an explanation. I'm not sure what to do. It's bad enough that you're my boss and my landlord. It gets even weirder knowing that you're old enough to be my grandfather—my *great* grandfather."

"Only chronologically. I stopped aging the day that my sentence began, but I understand your reluctance." His jaw tightened and his gaze strayed from her.

"Not reluctant. It's just a lot to consider. I've never thought about dating an older man before." She touched his chin and guided his attention back to her, regarding him with playfully narrowed eyes. "A chronologically older man. But I'm willing to give it a shot if we take it very slowly."

Hope arrived like a sunrise behind his eyes when he realized she wasn't rejecting the idea. "We could see how it goes. I'm definitely out of practice."

"Not according to that kiss."

A smile played on the edges of his lips. "Seventy-six years is a long time. We may have to relearn everything together."

"That sounds like it could be fun."

He lowered his mouth to hers in slow motion, giving her time to change her mind. She had no intention to do anything of the sort. Callie rose on tiptoe to meet him in anticipation of the kiss, a delicious roll of excitement building in her chest.

Out of the corner of her eye, she spotted almost too late something that dove through the air toward them with bat-like wings outspread. Her breath caught in a gasp of terror. Florian pulled her back from the side of the building as the creature collided with the barrier of the threshold in a growling buzz of energy, like an exploding transformer.

It screamed and clawed at the invisible wall. A face, human only in structure, contorted with hunger. Its glaring red eyes fixed on Callie. They watched in horror as its nails raked the outside, unable to penetrate. Fresh screeches were torn from a mouth full of jagged yellow teeth as sizzling weals grew against the pressure of its body on the barrier.

"What the hell is that?" Callie's voice rang with a note of hysteria.

"It's a harpy," Florian answered grimly.

Purple arcs of electricity crawled along grayish skin and across leathery, naked breasts smashed against the unseen barricade. It smoked and convulsed, its malevolent gaze never straying from her, and continued to claw at the protective shield. A corona of cinders sloughed off the corded body as holes seared through the membranes of its wings and it exploded into oily, smudgy flames. The monster disintegrated into spark and ash.

Callie's whole body trembled. Florian put his arms around her in reassurance and they both stared, wide eyed, as the embers of the incinerated creature oozed down the barrier in clumps to drift in slow showers toward the alley below.

His voice broke unevenly in Callie's ears. "I've never heard of a hunter doing that before."

The panicky impulse to flee, that she'd been tracked down, shrieked it was time to move on. She fought the racing of her heart with measured breaths. "I thought Bridget said they couldn't see me here."

"They can't."

"But it was looking right at me!"

Florian shook his head in denial. "I know, but I was told that can't happen. This has never happened."

"Well, it just did." She had no warning, no sense that the thing was coming. It frightened her.

"It couldn't cross the threshold. We're still safe." Florian's voice grew steadier.

Another minute passed before she accepted he was right. Whatever protected the threshold had destroyed the harpy despite its fatal tenacity.

"Are they always this determined?" Her voice broke despite the struggle to regain her composure. "I mean, I've been inside for three days, except when I was on the delivery dock. Has it been hanging around that long?"

"They primarily track by scent. I think it must have been close by when you leaned through the barrier. Eventually, they will give up when your scent fades. It may take a good rain to do that. It was one of the advantages to living in Ireland, which is why Gran and I survived so long. Here in the Midwest it could be some time. Best that you not go outside the barrier until we're certain there aren't any more lurking about."

"Don't worry. I don't want to look at anything like them up close, ever again." She shuddered and took comfort in the warm embrace of Florian's arms.

"I'm sorry to interrupt, kids."

Startled, they turned in surprise. Hermes stood a few feet away. Armor gleamed against his chest and arms, a winged helmet in hand. His caduceus staff rested in the crook of his elbow, no mere symbol of office but a far more fearsome weapon than Callie would ever imagine or had seen depicted. The curves of the snake-shaped blades gleamed with razor sharpness, the wings axe-edged.

"Hermes?" Florian's voice rose slightly in question. "Has it already started?"

"Not yet. But it will." Hermes's usually cool, unruffled demeanor was broken by a grim countenance. "Florian, I need your help. Can you come downstairs? Please?"

1 9

FLORIAN EXCHANGED an apprehensive glance with Callie as Hermes disappeared. Neither said a word as they hurried back inside. Exiting his apartment door, he sidestepped to avoid a collision with his grandmother. Bridget's arms overflowed with sheets and towels.

"You'll need to milk the cow, Florian," she said in passing as she climbed the steps. "They look hungry."

Florian's attention was drawn by a change upstairs. Opposite Callie's blue door, an extra stretch of landing bridged to a yellow door at the end. Beside him, Callie gaped.

"Looks like we have a new guest," he told her, and turned his attention to Bridget. "Don't worry, Gran. Pete delivered groceries this morning, and there's plenty of milk." He exchanged a quizzical glance with Callie. "Shall we go find out what Hermes wants?" In all the years he'd known him, Hermes had never asked for help—or said *Please*.

Downstairs, an anxious Hermes waited for them beside the bar. "I don't have much time, and I think tonight's crowd is going to be early to get a ringside seat." More serious than Florian could remember ever seeing him, the messenger wore lines of care that softened his typically ironic expression. He laid the lethal-looking weapon atop the counter and placed his helmet beside it. "I didn't know what else to do. I'm taking a risk with this, but I can't bear the thought of anything happening to them. I need a favor, Florian. I don't ask it lightly. I'm asking as a friend, not a god, or your lawyer."

Florian, startled, nodded as Hermes continued, "I told you I have certain interests to protect. I won't be able to keep them safe during this little squabble."

He held out a vambraced arm. From the shadows of one of the booths emerged a man and a young girl who stared at Florian and Callie with trepidation. Hermes moved to encircle them in his arms with a tenderness all the armor in the world could not disguise. "This is Marios, and our daughter Eleni. Athens is likely to be ground zero, and I won't risk their being harmed. Will you give my family shelter, Florian?"

"Yes, of course." Florian's response came almost before he fully realized what Hermes confessed: the god was protecting his human family in the same way Ares once protected Florian, in violation of the contract. Keeping them safely hidden from the hunters. If this was discovered Hermes stood to lose his freedom to move in the human world. His family would be left to flee the merciless creatures stalking the gods' descendants.

Callie clearly understood this family's plight, perhaps better than anyone. She had lost her own mother far too early. Her gaze traveled from Eleni to Marios, lines of worry between her eyes.

"There should be a key under the drawer in the register," he told her softly. "Will you show them upstairs?"

Callie retrieved the newly manifested key and smiled at the man. "Hi, I'm Callie. I live here, too."

"My English is not so good." Marios apologized haltingly in a charming but thick Greek accent, which made him difficult to understand. Hermes waved apologetically.

"I forgot, *agapimeni*." He leaned in and gave Marios a lingering, gentle kiss on the mouth, and on the forehead of his daughter. "That will do it. Callie will take you upstairs. I'll come back and take you home as soon as all of this is over."

"Thank you." The man spoke again, this time in unaccented, perfect English. "I'm pleased to meet you, Callie."

"And you." Callie's eyes widened, surprised. She motioned to the stairs. "Come up and I'll show you where you'll stay. Bridget is getting the apartment ready for you. It's the yellow door at the top of the landing. You can't miss it." She smiled at Florian, who grinned back as they realized her words echoed the exact phrase he used upon her arrival. "If you're hungry, we just had groceries delivered and I can get you something to eat."

Eleni turned an uncertain glance toward her father and he blew her a kiss, motioning that she was to follow Marios. Florian marveled at the change in Hermes. The acerbic, affected air of nonchalance was no longer on display, and his quicksilver eyes brimmed with love and concern as he watched his family disappear upstairs with Callie.

"I'm in your debt. I appreciate this more than I can express, Florian," Hermes said quietly. "You have my friendship and my eternal gratitude."

"This is what I'm meant to do as Doorkeeper. About time I got the chance." Florian reached for a bottle in preparation to mix Hermes's favorite drink, but the ex-god stopped him with a gesture.

"No, thanks. I'm not in the mood to drink today." He looked down. "This is going to get very ugly, very fast, Florian. I'm not sure how it escalated so quickly. Both armies are chomping at the bit. Michael and Ares have each assembled a group of malcontents who've been waiting for an excuse to duke it out. They don't care who's in the way."

Florian's stomach knotted. "What about Z? He's still bent on this reality show?"

Hermes shook his head. "Zeus is the most powerful of us, the most stubborn, the most prideful, but he's never been this reckless. Atlantis was an accident—unstable fault lines, a volcano, and really, really bad timing for a marital squabble over who should hold dominance in the new temple. But this? I have been his right hand, his loyal servant, and his conscience since the beginning. I was always able to get through to him. Now it's as if he doesn't even see what's happening. He's obsessed with this one thing. If I didn't know better, I'd say he was..." he stopped, his forehead creased.

"What?" Florian prompted gently, but Hermes grunted.

"Nothing any of us are strong enough to do. That's why he's the boss." He picked up his helmet and placed it on his head with a sigh. "I need to get back to make sure that idiot Ares doesn't pick the first fight. Zeus may be willing to test his theory about God intervening, but I'm not."

"Be careful," Florian found himself saying.

"Take care of my family." Hermes transferred the deadly caduceus to the crook of his arm. "Especially Eleni: she's gifted, so not too much ambrosia, okay? She needs to help her father and read a book instead of playing on her phone all day." He sounded so normal and paternal, so un-godlike, that Florian fought a smile.

"I will."

Hermes clasped Florian's wrist in a soldierly handshake. The armor was cold beneath Florian's fingers as he returned the pressure as best he could. Hermes entrusted him with a secret that could potentially cost the god everything he held dear. It was all too serious for the moment until Hermes grinned wolfishly.

"So, you and Callie looked pretty friendly."

Florian stumbled on his answer, heat rising in his face. "Maybe. I hope so. Yes."

"Saw that one coming. Later, Florian."

The messenger slipped between dimensions and vanished, but the sense of foreboding remained behind and drew cold fingers across the back of Florian's neck.

2 0

———————

By a quarter to nine in the evening it was standing room only. The bar teemed with immortals. The majority of the television screens displayed the Olympus Channel, still broadcasting a live shot of the mountain peak. The rest showed news channels, one or two of which promised to keep an eye on the developing story of a mystery cable station that appeared overnight, and speculated breathlessly whether the Russians were involved.

The crowd's mood read a bit nervous. Nobody took advantage of the pool tables or dartboards and the digital jukebox fell silent. Loud voices with occasional false, exaggerated laughter rang back from the walls. Most of the Greek pantheon's regulars did not arrive, except for Pan, whose vertical pupils fixed on Callie's chest or rear end every time she passed. Mercifully, he didn't grab tonight. One small tap at her thin shell of control was all it would take to erupt and savage him with whatever bludgeoning object lay at hand.

Aphrodite was also present. Breathtaking cleavage threatened to spill out of her sapphire dress as she leaned over the bar toward Florian. Hephaestus was nowhere to be seen, obviously embroiled in war preparations. Callie spied on her through narrowed eyes as the goddess flirted shamelessly with Florian, touching his arm any time he came near enough to touch. To his credit, he appeared as cool and unmoved by her as always, but it was starting to piss Callie off. How, exactly, did one tell a goddess to stop touching her ex-lover who was now your new potential boyfriend?

She slid through the crowd with her orders. Since her small meal of ambrosia earlier in the day, she had noticed an increase in mental alacrity and her energy level went through the roof. The stuff worked better than caffeine. She'd had no visions thus far but her early warning system built up pressure and steam, never quite absent from her conscious mind.

Puck flickered in and sauntered through the press of bodies, wearing his twenty-something emo incarnation and surveying the crowd with an amused, condescending smirk. He was the first of the fairies she had come across, though every other pantheon had representation in this crush of Amaranthine. Nobody else paid attention to him. He noted Callie's acknowledgement of his arrival with his usual ironic, romantic salute. She nodded back but didn't approach. The strange, uneasy feeling she developed in his presence was back, and she didn't want to talk to him now.

"It's starting! Turn it up!" someone yelled from the back, and a cheer rose. The crowd surged toward the giant screen at the front of the bar, and Florian keyed the remote for volume. Callie stopped. Her heart pounded with dread as the shot of the mountain peak faded. A sonorous voice spoke over the blackout.

"Tonight, we broadcast for the first time *Live from Olympus*, commercial free and without interruption."

"Because nobody would sponsor this crap! Who wants to look at Zeus walking around in his pajamas?" a heckler shouted at the television. Laughter went up in a brief flurry, trailing off as a marble throne room came into focus on the screen. Seated in the enormous chair was a radiant figure, the light too bright to discern his features at first and then dimming enough to allow a clear view of the powerfully built, broad shouldered, bearded man sitting in the high seat. Draped in a blindingly white chiton, he resembled nothing close to the incarnation of the hippie biker guy Callie met on her first night, but more like the Greek statues in museums depicted him: lean, hard, and warlike.

"Damn, dude hasn't looked that buff in centuries," Pan muttered. Someone shushed him.

"Good evening." He spoke, his voice deep and compelling. "I am Zeus. Many of you will have seen me in something like this form in your history books, museums, and films. It has pleased me to appear in many disguises over the millennia, but I suspect most of you today will remember me like this."

His body morphed into the sleepy-eyed, gray haired rock star, and the voice which issued from his lips was the mildly slurred, Californian drawl associated with the celebrity icon. "I took this persona in 1961 and man, it was a wild ride from then on. The sixties were awesome, weren't they? But when we take on human bodies we're just like you, and we have to pay the price of the abuse to which we subject that body. I'm afraid I didn't present a very good role model, unworthy of the adoration so many of you gave me. I want to make it up to you.

"Tonight, and every week thereafter, we will be running broadcasts where you'll learn that while you may have always considered stories about me myth and legend, I and my kind still walk among you in human disguises. Some you will recognize. Some you won't. But I understand I need to prove who and what I say I am: a god of the ancient world, and now a god of your modern world. Lightning and thunder have always been my element."

"Yeah, mine too," somebody, probably Thor, grumbled.

Onscreen, Zeus raised his arms. "For the next few minutes, I will show you my presence."

The room fell quiet in expectation. Callie waited. And waited. She exchanged a worried glance with Florian, who stood motionless behind the bar.

Nothing happened.

"Damn it, he's lost his touch." Aphrodite sighed and shifted, crossing her shapely legs. "Make me another strawberry daiquiri, Florian. Double rum and extra whipped cream. This is killing me."

"No. Look," Callie said, her attention fixed on the glass windows fronting the establishment. Ghostly flickers of what appeared to be heat lightning built in the west and moved rapidly toward them. She elbowed her way through the crowd and opened the door, careful not to cross the threshold. A rumble of thunder grew with each passing second. The rolling storm passed overhead with contained violence, forked shafts leaping from cloud to cloud. In less than a minute it was gone, rumbling its way over the horizon. The clear night sky reappeared, the first stars of evening visible through the haze of city lights. A smell of ozone lingered in the fitful summer breeze and lifted Callie's ponytail in its currents.

Stunned silence reigned in the bar, broken abruptly by raucous hoots and claps.

"Not bad for an old god!"

"Way to go, boss!"

"Shut up, he's talking again!" Aphrodite flapped wildly.

The figure on the screen lowered his arms. Callie closed the door and stood with her back to it, her heart pounding as she listened.

"Now, I get it that even this won't be enough for some of you to truly believe. But I'm not going to hold it against you. A lot of us over the millennia have judged you on the strength of your belief and required proof of your faith. I'm not demanding sacrifices. I'm simply asking you to like our Facebook page, or follow our Twitter. You can message me directly, if you like. I'm going for open communication between gods and mankind here. No more wondering if we're listening to your prayers and supplications. We're here. We want to hear from you, and we will answer you."

A mutter of admiration for Zeus's pronouncement rumbled through the room. "Whoops, was that a gauntlet I heard hitting the ground?" somebody joked.

"No, it was my beer. Hey babe, get me another one, willya?"

"I guess now we'll find out if they're serious about the contract." This voice held some uncertainty.

"Babe, the beer?"

Callie acknowledged the speaker absently, her attention still on the

TV as she made her way to the cooler. On screen, Zeus took his seat on the throne and invited viewers to enjoy the show as it segued into a more reality trope-ish format. It was absurd enough to see a hippie-biker in a chiton waving at the audience from his marble throne that she could hope Michael and the angels wouldn't take it as a plausible threat.

One of the news channels started reporting on an 'odd global weather phenomenon'. It garnered little attention as the crowded bar continued to watch Zeus's show, and as far as she could tell, the only one watching that screen besides herself was Florian. He craned his neck, trying to see around the press of bodies as he put together Aphrodite's drink, tossing strawberries into the churning mixture in the blender.

With intense annoyance, Callie noted the goddess watched him hungrily, murmuring something, and she caught the tail end of the conversation as she opened the cooler to retrieve the clumsy Amaranthine's replacement beer.

"When he puts me on his show, I'm sure my restrictions will be lifted. I can leave Olympus. I'll be able to go anywhere I like with whomever I like instead of being chained to Hef." Her voice rang with an ugly note.

"How nice," Florian muttered, not really listening. His eyes were on the screen.

"So I thought maybe we could go to my chateau in France again. You remember, the one with the furs and the huge bed?"

"Oh." Florian became mindful of where the conversation was leading as he poured the daiquiri into the waiting glass. "No, I don't think so."

"Why not?" Aphrodite couldn't take the hint, unable to believe he wasn't interested in picking up where she'd dumped him. "All Zeus has to do is announce it on his little show and we're off."

"Well, for one thing, my sentence is still in effect. I don't particularly want to test out what happens if I cross the threshold. Besides, Ares wouldn't take it lightly."

Neither would I, Callie thought murderously.

"Oh, pooh. Once I'm out in the world again, I can handle Ares." Her eyes glinted. "But as for crossing the threshold, you're right. That's out of my hands. But I can just zap us into the closest doorway. Poof. No crossing. That might work."

Callie gritted her teeth and grabbed another bottle of Boulevard Wheat from the cooler. She found it difficult to decide what peeved her more: Aphrodite's preoccupation with herself or the fact the cow was trying to encourage Florian to make a potentially fatal jailbreak.

She delivered the beer and took up a place at the back of the empty game room where she could see the news channel. Speculation about the strange thunderstorm already buzzed across the feeds as anchors scrambled to get meteorological experts on the air. Back on the largest screen the format of the show had changed to a confession-cam interview with Eros in his porn-celebrity guise, interspersed with a meeting in which a fatherly Zeus counseled him in the adult film business. It played like a parody. People were supposed to believe this?

But her early warning system grated down her spine, a raw nerve. Something was happening. Something terrible.

21

"Maybe Florian should sell popcorn. It might make this more interesting."

Callie jumped. A smiling Puck stood at her elbow. She took a step sideways to increase the distance between them. The hair on her arms prickled, like she stood next to a live wire.

"Do you think it's enough to make people believe again?" He leaned against one of the empty tables casually, head cocked as he waited for her to respond.

"The show is satirical enough that maybe no one will take it seriously," Callie admitted, rubbing her goose bumps. She took another step away with the pretense of getting a better look at the screen. "Having famous celebrities screams Hollywood production."

"Hmmm. You're right." Puck frowned and crossed his own arms. "I didn't think about it that way. But like the almighty Zeus said, we're not talking about belief, are we? The real issue here is intent: Zeus's intent to violate the contract against divine intervention and material apparition. Do you think this is enough to cross the line?"

"I hope not. But I'm afraid so."

"Why afraid, love? What's so terrible?"

Callie stared at him, aghast. "You know Ares and Michael are going to war over this, right?"

Puck gestured dismissively. "They used to fight all the time, back in the beginning. Back about the time they wiped out the dinosaurs."

"They killed the dinosaurs?" Dizzy, Callie wondered if there was more than one of the 'last' times that Hermes let slip.

"When they opened the first threshold between dimensions. That was unfortunate. I liked those big ones with the little arms and the giant teeth." He tucked his hands in at chest level, clawed playfully, and roared with a grin. Puck shook his head in regret. "Then the other bunch came. When they tried to open a threshold in Mesopotamia it caused the big flood. Clumsy bastards."

Callie shivered as an echo of the tsunami vision she and Bridget shared returned unbidden to her thoughts. Puck continued, "That one took out the breeding grounds for my favorite creatures. No more unicorns, no more dragons or griffins. A shame. I loved those, so bloodthirsty and fierce! I managed to save a few and relocate them, but not enough to last forever."

Something was happening on the news channel, the anchor speaking in urgent tones. Callie couldn't tell what they were saying. The Amaranthine, already bored with Zeus's reality show, drifted back into the booths and the gaming area.

"Now that you know they exist, how do you feel about asking for intervention?" Puck examined his black-polished nails.

"I don't know." Callie hazarded, distracted by the screens. "I've never been much of a believer in anything religious. I loved the stories, the art, and the poetry for what they were, more than believing the gods were real."

"And now that you've met them?"

"I can't imagine asking any of them for anything," Callie admitted.

"Good, because they're not really gods, you know. They're a bunch of idiot scientists who came to this planet looking for energy, stumbled into our paradise and never fucking left." His sharp features took on a fiercely indignant expression as he spoke, his eyes on Zeus's nattering figure projected on the big screen. "Word got out. Others followed, stomping all over the place. Then they started competing for the attention of you lot. It used to take something small like a volcano or an earthquake, but now it takes computers and text messages and cat memes. Things are too fucking complicated."

She wanted to listen, realizing this was important, but the silent cacophony of her early warning system made it impossible to concentrate.

"It's a rare beast, a practical romantic like you, Callie. But you're something even rarer than that, I think."

"What's that?" she asked automatically.

"I'm not sure yet. But I'm going to find out." His voice, soft and thoughtful, held the edge of something sinister.

As the images on the screen became more definitive, she could no longer pretend to listen. Something was definitely happening on CNN—something major.

"Sorry. Excuse me." Callie ran to the bar and grabbed the remote, changing the main screen to the news channel. A moment of protest erupted from the few still engrossed in the show until what unfolded caught their attention.

"An enormous explosion and fire in Athens has apparently leveled the Acropolis and the surrounding neighborhoods are heavily damaged," the reporter was saying. "This raw footage from a cell phone camera is all we have at this time, but crews are on the way and we will hopefully have something by satellite very shortly."

An immense fire atop the rocky hillside vomited flames into the pre-dawn sky on a grainy, wobbly recording. Her hands over her mouth in horror, Callie was able to make out huge, toppled columns.

The same columns she had seen in her visions.

Screams and the sound of running feet came in clearly on the audio, voices shouting in Greek. Glass sparkled in the streets, and fleeting glimpses of lifeless bodies filled her with horror.

It happened. Her vision was proven true.

The anchor said early reports pointed to a meteorite, as the explosion seemed airborne. But in the fuzzy digital footage of the writhing flames, Callie imagined she could see the outlines of wings and swords and armored bodies grappling. The swirling fire looked like Ares' red cape. A racking shudder passed through her and shook nausea into the pit of her stomach. She swallowed.

"Holy shit. Athena is going to be pissed," Pan remarked.

"Oh, please, it was a wreck. She had another one built in Nashville, with modern materials," Aphrodite interjected, sipping her drink. "Turn it back on the live shot. I don't want to miss my parole announcement."

"Yeah, but that one isn't a threshold," someone protested indignantly. "Couldn't they have just taken out the doorway in Siberia? The place is colder than a witch's tit."

And the laughter rose.

For a moment, Callie feared another terrible vision intruded into her reality. It started as a giggle and grew into a malicious chuckle. No one around her reacted to it, but the sound, bouncing off the walls, was undeniably real. Even Florian, staring in dismay at the screen, didn't acknowledge it. She turned toward the noise as if in slow motion, almost afraid to see the source.

It was Puck, doubled over in merriment, the terrible dark mirth of his laughter rising until it reached the maniacal pitch that echoed through her visions.

22

THE LAUGHTER WAS STIFLED as he realized she stared at him. Puck struggled to assume a serious expression, his mouth twitching.

"Sorry," he managed before he burst out giggling again. He waved apologetically. "It really isn't that funny. See you later, love."

He strode through the crowd toward the door, still chuckling. No one acknowledged him at all, even in a condescending way. Florian, who knew all his patrons by name and made a point to greet them, never spoke to Puck on exit or entrance. Stunned, Callie stood frozen in shock until Pan tapped her on the shoulder, leaped quickly out of swinging range, and asked for a drink.

The rest of the night passed in a blur. The show ended at ten, going back to the Olympus Channel live shot of the mountain, still in half-twilight though the city was dark and quiet outside the windows. The news channels all picked up on the Athens story and as better footage came out the grisly toll became all too clear. Florian was worried about her and kept trying to engage her attention, but she stayed busy, afraid to think about it for too long.

The mood in the bar remained subdued, ebbing with the steady outflow of patrons. Snatches of conversation stood out. The Amaranthine liked the human world and all the luxuries and trappings it held.

Primarily they fretted their convenience would be interrupted by the war. Aphrodite wondered aloud if the fall fashion shows in Paris would be disrupted, because she was certain she would be able to attend this year even though Zeus hadn't announced he was lifting the ban on divine intervention yet. Pan hoped the Glastonbury Music Festival would go on as planned.

Not one of them seemed to care about the human casualties in Athens, or how many lives might end worldwide when the battles spread.

And Puck—*Puck!*—was involved somehow. Was he connected with the faceless person who fanned the conflict from behind the scenes? If her visions continued to hold true, the next event would be a disaster of literally biblical proportions.

Late hangers-on finally wound down their party about two-thirty in the morning. At last, the bar was empty. All the TV's showed the silent mountain shot, save for one in the corner someone had hijacked to watch a rerun of *Duck Dynasty*. The main screen still showed CNN, where reporters relayed the grim details from Athens as they became clearer in the growing light of dawn. A smoldering Acropolis lay shrouded in gray, hazy smoke, and dazed people wandered the streets of the neighborhoods below, some wailing as loved ones were pulled from the rubble of their shattered homes.

Unable to look away from the horror, Callie stared in numb acceptance at the screen until Florian's decisive punch of a button. All the televisions snapped at once into blackness and silence. He came up behind and wrapped his arms around her. She leaned her head back against his chest and let him hug her.

"How many people lived in the threshold in Athens?" She swept at her eyes, stung by the hot, red miasma of despair rising in her chest. "Do you know?"

Florian sighed heavily. "For certain, no. The Doorkeeper. Possibly their family, and perhaps less then ten people like us." He stepped back and turned her around, his hands gentle on her shoulders. "You couldn't have done anything to stop it, Callie."

She met his gaze stonily. "Maybe I could, if I was able to control my visions."

His face went blank. He let his hands fall to his sides. "You can't be thinking of using ambrosia."

"I have to do something!" She spun away from him and leaned over the bar and took measured breaths fighting the urge to scream in frustration. Florian sat in the stool beside her, his gaze on the floor.

"You've seen Gran. If something happened to you, too, I'm not certain I could bear it." His shoulders drooped. Callie swallowed against the lump in her throat.

"I know. But I can't just sit here and watch another disaster unravel when I might be able to stop it. I don't know how."

"I want to help, however I can. Gran always said sharing a burden makes it easier."

Three to share the burden. She straightened in a slow movement and stared at Florian. His eyes narrowed in lines of worry.

"What is it?"

"I need to think." An idea shouted at the back of her mind, one that would require research. "Will you fire me if I go upstairs without cleaning tables?"

"No." He stood, his expression softening. "But I think you're taking advantage of me and the fact I may have a mad crush on you."

Warmth fizzed between the heavy, blunt-edged boulders lodged in her chest. Her mouth turned upwards despite the weight in her soul. "Most definitely."

"Just this once, then. I did it by myself for the last twenty five years, so I think I can handle it tonight."

"Thank you." She hugged him again. His arms went around her, his concern and fear betrayed in the taut muscles of his back. Florian held her locked in the warm embrace until she pulled away with resignation.

Callie hung up her apron on the hook behind the bar. At the entrance to the stairs, she paused and turned back. "Florian, did you see Puck here tonight?"

Brows knitted in thought, he shook his head. "No, I don't think he was here. I would remember pouring more tequila."

Callie nodded slowly, considering. He eyed her suspiciously.

"Has he been bothering you? I told him to leave you alone." Florian's frown darkened his countenance. "Fairies can get out of hand. They feed on human energy like the Amaranthine do, but it's more physical than emotional. They'll drain someone until they waste away if it goes too far. The bad thing is, a person finds it pleasurable and doesn't mind until it's too late to survive. Titania and Oberon are very good about keeping the others in check."

"They're energy vampires?" Callie rubbed her arms, vaguely disgusted. "So when they kiss my hand, like Puck does, they're sucking energy off me?"

"Something like that." Florian hefted a tub of sticky beer glasses onto the bar above the dishwasher and began to load them inside. "They get more of a rush from ambrosia and alcohol, but it's a different kind of high from a human, I've been told. I'd hate to play the cold iron card but Stefanio said I might if any of the fair folk got out of hand. I'm assuming he meant Puck, too."

"Why wouldn't it include him?" Callie inquired, her interest sharpening.

"Well, he's their clan chief, the oldest. Sunshine and Ron are the acknowledged king and queen, but Puck's the most powerful."

"Then why isn't he the king?"

"Some questions you'll find aren't wise to ask, and I never have. Call me a coward." Florian grimaced. "Remind me to make you a list. When you ask those things, my establishment gets struck by indoor lightning or my tables and chairs get broken. I haven't found a repairman or builder who can cross the threshold yet."

"Duly noted," Callie assured him. "Good night."

IN THE DARKNESS of her room, she huddled in the huge armchair and let her mind churn guilty circles around the disastrous events in

Athens. The only other visionary she had ever met was Bridget, and she could not ask her for more reliable information. Finally she opened her laptop, the display's glow the only light in the room, and pulled up a search engine.

Controlling your visions returned a lot of new age-y advice about dream journals, banners screaming SIGNS YOU MAY BE CLAIR-VOYANT, and offers to sign up for a free course on how to make the most of her psychic powers. Time was too limited for that. Skimming through some of the other results, though, a word jumped out and made something click in her mind.

Delphi.

More metaphysical nonsense populated this site, but the core idea grew. She needed real, academic information. Callie attempted to access her college's server and waited as the wheel spun down. After a moment the screen accepted her password. Evidently, she hadn't been dropped yet. Certain her parents had a hand in that, her heart ached.

Messages from concerned friends asking her to contact them blinked on her server chat window, dated more than a month old now. With a jab, she minimized the windows before she could see too much of the pain caused by her abrupt departure.

In the search engine's query box she typed in *Delphi*. Arguably the most famous of Oracles, the site was dedicated to the god Apollo. Research deduced that the priestesses inhaled vapors, presumed to be naturally occurring volcanic fumes, which fueled their visions. However, her recent conversations with Florian regarding the misuse of ambrosia brought insight into sharp focus: in its distilled form ambrosia was white and vaporous, and in large amounts, toxic to human descendants of the Amaranthine.

She suspected Delphi's highly revered status was due to the accuracy of visionaries fueled not by volcanic fumes, but by ambrosia.

In the cleared field she typed: *Dodona*. Often overshadowed by the more famous Oracle at Delphi, Dodona was a site dedicated to Zeus, but ancient kings and seekers of knowledge went there as well to commune with the gods and receive advice from the Oracle. She reviewed the information with a clinical eye, pulling out theories and facts she now suspected to be important.

At Dodona, the will of the gods was communicated by not one, but three women.

Three to share the burden, always three. Past, present, and future. Bridget's words echoed in her memory.

Unsettling accounts were unearthed by her electronic digging, stories of Delphi priestesses who died in convulsions after breathing in the vapors. A little too close to home. But in Dodona, she found no records of fatalities in any translations available on the college server. Was it because no ambrosia was inhaled, or due to the combined strength of the three individuals?

She typed in the first letters of another search, but a chat window popped up with a digital *bloop* and startled her.

Dr. C. Davies (online): CALLIE?

She'd forgotten to disengage the chat function after minimizing the windows. Up early to check her messages before summer classes, Mom discovered her online status.

A moment's hesitation passed as she wrestled her leaping heart and the panic of guilt. She typed back: *Hi, Mom.*

Oh, thank god. Are you all right? Where are you? Caroline's worry shivered from the screen in palpable waves.

I shouldn't say now. I'm okay.

Callie, what happened? Your letter scared us. The apartment was destroyed. Siobhan was talking about demons. Are you in trouble?

Not at the moment, she lied. *I can't explain without sounding completely crazy. I'm sorry I had to leave, but it was the only way to make sure you and Dad were safe.*

Safe from what? Callie, what is going on?

Tears gathered in accusing drops of shame. *I'll tell you when I can. I love you both so much. Kiss Dad for me.*

She hastily logged out, but not before another message popped up. *Callie, we love you. We know you are*

The laptop slammed shut without reading the rest. It was all she could do to keep herself from logging back on.

2 3

THE TEARS WOULDN'T STOP. A blind toss landed her computer on the bed when she stalked out the doors leading out to the garden, sniffling miserably.

The snowcapped mountains across the threshold glowed with pale, lavender midnight sun. Halfway down the stone steps she sat and glared at the peak which concealed the home of the old gods. Not that she could get close to it, but the thought of walking into the marble throne room and slapping some sense into Zeus was tempting. Her faltering laugh at the imagined scene was too much like a sob, and she covered her mouth.

"Did you have a bad dream too?"

Callie yelped in surprise. A pair of gray eyes, illuminated in the pale oval of a face by the light of a cell phone screen, looked back at her from the bench beneath the tree. At first, she couldn't see anything but a dim, legless shape on the bench. She recognized the girl was sitting in lotus position only after a long, heart-stopping second and wiped her eyes in haste, descending the rest of the steps into the garden.

"Eleni! I'm sorry, I didn't know you were there."

"I couldn't sleep." Her soft voice, high and thin, her speech unaccented, made it difficult to believe that only hours ago she didn't speak English at all. Peppy, repetitive music droned from her cell phone.

"What are you playing?"

"*Neko Atsume.*" Eleni sighed and put down the phone. "I have twenty cats now. I want a real one, but we move a lot."

She moved to the bench, where Eleni unfolded herself from the criss-cross pretzel of arms and legs and made room for her to sit down. The girl was long limbed, at the awkward tween-ish stage where puberty started to claim the softer edges of childhood. "Is it hard to sleep in new places?" Callie asked.

The girl shrugged and picked at the hem of her pajamas with sparkle-polished nails. "No. I'm used to it."

Callie took a tremulous breath. "We moved a lot when I was little, too."

Eleni looked up at the purple sky. "We never stay very long. How long have you lived here?"

"Only a few days," Callie admitted. "This is a safe place, though. I think I'll be here for a while."

"I knew it would be. It feels good." Eleni's face crumpled in the twilight. "I hoped the bad dreams wouldn't come here, but they did."

"What did you dream about?"

The girl's bare feet kicked against the grass. "That Papa's doorway blew up. The one at the Acropolis."

A frisson of fear and wonder shivered through Callie. "Do you mean the Parthenon in Athens?"

"Yeah."

Callie's pulse sped up. "Eleni, I dreamed about it too," she confessed.

"You did?" The girl looked at her sideways, suspicious.

"Bridget and I both have dreams like yours. Are they always true?"

Eleni twitched one shoulder again, winding a lock of long, brown hair around her fingers and avoiding Callie's intent gaze. "Daddy doesn't like me to talk about them. They scare him."

"They still scare me, sometimes. I've had them ever since I was a little older than you." Her voice dropped to a whisper. "Mine came true tonight, too."

"The one about the Acropolis? It's really gone, isn't it?" Eleni's lower lip trembled. Tears made wet tracks down her cheeks. "If the door's broken, Papa won't be able to come visit us in Athens again."

"Hermes will find a way to come to you, no matter what happens," Callie soothed the child. She reached out and took her hand.

The mistake became clear a moment too late as energy pulsed between them.

Eleni cried out in surprise. The vision of a flooding Rome took them, sharper and more detailed than the one Callie experienced with Bridget. The hysterical laughter rose higher. Callie now held certainty it was Puck, but he remained hidden. The figure silhouetted against the burning hilltops was female, but she still couldn't zoom in on the face. Just as she thought she might be able to focus, Eleni yanked her hand away. The vision ended.

The girl stared at her with wide, frightened eyes. "That hasn't happened yet, has it?"

"Not yet," Callie breathed. Again, the shared Sight triggered no seizure, just as with Bridget.

"I never had a dream that hasn't happened yet. It's always right now in my dreams," Eleni said quaveringly. "Was that Rome? We used to live there, but I don't remember so much water. I loved spaghetti. Will there still be spaghetti when Rome's gone?"

"Eleni?" A voice floated through the garden, making them both look up.

"I'm here, Daddy," the girl answered.

Marios appeared in pajama bottoms, his dark hair tumbled in the breeze. "Darling, what are you doing out here?"

"She had a nightmare," Callie answered for Eleni, and moved aside so Marios had room to sit.

"Oh, my dear," Marios swept the girl's hair back, crooning. "It was just a dream."

"No, Callie told me it was true! She dreamed it too."

Even in the dark, Callie recognized the daggers being thrown in her direction by Marios's narrowed eyes, and she spoke softly.

"It is true, Marios. The Parthenon is gone and the Acropolis is burning. You can look on the TV. People were...badly hurt." She amended her words for the sake of the child, but Marios interpreted her pause and cursed beneath his breath.

"You had this same dream?" He eyed Callie with dismay over his daughter's head.

"Yes. Bridget and I both had other visions. Eleni and I just shared one which hasn't happened yet."

"No, this can't be true." He shook his head.

"It is. And in the visions, I think I saw who is responsible for starting all this." Hope nudged Callie's spirits, and her voice quickened in excitement. "Eleni has seen them now, too, and maybe together we can—"

"No." Marios gathered his daughter and her cell phone with sharp, protective movements, and stood. "She's too young for such a burden. This gift is a curse for her."

"It isn't fun for me either." Callie rose and faced him in accusation. "Marios, terrible things are happening, and more people will die if we don't try to do something."

"No. I'm sorry." He turned and walked away, tugging a reluctant Eleni with him. Over her shoulder, Eleni glanced at Callie, her expression more thoughtful than frightened. The darkness swallowed them up, the slam of their terrace door an emphatic end to Marios's side of the conversation.

She buried her head in her hands. As long as her visions still remained true to their usual pattern, only a day or two was left before the war between gods and angels brought cataclysmic destruction to the city. Since she experienced the portent of Rome's annihilation with both Bridget and Eleni separately, she could not be sure. Thousands, perhaps millions of lives were in danger. Her research suggested that without the help of two other gifted individuals, the only way to elicit a more detailed vision required inhaling vapors of ambrosia.

Despite Florian's warning, the idea ricocheted inside her head until it was impossible to ignore: the ambrosia had helped Bridget see what she wanted. It might help Callie learn who fanned the flames in her visions.

If she continued on Bridget's path, was she destined for the same kind of madness?

Averting the horrors she'd glimpsed would be worth the risk. The hard part would be convincing Florian to let her try.

It might be best if he didn't know at all.

Sleep came with difficulty. When she woke about midday, it was to the sound of laughter—not the hysterical cackle from her visions, but the sweet, pure laughter of a child.

She peered through the lace curtains at the sunlit garden below, where Marios chased Eleni through the trees and raised beds, the girl giggling at her father's half-hearted attempts to catch her. Callie turned away with a wistful smile. Marios was right, for the most part. Kids shouldn't have to witness horrible things. They should be playing in the sun.

Showered and dressed, she made some toast and fretted over her plans to use ambrosia. She took her breakfast out on the terrace, and Eleni waved gaily when she glimpsed Callie. She waved back. Marios chose that moment to usher Eleni in for lunch and glanced uneasily at Callie as he shepherded his daughter to their own door. With Marios acting as if she were trying to corrupt the kid, Callie wondered how she and Bridget and Eleni could hope to work together. In search of something else to distract her, she went downstairs.

Florian, of course, was in place behind the bar. So were a small number of weary, armored gods and goddesses, unusual at such an early hour. Hephaestus squeezed into a booth alone, nursing his favorite brand of whiskey, scarred face stained with soot. Mercifully, his wife was nowhere to be seen.

Athena, whose ancient temple was built to house the threshold so violently destroyed last night, occupied one of the high stools with her helmet on the next seat. Callie recognized her as Hollywood's current golden girl, but her famously long, box-braided hair was now shaved close to her head in a warrior's crop, dark features fierce, beautiful, and monumentally angry. Hermes sat at the other end near Florian, who prepared something from ambrosia. No one was talking, the televisions dark and silent.

Knotting the strings of her apron, Callie leaned on the bar opposite Florian. "Anything I can do to help?" she asked in hushed tones.

Warmth and greeting rose in his eyes, but his serious mien didn't change. "Not really. If anyone else shows up, you can take orders if you like, but I don't think it will be very busy. You still get a day off this week. You aren't required to work every day."

"Don't know what else to do at this point," she admitted, leaning on the bar with her chin resting in her hand. She watched Florian put the finishing touches on the item taking shape beneath his fingers: something decadent, and densely chocolate.

"How are the new tenants settling in?" Hermes inquired carefully, his voice rough and fatigued. Callie glanced surreptitiously at the other Amaranthine and answered in kind

"They're doing well," she assured him. "They were out in the garden this morning."

She suddenly wondered if he would be willing to help her. As Florian took the plate of chocolate to Athena, she whispered, "Hermes, what do you know about Oracles?"

His head shot up, mercurial gaze piercing her. Barely audible he asked, "Eleni? Did she get another vision?"

"Yes, with me," she whispered back. "Both of us shared the same vision at the same time last night. And it happened to me with Bridget yesterday."

His face went pale beneath the sweat and soot before inexplicable relief soothed the tight-drawn tension of his features. Hermes glanced around for a second and motioned her to follow him into the still-dark gaming area where they could talk more privately. They slid into a shadowy booth. His armor rattled as he leaned toward her.

"Do you have epilepsy? Seizures that come with your visions?"

Unprepared for that question she stammered, "Yes, alone, but not with the others. Why?"

Hermes breathed out in wonder. "That's the hallmark of a true Oracle. It sounds like you are Delphi-gifted! We haven't had a real one in, what, fifteen hundred years? What did you see?"

"I saw what was going to happen at the Acropolis my first night here. I've had visions ever since I was thirteen, and Bridget, too. But Eleni is so young."

"Eleni is a prodigy. Normally our children's gifts don't develop so early, but she's special. Marios's family is known for producing gifted individuals. They possess strong, recessive Amaranthine genetics." Hermes ran a hand over his face. "Marios was still transitioning when he became pregnant. Eleni was an unexpected blessing to us, but she has nightmares, daymares...she's traumatized by what she sees. She doesn't suffer seizures but the visions are uncontrollable."

"She had a nightmare last night. She watched the Acropolis being destroyed." Callie hesitated, and said, "Hermes, Rome is going to be completely obliterated in the next battle. Bridget and I experienced the vision together and then Eleni and me. We all saw the same thing."

His head shot up. "Rome?"

She nodded affirmatively. "This has to stop."

His laugh crackled with bitterness. "Yeah, how do you propose I stop Zeus, one of the most infuriatingly stubborn beings in the universe, from doing exactly what he wants? I gave him the battle report this morning. It was like he wasn't even listening. With the threshold in Athens gone, Rome is the largest one left, and God's highway too. If it's destroyed, we're all going to have a very hard time passing in and out of the human realm. Everyone else made it very clear they're not involved in this pissing match, and using their door-ways won't be an option. So much for the divine intervention Zeus wants to reinstate."

"Did Eleni tell you anything about her visions? About the laughing man?"

Dismissively, he shrugged. "Yeah, a lot of people are probably laughing at us right now."

"No, Hermes. I heard Puck laugh last night. The same as in my visions, but I saw a woman too." She leaned forward. "I think he's somehow influencing Zeus."

"Puck. You mean the fairy, Puck?" Hermes gaped at her, incredulous. "Callie, compared to Zeus, Puck is nothing. They may have been here longer than the Amaranthine, but when it comes down to brute strength? No way." He shook his head vehemently. "This might be the most ridiculous idea Zeus ever had, but I think it's his own idea." His brow creased uncertainly, and Callie recognized it.

"You're not sure. You said before he isn't acting like himself. He's not listening to you. Would he listen to Hera?"

"Hera." He sat up straight. "You said a woman, too?"

"Yes. I can't see her face clearly in the vision. What are you thinking?" Callie asked. Hermes shook his head.

"It just occurred to me that so far, Hera's been uncharacteristically passive about this whole enterprise. Which is never good." One finger tapped his lips. "In the meantime, here's an idea. I don't like it, but I think it can slide through a two thousand year old loophole that concerns you, Eleni, and Bridget. Unfortunately, it also involves Apollo." He ran his restless hands through his hair. "He's become a real asshole, but prophecy is his specialty, not mine. I'll send him to you. Three is the magic number if you're going to do it safely, but Bridget is—well, to put it bluntly, damaged. I can't guarantee it will work the same way or if she should even try."

"Florian told me what she did." Callie bit her lip. "Do you think I could use ambrosia like they did in Delphi?"

"It was always a dicey prospect. You might be strong enough, or you could end up like Bridget. Or, you might die. I don't think Florian would forgive me for either one, so don't do anything until Apollo shows you how." Exhaling heavily, Hermes sat back. "Marios is going to take some convincing, too, and I can't talk to him here until this is over, not without risking my exposure. If they find out I'm protecting my family?" He shook his head. "I'm not ready to face those consequences. I'll leave it up to you. Show him this."

He closed his hand. When he opened it, a small silver coin with a caduceus engraved in subtle relief appeared in his palm. "Be careful where and when you start this conversation, okay? I can't protect them if I'm banished from the human world, and you never know who else is listening."

"I'll be careful," Callie promised him. He placed the coin in her hand and closed his fingers over hers, holding it there as he confided in low tones,

"I'm in contact with others on both sides who aren't happy about the way this is playing out. We've been talking, and we're going to see if we can convince people to stop this. Apollo will need to confirm your status, but if we have an Oracle again?" Hermes grinned at her. Hope glinted in his eyes. "Now, that's something humans and Amaranthine can put their hope and faith into, and something Zeus would be willing to work with. You might be the key to our comeback, High Priestess. Call me, and I will come when thou biddest."

He inclined his head respectfully, leaving Callie open-mouthed and ready to protest in bewilderment as he vanished. His words held the gravity of a pledge. What had she just gotten herself into?

Unexpectedly, Hermes stumbled back into existence in front of her and swore.

"Well, that ruined my dramatic exit. What the fuck?"

"What happened?"

"Not sure. The doorway bounced me back. I heard this is happening quite a bit in the last couple of days, but a first for me. I'll try again."

This time, he stayed gone. Sliding out of the booth, she put the coin in her pocket. Back in the main room of the bar, no one had moved. Athena picked delicately at the chocolate dessert in front of her, and Hephaestus brooded over his whiskey. Florian was absent. The door to the back room still rocked back and forth as if he'd passed into the storage area. She made her way around the bar and pushed through the door.

The long, windowless room, nearly pitch-dark save for the light that waxed and waned with the swinging door, seemed to be empty. But a shape moved against the shine of the newly delivered Guinness kegs, a faint, odd luminescence edging the aluminum vessels. The hair on her arms prickled. She fumbled and couldn't find the still-unfamiliar switch in her haste to banish the gloom.

"Florian?"

The figure startled and moved quickly away from the kegs. No sound of footsteps on the concrete warned her of approach until his shape stepped noiselessly out of the shadows.

She jumped, a high-pitched screech forcing its way from her throat. Deep, amused laughter rolled out and echoed in the windowless storeroom.

"Did I scare you?"

"Yes!" She laughed nervously and rubbed her goose-bump covered arms. "What are you doing back here in the dark? I can't find the lights."

"I was waiting for you." Roughly, he pulled her close, trapped against his chest. One hand gripped her ponytail and his lips moved in demanding hunger on hers. Desire crawled along Callie's skin wherever he caressed her and moved toward her mouth, where he drank her kiss like a man too long in the desert. Her senses reeled with a strange, disconnected desire which buckled her knees and threatened to sweep her away, the heat of arousal building between her legs in delicious anticipation.

Internal warnings brayed soundless alarms.

This wasn't Florian.

Ice crystals of terror flooded her veins and pricked sharp, cold edges through her skin. Rigid, she frantically pushed away from him. With an annoyed growl, he stopped kissing her.

Callie tried to squirm out of his embrace as a bizarre shift of mass and clothing took place against her body. Florian's t-shirt disappeared to be replaced by black leather. His frame shrank and became lean, wiry, and half a foot shorter. In the dim light, a familiar face grinned at her, his arm tightening around her waist.

"You're becoming a problem, love."

Callie struggled and tried to scream. Puck clapped his hand over her mouth and picked her up. She lashed out with fists and feet, but he was preternaturally strong and immune to her pummeling, her nails sliding off his skin. He carried her out to the loading dock entrance, kicked it open and threw her onto the concrete outside. Cement grated a layer of skin from her palms as she skidded toward the edge, the sharp pain forcing a cry between her gritted teeth.

Puck slammed the door and leaned against it, arms crossed petulantly over his chest.

"I tried three different warding spells, shadow travel, and glamour, and you are able to see through all of them, Callie. You're endangering my business." He stalked furiously from one end of the loading dock to the other as Callie huddled on the cement, nursing her abrasions. Finally he rounded on her and crouched only inches away, swirling eyes dark with rage and startling in his youthful countenance. "Ever since they signed that bloody contract, I hoped this would happen, and now you are fucking it up!" He screamed the last words into her face, and Callie flinched.

"Can you imagine what it feels like to be the most puissant race in existence and never be acknowledged for what you are?" His whisper held velvet edged with shattered glass. "We created magical creatures. We made places of breathtaking beauty, and they destroyed them in their squabbles over who was more relevant, whose little cults had more sheep in the fold, who had the most statues and monuments and temples! And *we*, we who were here before them, older than any of those barbarians who called themselves gods, are treated as less important, as no asset." The last three words were hissed in a venomous imitation of Gabriel's polished speech.

"It was you in the shadows and the sunbeams. You spied on the war council!" Cold flooded Callie as she realized. Puck snorted.

"Just when I think I can deliver the final push to send God and Zeus over the cliff, you show up. If you are what I think you are..." He grabbed her bloody hand, his nostrils flaring as he brought it to his face and inhaled deeply. Callie's head spun as the huge draught of energy crawled off her skin, sucked into Puck's lungs.

"Oh, ho!" he crowed. His tongue darted out and he gave her palm a long, lascivious lick. She tried to pull away in disgust. His fingers tightened with bruising force on her forearm; his eyes rolled back and showed white as he moved her blood around in his mouth like wine. They snapped open, a triumphant grin slowly spreading over his face, and he chortled. Puck started to look less human by the second, features angular and elf-like. His skin took on a luminescence that was beautiful and at the same time, terrifying.

"No wonder you give me such a hard-on. You're a bloody power-house! Three quarters Amaranthine, and I bet you're having visions, aren't you? Maybe even a real Oracle." He made a *tsk tsk* sound. Puck jerked her to her feet, and Callie found her tongue.

"I will find a way to stop this."

"Yes, you might," Puck agreed. "But you've drawn someone else's attention. I can't afford to be exposed, and I want to bring the bastards down."

He threw his head back to face the sky. A screech erupted from his throat, molten and painful in her ears. It burrowed its way into Callie's brain and spurred her pulse into frantic overdrive.

The flap of immense wings echoed off the brick walls of the alley. With a snarl the banshee landed on the cobblestones outside the threshold, its back to Callie: a dark, night-terror reflection of an angel, with shadow-hued wings and strong, naked ebony limbs. Its feet ended in the talons of a raptor, which flexed and struck sparks against the cobblestones.

The face as it turned was almost beautiful in its oil-slick sheened skin, moon-pale eyes wide and nostrils pulsing in search of the prey it could scent but not see through the barrier. Its mouth opened to reveal row upon row of sharp, deadly teeth, a hiss of breath escaping from its throat. Callie froze, the paralysis of nightmares numbing her limbs.

"I told you how much I loved the bloodthirsty beauties, didn't I?"

The banshee's head turned sharply in Puck's direction as he spoke, cocking in almost dog-like alert. "Always one of my favorites, the banshee. They're bloody brilliant, so much smarter than the harpy that fried herself against the barriers. I created the hunters to feed on Amaranthine energy, but they are hard to catch. Their bastard offspring, though?" He shrugged. "They've almost cleaned out you vermin on this continent. She wails because she's hungry and her sisters are gone. She's the last of her kind, but a good, gifted meal might help her last another few hundred years." Puck yanked Callie to her feet and propelled her to the edge of the dock.

He wrapped one freakishly strong arm around Callie's waist and his hand seized the back of her neck. He forced her forward until the fuzzy, electric tingle of the barrier pricked her nose.

Captive there at the fragile membrane between threshold and human world, she struggled to free herself from Puck's immovable grip. Fear numbed her senses as the creature lifted its head in search of her scent, drooling, and shuffled closer to the point where Puck held her. Talons clicked on the cobblestone drive.

"Take a good look at my darling girl. Isn't she pretty?" Puck whispered in her ear. "I'm sorry, Callie. I really am growing fond of you. But if you tell anyone what I've been up to, I will not hesitate to serve you to her as a main course. Keep your mouth shut."

She stumbled backward against the release of the strong grip that held her. Callie looked around wildly.

Puck had vanished.

Only a few feet away, the creature's head swiveled in a sharp arc with the sound of her uneven stumble on the dock. Her eyes riveted on the banshee outside the threshold, she took slow, quiet steps backward, heart thundering with the urge to flee.

A vicious shove hit her between the shoulder blades and sent her flying.

The explosive frisson of crossing the barrier in midair stunned her even before she landed with bone-jarring force on the cobblestones. Her head struck the ground. Pain lanced through her on impact, disoriented as much by the fall as the transition from threshold to outside world. Waves of vertigo kept her from rising.

A horrible scream pierced the alley and bounced back in terrifying echoes from the brick walls. Callie struggled to clear her graying vision as the dark shape loomed over her.

The scent of leather, carrion, and feathers choked her as one taloned foot came down on her shoulder and pinned her to the ground. The slavering mouthful of sharp teeth bent toward Callie, the banshee quivering with eager appetite. Terror vaporized the scream bubbling in her throat.

FLORIAN BLINKED in confusion and shook himself, trying to clear the cobwebby strands of disorientation from his mind. Why had he left the bar when patrons were inside his establishment? The urgent conviction he had something important to do dissipated as soon as he'd entered his apartment, but he had the odd feeling he'd been standing there for several minutes.

Downstairs, Florian recognized the unmistakable slam of the steel back door. Puzzled, he turned to descend the steps until the click of another door opening on the second landing made him stop. He looked up into the eyes of his newest tenant. Marios's tight-lipped expression spoke of worry and concern.

"Is everything all right?" he asked.

"No, Eleni is upset. She keeps asking for Callie. Do you know where she is?"

"Yes, she's downstairs."

"I think I need her help. Eleni has visions. Something is happening. She's frightened and not making sense." He cast a glance back at the open door, uncertain. "Callie said she gets visions, too."

"I'll ask her to come up."

"Thank you." Just as Marios turned to go back inside, the ear-splitting shriek of the child's voice rising in terror came from the apartment. Eleni ran out to the landing, her eyes wide, sobbing in terror, and tears streaked her face. Marios knelt before her, trying to soothe and calm her, and Florian froze as Eleni's eyes focused on him, fighting her father's attempt to gather her in.

"The monster! The monster is here!" the girl wailed. "Save Callie!"

Florian didn't hesitate, pounding down the stairs three at a time. As he turned the corner into the bar, he plowed into Athena and Hephaestus, grim and startled.

"Callie's in danger. Where is she?" he demanded. Athena made a motion toward the storage room, bewildered.

"She went back there a few minutes ago."

A scream filtered into the bar: unearthly, inhuman. Florian knew that sound.

It was a hunter.

The Amaranthine identified it too, and followed in haste as Florian shoved through the swinging door toward the sound, praying—not knowing to whom—he wouldn't be too late.

He ripped open the steel door. The dock was empty, but in the alleyway, a nightmare unfolded in broad daylight with Callie pinned beneath the claws of a banshee.

A resounding shout echoed off the brick walls lining the backstreet. Sunlight illuminated the alley in a searing splash of brilliance and he staggered blindly, his arm in front of his eyes. The banshee screamed and took flight. Callie cried out in pain. The flap of wings faded into the distance, a final wail lingered above the buildings. As the creature disappeared Florian lurched forward, his vision still full of light-dazzled blobs.

Hephaestus's massive hand enveloped his forearm and yanked him back before he could jump down into the alley. "Stop right there."

"She's bleeding!"

"I'll get her," Athena said firmly, and vaulted over the rail. She jogged to Callie's side in a rattle of armor.

"Back away from that barrier before you go through it," Hephaestus growled.

Callie raised up on her elbow as Athena reached her. "I'm okay, Florian. I just want to get inside," she said, her teeth chattering. "Please be careful."

His pulse hammered with the comprehension of what he'd nearly done out of fear for Callie. Florian reversed carefully until his shoulders met cold steel and realized someone else stood framed in the doorway.

The stranger sauntered casually to the edge of the dock and shoved his hands into the pockets of his soiled white medical coat. "Don't everyone thank me at once for chasing off the banshee."

Hephaestus eyed the newcomer sourly. "You haven't changed."

"If you chased it off, then *I* thank you, " Florian said fervently. "I owe you a drink on the house."

"That'll do for a start, I suppose." The Amaranthine's face turned toward him, but his gaze was riveted on Callie as she wobbled unsteadily toward them, supported by Athena. "So you're the Door-keeper, yes?"

"Florian." The shoulder of Callie's shirt was torn and bloody, her skin marked with claw tracks, proof of just how close tragedy had come. Why had she gone outside the barrier?

As Callie reached the midpoint of the alleyway, the stranger leapt lightly from the dock and ignored Athena's suspicious glare. "Let me look at that shoulder."

"I'm sorry. I don't know you." Florian saw Callie wince as the individual examined the deep scratches.

"No, you don't." He probed her wounds. "These aren't bad. I really don't have time for this. Let's go inside and get it over with. Hermes sent me."

"You—you're Apollo?" Callie gaped as he put her hands around her waist and boosted her upwards. Hephaestus stooped and caught her under the arms to draw her onto the dock.

"You're a genius. But I guess, given the circumstances, you could call me Dad."

Callie staggered forward in mid-step as she crossed the barrier and he released her. Florian moved hastily to catch her as she fell.

"What?" she managed to say before she fainted.

Cradling the threshold-stunned Callie in his arms, Florian stared at Apollo, unable himself to form a coherent thought. The reclusive Amaranthine stood below the dock with hands on hips and gave a beleaguered sigh, shaking his head.

"Damn. My first Oracle in two thousand years and she's already a pain in the ass," he grumbled.

2 6

STARING ACROSS THE BOOTH, Callie struggled to attach the weather-beaten, middle-aged face to any stories she knew of Apollo. God of the Sun, music, medicine and prophecy: nothing prepared her for the person sitting impatiently on the opposite side.

Slate-blue eyes and disheveled ashen hair mirrored nothing in her own features. Stained, rumpled khaki clothing and the once-white lab coat he wore spoke of weeks without washing. So did his body, odd for the Amaranthine. Even the goat-guy smelled like clean livestock. He noted her expression and shrugged irritably.

"What? I'm researching medicine in the Amazon, and I'm at a critical juncture. If it had been anybody but Hermes asking, I would have told them to go screw themselves. You already threw off my timetable with the rescue and being inconveniently sensitive to barriers, so let's get on with it." He reached over the table and tried to touch her face, and Callie avoided his reach, gaping incredulously.

"Wait a minute. You can't say, 'Hi, I'm your Dad', and not expect me to have some questions."

"Oh, Zeus's balls." In disgust, Apollo knocked back the scotch Florian had poured for him. "This is why I don't make a habit of introducing myself to my offspring. Yes, I'm your 'father'." Sarcastic quotation marks were added with his fingers. "I donated the biological material which produced you."

"My mom was only seventeen!" Outrage sang in Callie's ears, but he scowled in affront.

"Relax. So was I, at the time. I'm not a pedophile. This shape works for what I'm doing now. Back then I was in a boy band, doing the music thing, and she was half Muse. We dug each other and we hooked up. It was only natural."

"Half Muse?" Callie sat up straight.

"Yeah. I guess I should have known our kid would be gifted."

"The hunters got her when I was four." Callie didn't hide her venomous accusation. "Didn't you know? She died leading them away from me. Didn't you even care?"

He stiffened, and took another drink. "I was somebody else by then. The boy band thing didn't work out as well as I'd hoped. Marky Mark ruined it for everybody." He rolled his eyes. "Now he's an actor. I weep for the future."

He leaned forward. "Listen, I'm sorry, but this thing with God and Zeus is a little more important than your hurt feelings because I didn't stick around. You inherited some considerable power, and if Hermes is reading the contract right, you might be able to settle this fiasco with a win/win situation. I can show you the safest way to use it. If you're lucky, the kid and Mrs. Alzheimer can help you out and take some of the energy off your nervous system so you don't burn up or spaz out."

Callie's mouth dropped open. "You *are* an asshole."

"But I'm the asshole with the knowledge you need, and you're running short on time. My incubations will be reaching peak mitosis in about fifteen minutes, and I'm leaving whether we're done or not. So, what's it going to be?"

The infuriating challenge in Apollo's eyes made her want to refuse, no matter the consequences. For a minute, Callie stared back. She dropped her eyes first.

"Please teach me," she finally muttered.

"At least I got a 'please'." He sat back. "You're Delphi-gifted. That means you can probably do this on your own, but not without risk. It is impossible to accurately measure a safe dose of ambrosia vapors to inhale." He narrowed his eyes at her. "It's like playing Russian roulette with your central nervous system, so if you're okay with that, go ahead."

Callie stifled a gulp and glared at Apollo in stony resolve. She'd be damned if she showed this callous jerk any fear.

"Never do it alone, and never more than once every couple of days. You need to use the Dodona method as often as possible, which takes all three of you. There's still a risk, but not as prevalent. Because you're my offspring, you possess the strongest gift. You probably read people easily, and when you touch other visionaries, you connect with them, yes?"

Callie nodded wordlessly, and Apollo continued, "Before you breathe in the vapors, you need to hold their hands for a few minutes and let your gifts work together. It's called synchronizing. You're the only true Oracle. You're the only one who can inhale the ambrosia. The other two are gifted, but they're not you, and the old lady would die if she tried it again."

"What does it mean, I'm an Oracle? That I'm psychic?" Callie asked, confused.

He snorted derisively. "An Oracle isn't new age psychic bullshit. It's someone who has the ability to tap into events in time that haven't happened yet. You read people because you can sense their probable futures. If they're going to do something important, bad or good, shifts in time come off the event. Hone in on those shifts and you will be able to direct the vision down any potential time stream to find what you want. When I was younger and randier, I produced more Oracles, but more of our offspring survived. Strong blood like yours is hard to come by these days."

"If I'm so strong, how come my nervous system shorts out every time I get a vision?" Callie tried to cross her arms and winced as the deep rakes left by the banshee's talons reminded her they were there.

"Because the human part of your brain can't process that much information at one time without switching off other parts. This is a rare gift, even among the Amaranthine." He reached for her again, and stopped in mid-motion, his mouth quirked in a sarcastic smile. "May I? I'm going to download your instruction manual."

She nodded and shut her eyes, her face tight with apprehension. Apollo laughed softly. "Chill out. This isn't going to hurt. It might feel a little weird, though." Fingers, warm and rough, touched her forehead between the eyes.

The sensation akin to an electric charge pushed into her brain and fizzed its way along nerves and synapses with carbonated energy. She gasped in surprise and her eyes flew open as new information and memory settled into her consciousness like bits of glitter in a web. With a smug half-grin, he sat back.

"Neuroscience." A shrug of false modesty twitched his shoulders. "I have mad skills."

Callie swayed in her seat as knowledge took root and grew, crystals of data that spiked and flashed in her mind. "Whoa. I need to read Stephen Hawking, or something."

"Don't overthink it. It'll come naturally, now. Anyway, Hawking is one of us. I think he's coming home soon, so just ask him." Apollo slid out of the booth. "Before I go back, let me fix those scratches and look at your head bump."

With surprisingly gentle fingers, he palpated the tender bruise on the back of her head, his eyes closed. She watched his expressionless face, her emotions in turmoil.

So this was her father. An immortal dickhead, who'd abandoned her teenaged mother and an infant Callie to face monsters created with the sole purpose of eating people like them. Anger and disappointment flared, but as his fingers pressed harder against her skull, she couldn't suppress a small grunt of pain.

"Not bad. No fracture or concussion. The lacerations are superficial, but who knows what her claws have been in. I'll take care of it."

"Isn't that breaking the rules about intervention?" Callie couldn't help but ask.

"Threshold rules are a little vague. Besides, you're barely human. In the old days, you would have been the highest of priestesses, able to move between dimensions, advisor to both Amaranthine and humans. You're technically a demigod." He snorted softly as he laid his palm over the scrapes and left it there. "If there were such a thing as gods, anyway."

"You mean—" Sharp remembrance of Puck's words from the previous night echoed in her thoughts. "You really are some kind of explorers?"

He looked at her with a strange expression, his eyes newly interested. "So you figured that out already. Good girl. It's best to get that sentimental idea out of your head." Warm, itchy sensations rippled across her torn skin. "Welcome to your alien DNA."

Callie's head reeled. She could have accepted being a demigod, she decided. But an alien? It would take some getting used to.

He released her arm. Where the furrows once were, the skin shone newly pink and unblemished, the only telltale sign of injury in the crimson-stained shredded arm of her t-shirt. He repeated the process with her scraped palms.

"That's it." Apollo let go of her hands. "Any more questions for dear old Dad before I disappear into the rainforest again?"

Callie remembered with a start. "You said I can move between dimensions?"

"Hah! Right. You'll chap some hides. Nobody's kid has been able to do that for a while, either. I wouldn't try it without a psychopomp since you seem to be overly sensitive to the thresholds. Your pal Hermes can show you around." Apollo turned to leave.

"Just one more." Callie slid out of the booth and hesitated as he faced her. "I don't know my real mother's name. Do you remember it?"

He raised an eyebrow. "All the questions in the universe you might be asking me, and this is it?"

"Yes. She died protecting me, and I never knew her name." Callie blinked back angry tears. "Contract or no contract, I can tell you wouldn't have protected her. You don't care. But do you remember?"

Apollo shook his head. "Okay, this is why I don't take permanent human bodies anymore. Emotions are so messy. They complicate things. You've got one hell of a job ahead of you as Oracle, a lot of responsibility and sacrifice coming, and you can't let emotions get in the way. You'll see things you don't want to see about the world and about those you love. Your job is to give the information whether or not you like the outcome, so here's some free advice: grow some thicker skin."

He stalked away. Before he turned the corner, he stopped short. His broken voice, thick with unexpected emotion, floated over his shoulder.

"Her name was Alissa."

She followed him, the edge of her anger blunted by confusion. He reached the main barroom where the others waited. Athena watched Apollo's approach with resentful, accusatory eyes. Florian's taut stance relaxed when he saw her trailing after, but Callie did a double take when she registered the presence of Bridget, still and quiet in the corner seat and oblivious to the tension riding the air.

At the corner of the bar, Hephaestus stepped out to place his massive bulk directly in the disheveled ex-god's path. "Apollo, we need your help persuading Zeus to end this. Barring that, we could use your arrows in battle. We gave as good as we got, but our asses got kicked out there."

"Not a chance, Hef. My battle days are over, and Zeus made it very clear a long time ago that my opinion is neither wanted nor needed." He nodded towards Callie. "Meet your new Oracle Priestess, Calliope. She was named after her grandparent."

"Apollo," Hephaestus began again, his face flushing an angry red, but the other immortal went around him, flipping a lazy middle finger at no one in particular.

"Thanks for the drink, Florian," he said before he vanished. Callie seethed a moment over Apollo's indifference before a perplexed skyrocket of thought left a spark-trail through her anger.

She never told him her full name.

2 7

Oracle priestess or not, the Amaranthine didn't believe her.

Though all signs pointed toward Florian being glamoured to get him out of the way, none of them saw Puck in the bar or outside in the alley.

"I'm telling the truth!" Callie insisted, looking from face to face. "I didn't throw myself to a banshee!"

"Not saying you did. But a fairy, somehow able to influence Zeus against his will?" Hephaestus growled, unconvinced.

"Delusions of grandeur." Athena dismissed the idea with a wave.

"I don't think he's working by himself. He was gone, I swear, and then somebody pushed me over the barrier. In the visions I had with Bridget and—" she stopped herself from naming Eleni in front of Hephaestus and Athena—"and alone, there was a female figure."

"Sunshine?" Even as he said it, Florian looked doubtful, and Callie shook her head impatiently.

"No, I'm sure it isn't Titania." She hesitated. "Although there was someone here with him on Wednesday, and I couldn't see who or what they were. I haven't managed see the other person clearly in the visions either, but there were only two of us linking at the time." She glanced at Florian. "Without ambrosia."

His body went rigid.

"I will be the only one to inhale the vapors. Apollo said that is the best way, and it will be safer."

"Can you truly say you won't be in any danger?" Florian's worry eroded a deep canyon across his forehead and dulled his eyes.

"Thousands or even millions of people will die if I don't try." Fear left a sharp tang in the back of her mouth. She swallowed hard. "If there is a chance to stop it, the risk is mine to take, no one else's. This is what I'm supposed to do as Oracle."

"What about Gran?" he questioned. "I'm not certain she's up to this."

"Oh, I most certainly am." Bridget's voice startled them all. The blue eyes she turned to her grandson were crystal clear and determined. She bobbed her white head at Callie in encouragement. "I may be a few biscuits short of a tin, but I can shoulder my part of the burden."

Callie rewarded Bridget with a grateful smile before turning to the waiting Amaranthine. "Our vision showed the city of Rome being completely destroyed in the next fight. I feel that it means the threshold as well, just like Athens." She stood up straight, meeting Athena's gaze in challenge. "Is that enough incentive to delay the battle?"

Athena blinked, dismayed. "That may do it. Even Ares will listen if we tell them an Oracle prophesied an unfavorable outcome, though he won't like it."

"Hermes went to try and rally those not committed to the cause. Let's see if he's been able to round anyone up." Hephaestus straightened to his full height, like an armored wall. "If you experience any more visions of importance, I give you permission to invoke my presence, priestess." He inclined his head in respect. "I will come when thou biddest me."

For the second time today, a god gave her leave to call upon them. None of her studies dictated the proper response, so she just bowed with as much gravity as she could manage. Hephaestus handed Athena her helmet. They both disappeared.

"Oh, so they'll believe I prophesied Rome's destruction, but nobody will accept Puck is behind it?" Callie huffed in frustration and flung her arms upward. "Evidently, I'm the only one who can see through his glamour and spells, so how am I supposed to prove this to everyone else without him killing me first?"

"Salt and iron will keep mischief outside the door," Bridget stated. Florian nodded, his jaw set.

"I can do that, but I think I need to talk to Sunshine and Ron first and tell them Puck tried to kill you. Too much segregation already exists between the Sidhe and the Amaranthine to simply ban them without an explanation."

"How can we send them a message?"

"I've never done this before, but I never needed to." Florian cleared his throat and spoke, his voice ringing off the walls: "Titania and Oberon, shining ones, by my right as Doorkeeper I beg you, come!"

A sleepy-eyed brownie rippled through the front door, looking grumpy but curious. "And just what might you be needing, Master Florian? Their majesties are otherwise occupied at the moment."

"I need to advise them of my intent to invoke cold iron and salt, Tom." Florian rocked back on his heels and crossed his arms over his chest. "One of your people violated the sanctuary of my threshold."

"Really?" The brownie sucked in his breath and mournfully regarded the regiment of bottles lined against the wall. "Salt and iron, now...isn't that a bit of overkill? None of us would be able to cross and take advantage of your hospitality. Surely this is some kind of misunderstanding."

"No." Florian leaned over him. "A newly recognized Oracle was granted shelter in my establishment, and someone tried to kill her today."

"An Oracle? Threatened? That is forbidden," Tom sputtered. "Who would be so foolish as to trifle with one of those?"

"Puck."

The brownie stiffened, eyes bulging, the whites stark and bright against dark irises. He ran for the door.

"Now you stirred the pot." Bridget clutched her hands together in expectation, grinning.

A moment later, Tom reappeared. Two naked figures with him pulled on gossamer robes and brushed disheveled hair away from their eyes. Titania drew the gauzy wrap over perfect breasts as she phased through the glass of the door, appearing to have been reluctantly interrupted from an intimate moment. Bridget crowed in delight and clapped as Oberon, still excited and upright, strode in and lazily belted his robe with a playful leer toward the elderly woman. He cast a smoldering look at Callie, who swallowed and averted her gaze, heat spreading across her cheeks.

"You accuse Puck of attempted murder—of an Oracle, no less." Titania padded over to Florian on bare, delicate feet, her nearly transparent robe doing nothing to conceal the lissome anatomy beneath. "I was not aware one was recognized in recent memory."

"It just happened today."

"Who? Granny Bridget?" the brownie asked, his face crinkled in deprecating confusion.

"No, not me, you shrewd and knavish sprite," Bridget quoted absently, and Tom stuck his tongue out at her.

"Who, then?" Oberon's shapely eyebrows made question-mark arches, but his queen's eyes were already turning to the answer.

"Callie is an Oracle?" Titania burst out giggling and dipped a mischievous curtsy in her direction. "My, how the mighty have fallen: their temple a bar, the priestess a waitress. I knew she carried a destiny, but this is delightful."

Florian exchanged an irritated glance with Callie, and she was glad not to be the only one who saw no humor in the queen's mirth. "Puck tried to feed her to a waiting banshee this afternoon," he said sharply. "We barely reached her in time. One of the Amaranthine chased it off."

Titania became solemn, and faced Callie with new gravity. "What have you seen, that your silence is a matter of life and death?"

"When I saw him this afternoon, he was doing something in the back room." Callie led them to the swinging door and showed them the kegs of Guinness stacked against the wall. "These were glowing."

Titania extended one graceful hand and skimmed it over the aluminum. "These have been infused with a strong glamour," she murmured. "What mischief does he author?"

"That's Zeus's favorite drink." Callie, confused, looked to Florian. "But Hermes says fairy magic isn't strong enough to affect him."

Titania did not answer immediately, her gaze locked with her consort's in a silent conversation. Oberon shrugged, and she turned back to Callie. "Ours is not. But his, perhaps."

"Strong enough to convince him to start a war with God?" Florian regarded the fairy monarchs gravely.

Oberon grunted. "Only his, or Mother's."

"Mother?" Callie gasped. "There is a female figure in my visions."

"Who could that be?" Florian's voice rose in query. The royal couple exchanged another silent look, and Titania shook her head, glancing pointedly at Callie.

"I think the Oracle can discover that on her own. Our word would be discounted by the Amaranthine at any rate, and Callie's visions will not. We forced her to abdicate her claim on this world when the Amaranthine arrived because our folk are too delicate to risk all-out war. Mother has never forgiven us. We cannot take sides now." She sniffed disdainfully. "Though it is tempting to let the barbarians destroy their means of entering this world."

"Too much has been lost forever," Oberon muttered. "Let them shatter the thresholds. The Amaranthine won't be able to come back."

"Nothing obliterated in this dimension by their violence restores us to our former glory," Titania objected. "We bear an obligation to protect what's left of our creations, and that we cannot ignore. How can we prevent this?"

"We can help protect the Oracle." Oberon turned back to the waiting Florian. "Salt and iron will keep Puck and Mother from entering. They were old when your world was new, and their energy is absorbed by the combination of those elements, just as ours is. With that counter in place they will be unable to pass the barrier from the human realm."

Florian nodded in agreement. "What about the garden?"

Oberon winced. Callie saw it. "That is outside our scope. We cannot guarantee her safety there, but I think it unlikely they would risk crossing from Olympus to do her harm."

"Until this conflict is settled, we will forgo the pleasures of your establishment." Titania pronounced. At her knee, Tom grumbled discontentedly beneath his breath. His queen raised an eyebrow, and he quieted, sniffling resentfully. Titania turned her attention back to Callie. "Settle it quickly, dear, or I may be forced to quell a riot."

"Thank you, shining ones. I'm in your debt once more." Florian bowed reverently, and Callie followed suit. He pulled a bottle of whiskey from the shelf and ceremonially presented it to Tom. "Please accept this as my pledge the door will reopen to the fair folk once the danger has passed."

"Generous, most generous." The brownie caressed the bottle with greedy fingers. "I will spread the word that there will be no more pinching of the Oracle, if you please. I won't allow such disrespect."

"Thanks, Tom." Callie favored him with a grin.

"Time is of the essence," Titania advised her again. "I suggest you confirm your vision, and bring the truth to light." She turned to Oberon, looking up at him with hungry eyes. "We return home. We have unfinished business." The fairy queen took her consort's hand and pulled him through the door. Tom trailed behind them, his adoration still focused on the bottle cradled like an infant in the crook of his arm.

"How do we do this?" Callie turned to Florian. Puck could slip back into the bar any time he liked until the wards were done. She found herself twisting her hands. It took conscious effort to still them.

"There are iron grates for the windows and door in the cellar. Stefanio took them down when he became Doorkeeper to give the fairies access to the bar. All we have to do is rehang them on the hooks, but they're heavy. I'll need your help." He fished a couple of boxes of the coarse salt used for tequila shots from the recesses of under-bar storage. "You and Gran start putting this in the windowsills and across outside doorways while I bring them up."

2 8

Two hours and many aching muscles later, Callie and Florian hung the last of the heavy iron bars. The iron provided warding and not defense, so the grates were merely suspended, with salt below them in the sills of the door and windows. The back door's reinforcement consisted of a strong iron rod slipped into waiting supports, the foot of the door awash in salt crystals that crunched beneath his feet as Florian slid the rod home. Callie did the downstairs entrances herself and sent Bridget upstairs to ward the windows and terrace doors of the apartments while she helped Florian with the heavy lifting.

"It's getting late." Callie glanced at her watch as they went back into the main area. "Do you think we'll get a crowd tonight?"

"Friday is usually a busy night, but I really don't know what to expect with a good number of my patrons at the front," Florian admitted. Despite the circumstances, he found a level of uncertainty refreshing. Able to predict drink and ambrosia orders for the last quarter-century, the past four days had been anything but ordinary.

"I need to talk to Marios and Eleni," Callie mused. She pulled something out of her pocket. Florian caught a flash of silver in her palm before she closed her fingers over it. "I have to discover who's working with Puck before the battle starts, and I can't put it off much longer." She hesitated. "If I can't convince them, I'll have to do this alone. Promise you won't try to stop me, Florian. There's too much at stake."

Every fiber of his soul vibrated against the risk, for selfish reasons, perhaps, but sound ones. But even he knew that she had little choice. If her visions might avert another horrific loss of life, he could not make this more difficult for her. He would be her ally, not the devil's advocate. Resignation weighed heavily in his chest. Finding his voice proved difficult when he spoke at last.

"I give you my word."

"Thank you." She stood on tiptoe and kissed him, the brief touch of sweetness enough to tantalize, but nothing more. He didn't turn to watch her go. The newly made promise already chafed. Movement and the sound of her footsteps on the stairs heralded her departure and he sank down on one of the bar stools to bury his head in his hands a moment, elbows atop the counter. A wave of exhaustion accompanied his reluctant acceptance of the truth.

He thought she was gone, but a moment later arms slipped around his waist. A cheek rested against his back. He straightened and put his hands over hers with a sigh.

"Under extreme duress, protest, and against my heart. But I give you my word," he amended his earlier statement.

"What a passionate declaration. Your word about what, exactly?" an unexpected voice purred.

Florian stood and removed himself from the unwelcome circle of Aphrodite's embrace, startled. "I thought you were..." he began, and thought better of it. The less his former benefactress knew of his budding relationship with Callie, the better. "What can I get you?"

"I think you know." She attempted to follow him as he retreated behind the bar, and he lowered the drop extension behind him to block her way. She laughed low in her throat and sat in the corner stool. A black bandage dress left nothing to the imagination, jewels sparkling in the hollow of her breasts and at her earlobes.

"Strawberry daiquiri, right." He hadn't had time to prepare any garnishes or fruit, and retrieved the casket of ambrosia, glad of the

excuse to stay busy. "You're not involved in any of the war preparations, then?"

"Please." She rolled her eyes and peered at him through flirtatious
lashes. "You know that's never been my function. Although, I may
have indirectly started a few." Aphrodite bit her lip and looked around
with a critical eye. "You've been occupied too. What's with the redec-
oration?"

"A little Sidhe trouble. It'll all be sorted out soon enough." He
shaped quick strawberries. "Hef and Ares must be working like mad."

"Yes," she pouted. "I'm all alone without a thing to do because Hef's
too busy to escort me anywhere." Her voice rose into a note of hysteria, lacquered fingernails biting into the edge of the bar. "I can't
believe Zeus hasn't lifted my restrictions yet. I'm about to go
stir crazy."

"Take it easy," Florian said with alarm as wood creaked and splintered under her nails. "That's solid antique maple you're savaging. I
can't replace that."

"Sorry." She tossed her head and took a deep breath to collect
herself. "So I overheard some gossip. What's this about a new Oracle
showing up? I didn't think Apollo had it in him anymore. Who is it?
Not your granny, I take it."

"No, not Gran. Callie."

For the first time he could recall, Aphrodite was stricken speechless, her succulent mouth a perfect, crimson O. Then an unexpected,
ugly laugh burst from her throat. "Your waitress? The pretty one? Oh,
poor Pan is going to be so disappointed."

"So? He can just go back to molesting squirrels."

"He'll get over it." Aphrodite's voice, suddenly too light and innocent, raised his suspicion. "But will you?"

Florian threw the strawberries into the blender with another
handful of ambrosia-crafted ice, taking a moment to answer. "What
do you mean?"

"Oh, come on. I saw you mooning over her." Her effort to look hurt
failed; a self-satisfied upturn at the corners of her mouth hinted she
held something in reserve she felt would force his hand. This wasn't a

promising start to the evening. Florian pulsed the blender's contents into slurry, added rum and squeezed a hastily crafted lime into the mix.

"I still don't understand." He poured the slush into a tall glass and placed it before her.

"The Oracle Priestess must be a virgin," Aphrodite said with barely contained glee. "It's tradition." She looked down at her drink and back up to Florian's stunned expression. "No whipped cream?"

THE FIRST SOFT knock went unanswered, though footfalls gave evidence someone waited on the other side. A minute passed, and she tapped again.

"Marios? It's Callie. I'm sorry, but I need to talk to you."

A creak heralded the spreading gap between yellow door and jamb. Half of a face and one dark, fiercely protective eye regarded her through the crack. Fishing the caduceus coin out of her jeans pocket, she showed the token to Marios. "I'm here on his behalf, as well as mine."

That dark eye closed briefly; a sigh whispered through parted lips. One glitter-nail-polished hand thrust itself against the outside of the jamb and the other forced the door open, a dark-haired head butting Marios aside. Eleni squeezed beneath her father's arm to engulf Callie in a bear hug. "I'm so glad you're all right!"

"Thanks to you." She kissed the top of the girl's head, silky hair against her lips. "You saved me, Eleni."

She had taken the time to change out of her bloody, shredded t-shirt, not wanting to alarm Eleni or her father any more than this conversation might. Mouth already pressed in a tight, thin line,

Marios folded his arms over his chest. Callie released Eleni and grinned at her, motioning toward the couch inside.

"Can we sit down?"

The man sat on the sofa and pulled his daughter into the protective half-circle of one arm. Sinking into the opposite cushion, Callie placed the caduceus coin on the low table in front of them.

Excitement lit Eleni's face as she picked up the coin and turned it over in her fingers. "That's Papa's mark!"

"Yes, it is. There's something important he wants me to talk about to you and your father." Callie waited for permission.

"Tell us." Resignation mourned in Marios's voice, his eyes hollow.

"You know something terrible is happening right now. There is a war between the old gods and the new ones. The destruction of the threshold in Athens was just the first skirmish. Eleni and I saw this vision independently. Together, we've seen another battle coming. This one will destroy Rome, its threshold, and kill thousands of people." She studied Eleni to make sure she wasn't frightened, but the girl simply watched her with solemn attention. Eyes downcast, Marios pulled his daughter more tightly into his embrace.

"Eleni, you and Bridget and I have an important gift. If we work together, we can have more powerful, accurate visions. We figured out who the laughing man is, but there's a woman too, and I think she's the one orchestrating the entire thing. It's important to discover who she is and stop her. Hermes thinks he's found a diplomatic way to solve this, but only if I act as Oracle Priestess." Callie leaned forward and touched Marios's arm. He met her gaze with reluctance. "I've received some instruction from my...from Apollo, and if Eleni links with me, I can teach her to control the visions."

"You can?" Wary hope kindled in Marios's eyes, and Callie nodded. Silence reigned for a long moment before the light extinguished, smothered by fear. He shook his head.

"I don't want her to see these horrible things any longer. She's too young for this."

"Marios," Callie began to plead, but the man cut her off with a sharp wave of his hand.

"No, I won't allow it. She should be a normal child: happy, able to play and laugh with other children instead of having walking nightmares! Train her not to have them, please, but I won't let her be used as some kind of fortune teller, even for Hermes."

"Daddy, wait." The girl's voice, strong and calm, startled them both, and Eleni pushed gently away from Marios so she could look at him. "I saved her! I could help her do that for all the people in Rome. Papa thinks so too, or he wouldn't have sent her to talk to us."

Callie could tell Marios wavered with Eleni's conviction, and moved to support it. "Hermes does think so, but I won't lie to you. This could be dangerous for me, but Apollo says you won't be harmed by what we do. Do you know what ambrosia is?"

A wrinkled nose displayed Eleni's opinion. "Yes, it's Papa's food. He let me try some once. It was gross. But he said when we came here that Florian can make ambrosia taste really good."

"He can! Ask him to make you some mint chocolate chip ice cream. The ambrosia can help me control stronger visions. It gives me extra power, but you and Bridget have to take some of that power away so the energy doesn't hurt me. You won't use ambrosia while we work, all right? After that, we can start to work on controlling your gift, so visions only happen when you want them to."

Eleni turned an eager face back to her father. "Daddy, this is important. It scares me, too, but I think I would feel worse knowing stuff is happening, if I don't try to help."

A shine grew in Marios's dark eyes, and he stroked his daughter's cheek. "When did you become so grown up? I don't know this young woman."

"I'm almost twelve," she reminded him seriously.

"When will you start, Callie?" Marios didn't take his gaze from his daughter.

"As soon as possible. The faster we find who is behind this, the better chance there is of preventing the battle."

The window behind them held late, amber sunlight. Slanted beams glinted in the salt along the ledge of the sill. Bridget had done her warding job well, but Callie hadn't seen her since she sent the elderly woman upstairs. "Eleni, will you find Bridget and meet me in the garden in about fifteen minutes? I need to get something from Florian before we start."

Marios didn't look happy, but nodded his assent. Eleni squirmed out of her father's protective arms and left the apartment door ajar in her determination to fulfill Callie's request.

Her father stared after her with an expression of sadness and resolve. With a tug on a chain hidden beneath the collar of his shirt, he sighed in resignation.

"She's the child of a god. I know she's destined for things I can't understand, but it doesn't make me any less frightened for her." A pendant emerged from his collar as he rubbed the chain back and forth against his thumb in absent movements. Callie realized it was a caduceus as Marios released the charm to fall against his chest. "Hermes tries to be an ordinary man around us, but he's afraid, too. He moves us in secret, like a rich man hiding his gold."

"I think that's a pretty accurate analogy. You're both precious to him."

"She is my world. I know I can't keep Hermes forever. But Eleni is my child, and I will do everything in my power to keep her safe. Can you understand that?"

Hesitant to tell the story, Callie realized the man in front of her would understand perhaps better than she did. "My real mother died protecting me. Mom and Dad adopted me when I was four. When the hunters found me, I left to protect them." A knot tightened in the back of her throat, and she shrugged. "We do that for love, don't we?"

"What about your father?" Marios's dark eyes studied her. "Is he like Hermes?"

"Not involved." Callie frowned. "I just met him today for the first time. Like he said, he donated the material to create me, but he's not my father. Richard Davies is." Even though her words held scorn, she found it more difficult to rouse the biting anger she held toward him earlier in the day. She didn't think Apollo was as detached as he claimed to be. He'd known her full name, and had come immediately when his friend asked. His actions spoke of interest, whether clinical or paternal. "How did you meet Hermes?"

"Through prayer, if you can believe it." Marios smiled tentatively. "I'm a doctor." Catching the chain between his fingers, the winged pendant dangled from the end so she could examine it. "I was given this as a gift when I completed my studies. As a joke, I started talking to him out loud, asking for guidance and skill whenever I treated a patient. After a while it stopped being funny and I truly felt he was listening to me, somehow. He heard me and helped me save someone's life. At first, I thought he was another doctor. After our daughter was born, he told me who he really was and what that meant for Eleni. He can't be with us all the time, but he keeps us safe."

Hermes had no qualms about violating the rules to protect his family, only about the consequences he faced if he was caught. Neither did Aphrodite, in her illicit affair with Florian. Callie wondered how many others secretly intervened in the lives of human beings when it suited them, and whether the contract was as inviolate with the angels as Gabriel declared.

The thought made her remember why she'd come, and she stood. "I have to get some ambrosia from Florian so we can go to work. I'll see you in the garden."

"You swear she won't be harmed?" Marios's voice stopped her before she made it to the door.

"I promise. All risks fall on me."

Descending the stairs, she passed Bridget's apartment. Eleni's clear, piping voice sounded inside, chased by the older woman's reply. It would be difficult for Florian to provide her with the first dose of ambrosia, knowing how it affected Bridget. The quiet despair in his voice had cracked her heart in half when she extracted his promise not to stop her.

When she reached the bottom of the steps, added complication sat there in the form of the one female entity who could be classified as her boyfriend's psycho ex. Her perfect curves undisguised by a painted-on dress, Aphrodite displayed her half-bared breasts in a forward lean and spoke to Florian in a soft, intimate voice. He appeared dismayed and uncertain, and she smelled trouble before either of them noticed her there.

Florian straightened as she rounded the corner. Aphrodite turned her head and smiled. "Well, if it isn't the Oracle Priestess! Congratulations on your promotion, dear." Her voice was too friendly. Callie wondered what she was up to.

"Thank you." She cast a cautious glance at Florian, who had trouble meeting her eyes. Oh, the goddess was definitely up to something. Her special senses didn't seem to work with any of the immortals, only Puck, who wasn't Amaranthine at all. But Callie was female, and could tell when another female was a conniving bitch. "I'm meeting Bridget and Eleni in the garden in a few minutes. We're going to try vision work." She faltered. "I need to take some ambrosia with me."

"Yes. Right." To his credit, Florian retrieved the golden casket without hesitation. "How much do you need?"

"About half a cup," Callie hazarded. "Maybe one of the salsa bowls full?"

Florian reached for one of the plastic bowls beneath the bar. Aphrodite waved dismissively.

"Oh, no! That will never do. If you're going to do this according to *tradition*—" she put unusual emphasis on the word, looking at Florian with a raised eyebrow. He flushed miserably, to Callie's mystification. "You'll need something a little more ceremonial. More like this." She gestured with graceful motions, and in her cupped palms appeared a flat, shallow porcelain vessel with a lid. The outside was painted in classical Greek style with the scene of an Oracle priestess, seated on her three-legged stool over rising vapors as she read the future for ancient kings.

"That's beautiful," Callie admitted begrudgingly. Aphrodite presented the dish to her with upraised hands and bowed her head briefly in respect.

"In celebration of your new rank. Waitress to High Priestess is quite an elevation for one afternoon."

"Um...thank you." She hoped suspicion was not too obvious in her voice and cradled the delicate vessel in both hands as Aphrodite cere-moniously transferred it.

"Consider me your first private appointment. I need talk to you as soon as possible about how to get out of my personal hell." A twitch distorted the side of her mouth as the goddess picked up her daiquiri and drained the glass of icy slush in an impressive show of brain-freeze immunity. "Well, I'll leave you both to your work. Catch up with you later, Florian." She cast him a hungry glance, and vanished as she spun in her seat. The scent of expensive perfume lingered in her wake.

"What was that all about?" Callie asked, befuddled, and Florian shook his head.

"You probably don't want to know right now." He avoided her eyes. "You have more important things to think about." Reflections skit-tered across his troubled face as he opened the golden box.

A twinge of foreboding lanced through her heart. It didn't arise from her warning system, but from the discomfort of knowing he kept something from her. She took the lid off the cup, the inside gleaming with gilt in the diffused light of the bar, and placed the vessel on the wooden counter. Argent vapors trailed from his fingers and descended in milky, iridescent spirals until the misty stuff reached the rim of the dish.

"Do you think that's enough?"

"I guess we'll find out." She replaced the top. Porcelain clinked against porcelain as the glow was veiled beneath the lid.

"You persuaded Marios, then." Florian stowed the box under the bar.

"Eleni was very eloquent. She did most of the persuading herself," she confessed. Florian laughed softly.

"Well, she is Hermes's daughter, after all." He met her eyes at last. "Be careful. Remember you can call on Hephaestus for help."

"Hermes too." Confidence buckled against a sudden wave of panic and a metallic taste flooded her mouth. Callie took a deep, uneven breath. "Will you come and watch? I'd feel better knowing you're there."

His eyes softened. She thought he was going to say yes, but at that moment a few patrons flickered into the room. They took seats in the booth by the window, and his face fell. He shook his head with regret. "I didn't realize it was so late."

"Oh." She hated the return of that businesslike distance between them and wondered what the hell Aphrodite had said to him. "I'll come down to help as soon as I can."

"No rush. Go save the world." He was serious when he said this. Callie nodded blindly. She picked up the ambrosia-filled cup and blinked against the sting in her eyes as she turned away. The creak of the hinge on the drop partition sounded as she approached the first landing. His footsteps pounded quickly up the stairs behind her.

"Callie?"

Unprepared for the fire and hunger of the kiss that followed, a small moan escaped her. The ambrosia balanced carefully between them was an obstacle preventing complete surrender to the delighted weakness that flooded her body. It was only their second kiss, but held all the shattering intensity of a farewell.

He leaned his forehead against hers a moment longer. Neither of them spoke, Callie's voice held captive in her throat behind a tangled knot of fear and guilt. They turned away at the same time.

Tears traced hot, salty tracks against her skin. Hastily she wiped them away and continued upstairs with reluctant feet. *This was the right thing to do.* The lives of millions hung in the balance. She was not the only one afraid, but she could not comfort him.

3 0

Eleni, Marios, and Bridget waited in the garden when Callie arrived. They watched the far-away mountain peaks with varying expressions of interest and concern. A dark thunderstorm obscured much of the third peak, sullen flashes of purple lightning leaping from cloud to cloud. A distant rumble reached their ears, low and ominous.

"I don't like thunder," Eleni said, shrinking.

"Someone's not happy," Bridget remarked absently. "The old sot or his wife, one."

"What does it mean?" Marios stepped closer to Eleni, but the girl moved away from him, curiosity piqued by the small vessel in Callie's hands.

"What's that for?"

"It means we're ready to go to work," Callie forced a bright smile for Eleni and held out the dish. "Inside this is the ambrosia I'll use. When you and Bridget and I join hands, we will link together, and we'll have a vision. I'm told I can control where we go and what we see, but this is the first time I've done it this way and I don't know what to expect, exactly." Appealing to Marios, she gestured with the cup. "Will you take this from me after I breathe in, so I don't drop it? I don't want to break it. It was a gift from a goddess and I have a feeling she can hold a grudge."

Eleni's father shrugged. "Can't you show her how to control the visions first?"

"We have something important to do before I can take the time," Callie hesitated. "I can't promise we will do it tonight, but I do promise that will be our next work together. Okay, Eleni?"

"Yes," the girl stated firmly. "We need to save all those people in Rome first. And spaghetti."

Callie grinned at her. "Let's sit down." The high backed stone bench beneath the trees, long enough that the three sat beside each other without difficulty, seemed made for this purpose. She sat in the center, with Eleni to her left and Bridget to the right. Marios knelt before them. Callie swayed with an odd sense of time stretching and flowing backward. *Acolytes knelt at the feet of a Delphi priestess, ready to catch her if she fell...*

She forced herself back to the present. Somewhere, she hoped Apollo's 'instruction manual' had a chapter on how to prevent these distracting little jaunts down time streams.

The glowing stuff swirled in the recesses of the ceremonial cup as she took off the lid. It rattled against the rim with her trembling hand. Her heart sped up. She wished she'd taken more time to prepare.

"It burns going up your nose."

Callie turned her head to discover Bridget smiling at her gently. "Try to take it in through your mouth. That may look like mist but it's more like drowning than breathing."

Seventy-five years ago, out of desperate love and fear for her grandson, Bridget once risked her life and sanity by inhaling the vapors. Gambling on a vision, she lost. Or had she?

Callie's mouth was a cold, dry tundra. "When you used ambrosia, did you know Florian would be all right, Bridget?"

"I saw him back at my side, but his journey isn't over yet. Danger, blood and heartbreak will come before he's done." Bridget's eyes focused on something far away, her pupils wide and black against the blue of her irises. "But in the end, the two of you will be together long after I'm gone."

Nerves threatened to sweep away her resolve. Ambrosia churned in the gilt interior and created disconcerting, impossible shapes. Callie startled when Bridget patted her knee.

"Just pretend you're going swimming," she whispered. The elderly lady winked at her. "Take a deep breath and jump."

Eyes screwed tightly shut, Callie raised the dish to her lips. The vessel tilted and she sucked in a mouthful of air and ambrosia.

It did burn! She tasted ozone and pepper, the sting of it in her nostrils. Her eyes watered. Aware of energy in every bronchiole, the ice and fire moved deeper into her lungs with each breath. Warm fingers brushed hers as the dish was taken from her hands. A cough racked her after another shuddery gasp. The pain dissipated. Heat flooded through her body as the ambrosia traveled in her bloodstream, flowing into her brain and organs and skin with the rush of her pounding heart. Reaching out blindly, she encountered Bridget's cool fingers and laced them through her own. Seconds later Eleni's warm, sweaty hand clasped her fingers on the other side.

The stretching, telescoping sensation of time grew more pronounced as several different time streams expanded before Callie's inner vision. Each one possessed an oddly distinct feel to it: events that were already in the past had an unyielding weight to them; writing chiseled in stone. Present events moved smoothly, like watching a film on screen. Real time unwound toward the dizzying fluidity of future tense, which broke off into myriads of pathways. Some of those pathways beat with a dreadful resonance, and she turned instinctively toward them, looking for hints.

Eleni's fingers tightened on hers as Callie narrowed down on a familiar, skin-crawling presence she sensed somewhere in the chaos of immediate time. Puck. It was difficult to home in on him, but persistence won out against a negative-magnet heaviness that pushed her away.

Arguing with someone. Puck's face, embarrassed and angry.

Time fast-forwarded from that point. This was a possible future—less than twelve hours away, if her sense of chronology was accurate.

Amorphous figures slip through the ranks of gods and angels and whisper in their ears. Ares and Michael rouse their followers toward a clash of supernatural power.

Hermes, his face grimy and despairing. Ares' human form transfigures into crackling white-hot plasma and streaks toward an equally terrifying bolt of energy. Lesser beings trail behind him like the tail of a comet. A retina-searing collision of nuclear magnitude, and the atmosphere burns. A hole rips in the fabric of space through which an ocean on the opposite side of the world pours through: directly into the city of Rome.

A woman stands in silhouette against a burning sky.

It took effort to will herself closer and focus on the face. Even as she did the woman's shape *blurred* as she drew something around herself.

"No!" Callie's own voice nearly startled her out of the vision. Despair outweighed her optimism. Time was running out, only hours remained before the battle erupted.

The ambrosia's effects tapered off too quickly. Although they protected her from absorbing too much energy, Bridget and Eleni siphoned power from her. Callie could still direct herself down the time streams but the clarity faded. Beside her, Eleni squirmed. Bridget's hand grew colder in hers. She sensed the older woman weakened with each breath. It was time to stop.

Callie let go of their hands, and with that, the vision. They wilted on the bench, utterly spent. Marios anxiously examined his daughter to make certain she was in one piece. Eleni leaned into his shoulder for a weary hug. Despite her own exhaustion, Callie steadied Bridget as she passed a frail, trembling hand over her eyes and swayed in her seat.

"I'm all right, dear," Bridget protested tiredly. Pale and sweaty, she clearly wasn't. Her fingertips and nails were tinged with an unhealthy, dusky purple.

Alarmed, Callie searched her face. "Bridget, are you sure?"

"No, no. I just need to rest. Stefanio will be wanting some help downstairs with my baggage." She was confused again, her breathing rapid and shallow.

"Marios?" Callie implored. Grim and professional, Marios took the woman's pulse and watched her breathing.

"We should take her to her apartment right away."

Callie helped Bridget stand. Between the three of them they managed to cross the terrace, and crunched through the salt line in front of the French doors to settle Bridget comfortably in her bedroom. Marios sat on the edge of the mattress and examined her feet and legs with a grave countenance.

"Her heart is failing," he said with a shake of his head. "She needs to be in a hospital."

"Nothing is wrong with me but an overabundance of years." Bridget waved in irritation. "Let me rest a while."

Marios turned to his daughter. "Eleni, will you get my bag, please?"

Eleni nodded and disappeared. Callie was unprepared for the quiet fury Marios turned on her when the child was out of earshot.

"You said there would be no danger to them!" Callie, shocked and dismayed into speechlessness, could only let the wave of fury crash against her. Marios continued, "It's too much for Bridget's heart to withstand, and I will not let you put Eleni at risk again. You will show her how to control her visions, but that's all. No more of this." He swiveled away from Callie in dismissal, his attention on the elderly woman.

She blinked back tears for the second time that day, a painful blade of guilt in her chest. She couldn't move, couldn't think until Bridget patted Marios's hands away and spoke.

"It was my choice, both times. Don't burden her with that too. She has work to do." Bridget's eyes, steely and sharp, pierced Callie, her entire being present as she struggled to maintain clarity. "The battle is coming. You have to stop this."

Despair collapsed inside her, leaving Callie hollow. "I can't see her, Bridget! How can I stop her if I can't prove it? They won't believe me!"

"While you were looking at the future, I watched what went before. She's there."

"And I was watching the right now part," Eleni said. Having returned as silently as a little mouse while Bridget was speaking, she gave Marios a medical bag. "He's really mad because the monster didn't eat you. He's afraid."

"We all saw something different?" Callie was taken by surprise.

"You'll have to go back." Bridget raised her head and said faintly, "Where has Florian gone? He can't go wandering about with those hunters outside."

Marios, his lips compressed in a tight line, glanced up from where he listened to Bridget's heart and breathing with a stethoscope. He shook his head at Callie solemnly. "I'll stay with her."

"I'll get Florian."

She flew downstairs into the bar, which was still spare of patrons. When Florian caught sight of her, his face lit up with a brilliant smile of relief.

It made it so much harder to tell him.

31

FOR THE FIRST time in seventy-five years, Florian shut down the bar.

As Callie delivered her urgent message, warmth drained from his head and limbs. Heavy cold settled in his stomach. Silently, he moved on leaden feet to the board where he listed his specials and scrubbed out the words with a bar towel. In the cloudy space left by his eradicated menu, he chalked stark letters: CLOSED.

Ignoring the baffled glances and mutters of the dozen or so Amaranthine patrons, he climbed the stairs to Bridget's apartment. As he reached for the doorknob his breath left him as if he'd been gut-punched, and he staggered. He took a few seconds to lean against the door and collect himself before he went inside.

Marios rose from the bedside and met Florian at the bedroom door. Eleni, curled up in a tight ball under Bridget's shawl and sound asleep in a winged armchair, didn't move. In the bed, his grandmother's form was so much smaller than he remembered, her chest laboring beneath the quilt.

"She's comfortable, Florian. She told me no hospital, but I don't think she's going to live much longer." Marios said gently, his features lined with concern.

"No." He could read it in the purplish tint to Bridget's lips and in her breathing. "She's one hundred and forty six years old. She's entitled to rest."

"If you like, I can stay," Marios offered.

"Thank you. There's a sofa in the parlor where Eleni can sleep. I'll call if there's need." He realized Callie's absence only then. She'd appeared shattered and exhausted when she told him about Bridget. He assumed she might have gone to her own apartment.

Marios gathered up the sleeping Eleni and left the room. Florian hefted the armchair closer to Bridget and took up vigil at her bedside.

He held his grandmother's cool hand. Her fingers were not soft, but calloused and used to labor. Always a hard-working woman during the nomadic years of Florian's childhood, she took whatever position she could find which would feed them both and put a roof over their heads. She scrubbed floors, made bricks, and mucked out stalls at a dairy farm. They stayed until the hunters found them and they were forced to flee. Traveling by river or by sea, or walking only in the rain through Ireland's countryside, she showed him how to confuse the scent trails the creatures followed as she had learned.

At one grand house, Bridget was a maid and cook for a family who didn't mind that her orphaned grandson tagged along to help with the baking. From that time, he could pinpoint the beginning of his love of preparing food, and Bridget taught him that too: everything she knew, until his thirst for this domestic alchemy surpassed her knowledge and drove him out to hotel kitchens and restaurants to beg the chefs for apprenticeships in his early teens.

He retained no memories of his mother except those Bridget gave him. She had been his mother, his guardian, and the one person in the world who would take back the prodigal grandson who left in anger to pursue a dangerous affair. Her love for him drove Bridget to push her gifts to dangerous limits and she never fully recovered, forever scattered and distracted by visions she followed like will-o-the-wisps through the fog.

She opened her eyes and squeezed his hand weakly. Florian did his best to smile at her, but the heavy weight in his soul dragged the corners of his mouth down.

"Oh, stop it, boyo." Her voice, stronger than he expected, held a tender note that chided him at the same time. "I'm not dead yet."

"I'm sorry, Gran. I was thinking about how much you did for me. I can't recall if I ever thanked you for it, fool that I am."

"Nonsense." She patted his hand weakly. "You have grown to be a fine man, Florian."

"Have I?" Uncertainty added a quaver to his voice. Trapped as he was in the limbo of the threshold while he served his sentence, he never really had a chance to find out the true mettle of his character. He feared he wouldn't measure up if it came to proving.

"Of course you are. The gods don't trust just any mortals, you know. Neither did my Stefanio, and he chose you."

"He chose me because he loved you, Gran." He swallowed hard. "He did it to save my life, for you."

"He didn't. He would never have entrusted his precious threshold to an *amadan*."

Florian's mouth tugged upward in a grin.

"And she's a fine girl. See that you take care of her." Bridget nodded meaningfully against the pillow.

"And you're still matchmaking." He took a deep breath. "I will, Gran. Although we might not be allowed to be together, now that she's the Oracle Priestess." The brief kisses they shared promised so many things. It would be difficult to go back to the monk-like mentality he'd maintained for so long after tasting what was possible with Callie.

"It doesn't mean you can't take care of her." Bridget's speech grew labored, uneven breaths interspersed with whispered words. "They'll try to use her to their own ends. She'll need you to make sure they don't take advantage of her."

"I'll protect her, Gran. No matter what happens."

"Good boy." She stirred fitfully. "Don't forget to call Pete when the time comes. He has all the arrangements. Stefanio says the ferry's leaving soon, but I'm tired. I need to rest a bit."

"I'm sure he'll wait for you, Gran. And I'll call Pete. Don't worry.

Go ahead and rest now." A painful lump rose in Florian's throat, and he kissed her forehead. She was already unconscious, her color ashen.

His thoughts full of memories, he considered praying but didn't know to whom he would address it. He left the prayer silent and unspecified, spoken only in his heart.

32

CALLIE REMAINED BEHIND, miserable and silent, until the door of Bridget's apartment shut. Then she went upstairs as well, not to follow Florian, but back out into the threshold garden where she collapsed on the bench.

The storm clouds, as gray and heavy as Callie's heart, still throbbed with ominous flashes and distant thunder over the mountains. Someone was mightily pissed. She wondered if Hera finally took notice of Zeus's comeback bid and was setting him straight.

Pain spiked between her eyes and she pressed the heels of her hands over her closed lids. Her insides churned with a hot-and-cold flare. Apollo said that her gift would just come naturally with his instructions, but Callie thought she must have done something wrong. She really had no idea what she was doing.

Even though Bridget made it very clear the risk was her choice, guilt boiled in a thick, scalding black wave. The whole effort had been a disaster. Still no evidence existed she could present to the Amaranthine that they would believe, or could identify the mistress of this chaos.

"Hermes!" She stood and pitched her voice to carry above the wind, trying to frame some kind of formal summoning, but what came out was a pathetic cry. "I need your help. The Oracle Priestess needs your help. Please."

The breeze picked up, whipping the trees and sending leaves fluttering to the ground. Hermes phased into being right next to her, a violent gust rocking her back on her heels.

"Callie?" His winged helmet glinted in the lavender twilight. "Is everything all right?"

"No." She swiped impatiently at her eyes.

"Eleni?" His body stiffened, all his attention on the dark terrace door of Marios's apartment.

"She's fine. Our casualty is Bridget. Marios says she's dying." Before he voiced the question forming on his lips, she rushed on. "The stories said you escorted spirits to the land of the dead. Any truth to that?"

"Well, yes, sort of." He cleared his throat. "When we first arrived here, we studied humans to make sure the energy you produce would be beneficial to us. I noticed when humans cease to live, you release a different kind of energy: one we can't consume, or even touch. It's more like our natural forms than anything else. These energy bursts go...somewhere." He shook his head. "I've followed them as far as I can. They go somewhere I can't cross, another type of threshold that keeps me on the outside. Some of that energy wanders a bit before it eventually finds the way out. Some never does. Like ghosts, I suppose."

"So something else exists besides our world and yours." Callie was undecided whether it comforted or unsettled her.

"Something," Hermes allowed.

She swallowed a sob. He reached out as if to comfort her, but she drew away. She didn't deserve his sympathy. "Will you make sure Bridget finds the way?"

Hermes glanced at the door, and back to Callie. He nodded solemnly. "It will be an honor."

They went inside. Florian rose and moved in stiff slow motion as they entered through the terrace door. She held him tight in wordless comfort when he gathered her in his arms.

"How is she?" Callie whispered.

"She's only breathing a few times a minute now. Marios says it won't be long." Florian's exhale held an uneven cadence as he released her. He nodded at Hermes. "He's in the parlor if you want to see him."

Hermes brightened. He took a moment to share a brief, sympathetic hug with Florian before he left the room.

Florian said softly, "Sit down. You look exhausted."

"No, I'm okay." Callie's heart was pierced with another dart of guilt as she noted the telltale redness of his eyes. "How are you?"

"I'm all right." He looked down at Bridget with a sad smile. "She had the presence of mind to tell me to call Pete to take her to the mortuary. She'll be buried beside Stefanio. They arranged it all years ago when he died."

"That's good." Callie fought against the thickness in her throat and blinked back tears. Her voice broke. "I hope they can be together again."

"I'm sure of it." Florian's fingertips brushed away a stray droplet on her cheek that had escaped despite her best efforts. "She told me to protect you. I promised I would."

She leaned into his touch, breathing wonder at the swell of emotion she couldn't yet call love, but perhaps its herald, despite the remorse eating at her insides. Bridget's words in the garden cast a shadow over the moment when she recalled them: Heartbreak, danger, and blood. She believed she had caused the heartbreak. What else waited in Florian's future? She now had the power to look and see, but feared what she might learn.

Hermes and Marios came to the doorway. So it happened that with the four of them beside the bed, Bridget sighed. Her lips curved upwards. She breathed the name of her beloved husband and her body relaxed, a tender smile still lighting her face.

No other breaths followed.

Marios moved forward to place his stethoscope against Bridget's chest. Florian gripped Callie's hand in expectant dread. She glanced at Hermes, whose eyes followed something she could not see as he nodded in affirmation.

"Will you open the door?" he whispered. Callie gently untangled her fingers from Florian's and hastened to unlatch the doors to the terrace, swinging them both open to the night and the purple twilight of the mountains across the barrier. Marios completed his assessment and confirmed with a sympathetic nod what they already knew. Florian smoothed the blankets and tucked them in gently over Bridget's still form.

"I'll be back when I can." Hermes bent and kissed Marios. The doctor creased his forehead minutely.

"Where are you going?"

"To keep a promise. Then back to try and hold things together." He crossed to the door and blurred into motion. The breeze in his wake fluttered the curtains and bedclothes in the room.

Florian stood in shocky silence beside the bed, a little lost. "What's happening?"

"I asked Hermes to make sure she finds her way home," Callie soothed him.

"Ah." Florian nodded, his throat working. "That's good, then. Remind me to thank him later."

"He knows."

Marios put a compassionate hand on Florian's shoulder as he turned to leave. "I'll be in the next room if you need me."

Callie recognized Florian was bewildered, almost childlike in his grief, uncertain what to do or where to go. She took his hand.

"I'm all right." He didn't seem to be aware of the tears, streaks of sorrow etched upon his face. Her throat spasmed in a choked sob, and she turned away to hide her own guilty tears.

"Take as long as you need. I'll go downstairs and call Pete." She took a step to move away, but he wouldn't release her hand.

"No, please stay with me. Just for a few minutes."

She guided him to the chair. He sank into it and gathered her into his lap. They became a comfortable tangle of arms, his head resting against her heart. His body trembled and she held him tighter as he wept for the woman who was his childhood protector, adolescent conscience, and who loved him unconditionally as only a mother or grandmother could. Her own tears mingled with his, tainted with shame and sour against her lips.

At length he released her and let her go make the call.

IN THE SMALL hours of night, she let herself out of Florian's apartment and into his deserted vegetable garden.

She'd led him to his bed without protest after Pete drove away to complete his sorrowful task. Florian's grief was silent, a pain too deep to navigate with words, and she held him in her arms until he fell asleep, his head buried in the curve of her neck. She disentangled herself with care not to wake him. Deeply asleep, he didn't stir as she covered him with a quilt.

She stood on the patio, the scent of rain carried on a fitful wind that agitated the trees in short, uneasy rustles.

Sullen flares of lightning in the southeast, beyond the dull curtain of the barrier, echoed the storms over Olympus. She stared across the threshold as amethyst spears of electricity plunged into the dark head of the mountain, its summit muffled in heavy swathes of gray. Why couldn't they take their deadly battles there, instead of here on Earth? *Why?*

"Why?" The scream erupted from her throat and rage exploded with frightening heat inside her. "Fuck you! You can't do this!"

The answering rumble of thunder from the real world drowned out her shriek. She ripped a green tomato from a vine and hurled it toward Olympus, and another. The pointed tines of a hand rake jabbed her palm as she groped for something more solid to launch. She lurched into the garden and as it expanded, threw the rake. Her arms came up in a shield and she flinched as the sharp tool bounced back from the barrier to imbed itself points-down in the grass. Sobbing in helpless anger, she plopped down on the ground near the bench where only hours before, everything had gone so wrong.

Behind the self-serving tears, her early warning system nagged with the sense of some catastrophic event looming closer in time until she could no longer ignore it. What was the purpose of these bullshit visions if she couldn't figure out how to control them to give her the information she needed? There was only Eleni and herself, and with Bridget's death, Callie could no longer justify asking the girl for help.

Sitting there crying wasn't going to accomplish anything, either. She allowed herself another moment of unbridled resentment and wiped her face with the back of her hands.

Something bumped against her shoe with a soft clink as she shuffled her feet to rise. Beside the bench she found the covered vessel Aphrodite had given her, left behind by Marios in his concern for the others. Callie leaned over and picked it up. The lid shifted. In the falling twilight, a flash of golden luminance from the vessel's gilt interior dazzled her. She lifted the top.

Ambrosia gleamed inside, the shallow dish about half full.

With sudden resolve she stared into the glowing stuff, calm and still inside. She knew what she had to do. Before she could think too much, she raised the bowl to her lips and breathed it in.

33

Ambrosia burned untempered in her veins without the presence of Bridget and Eleni. Callie fell, grass cool against her feverish skin as the avenues of time arrayed before her in dizzying tangles. Once more, the blocky, unyielding events of the past slid by, the fluid current time stream, and the hazy, splintered potentials yet to come. The cataclysmic events loomed closer now and made it easier to hone in. She found the horribly familiar event easily.

Water rushing. The sky on fire. Puck's laughter.

She'd seen that too many times. She turned her attention backward along the stream, against the current of possibilities into a sort of temporal rewind. *The white-hot explosion imploded back into itself. Ares and Michael reformed from comets into human guises. Puck's mouth moved rapidly as he argued with someone out of sight.*

"Where is he?" she whispered, looking back. She found him sulking, hunched deeply into an overstuffed white leather couch on what appeared to be a darkened soundstage. The currents of time slowed down as she reached present events, calmer waters. But she needed to go farther back.

She hit the time stream of the past without warning, sliding as if on ice along the surface of events now frozen in the glacier of history.

It took a moment to get her bearings. The argument she glimpsed earlier began—or ended, she realized, as the backward flow became more familiar. She willed herself to control the speed with which it unfolded. It was like operating some kind of cosmic remote control on steroids.

"...lucky that your pet didn't kill her on sight." A low female voice, dangerous and strangely familiar, berated Puck, glowering at the unseen person from beneath his brows. "Don't give me that look. This isn't the first time you were warned about them." Thunder rumbled above, echoing among the empty seats of the deserted studio.

"I didn't know he was going to do that," Puck muttered.

"Now everybody knows there's a new Oracle, or they will once that mouthpiece Hermes is finished squawking. We can't afford anybody finding out about your little side business. I told you it was a bad idea. But now I've decided an apocalypse might help me more than I thought, so you get to do damage control."

"Why can't you do it? I have been out in both camps listening for every hint of treason and pandering to that idiot whispering in Zeus's hairy ears for months. I'm tired from casting spells." Puck's voice rang with petulant protest but he got up from the couch.

"I have a show taping tonight. I'm going to be late and you still have that tragic little couple to interview." The woman's voice was maddeningly familiar, dark and silky, and made Callie want to listen to anything she said no matter the amount of venom infused in the words.

A sharp crackle, and a purple spark of static lightning zapped Puck in the seat of his tight leather pants. He convulsed and glared at the air.

"Fuck! Why'd you do that?"

"You're still here. Get to work. And don't let her do anything stupid or she's going to become monumentally inconvenient."

"Fine," he answered sullenly.

"Do it." A crash of lightning signaled an apparent dramatic exit, and silence followed. Puck stuck his tongue out at the emptiness and flung himself through an arched doorway, his face twisted in fury and embarrassment as he disappeared. Callie tried to follow his vanishing energy but he slipped away.

Something was out of kilter, though. Her chest hurt. It prevented her from concentrating. Irritation turned into panic. Something was terribly wrong.

Startling, sharp pain in the form of a slap shocked her out of the vision state, and Callie sucked in a whistling breath, and then another, before becoming racked with violent coughs. She curled up in a ball on the grass, taking in one shuddering breath after another until the fire in her lungs eased, and her pounding heart slowed to a more normal rhythm.

"You forgot to breathe, genius."

The acerbic voice startled her and she sat up. Surprisingly gentle hands aided her to an upright position as Apollo crouched on the turf beside her, his mouth a thin smile.

"Didn't you read rule number one? Never use the Delphi method alone. This kind of thing tends to happen."

"I...I didn't."

"You didn't read the instructions. Kids these days." Apollo shook his head. "If it isn't in an email or a text message, you ignore it. I thought you were going to work with the others."

"We tried it. It didn't work." Callie shook her head. "We all saw different moments in time, and now Bridget is..." Hot, red lines of regret traced fine glaze-cracks through her heart. She knuckled burning tears out of her eyes. "She died."

"Did you take time to synchronize with each other before you inhaled the ambrosia?" He thumped her forehead with a gentle fore-finger. "Why did I bother to give you instructions if you didn't access them? You also need a couple of days to burn off the ambrosia before you make multiple attempts. You'll fry your nervous system and end up crazy, or dead too."

Callie began to fold in on herself, a crumpled ball of misery. "It's my fault she died."

He thumped her forehead harder this time.

"Ow!" Forcibly dragged from the quagmire of self-recrimination, Callie just stared at him.

"Knock it off." He folded himself down to sit beside her on the ground. "Not synchronizing isn't going to kill anybody. It just gives you three vantage points. She was very old and she barely survived an ambrosia overdose the first time. It had nothing to do with you."

It didn't relieve the guilt, but his callousness gave her a new focus. Callie found herself glaring at him. "Why did you come back?"

"I wanted to make sure you didn't do anything stupid, like use the Delphi method alone." He bumped her shoulder with his.

Despite his sardonicism, she recognized genuine concern. She still didn't know how she would come to terms with the fact he cared, but wasn't about to pass up an opportunity. "I have to find out who is behind this. I'm sure I know her voice, but I can't see her face. This whole war is a setup, an inside job. I have to make them listen to me."

"You're the Oracle Priestess. They'll listen."

"What the hell does that mean, anyway?" Callie ripped up a handful of grass blades and shredded them irritably. "Hermes and Hephaestus have given me permission to call on them. Even Aphrodite is acting like this is a big deal, talking about tradition and making me ceremonial pottery."

"It isn't only the human world's past and future you can see. It's *our* past and future. Advisor to gods and humankind, Callie. One hell of an influential position, and something nobody else can do but you. Not even me. I can't see our future, but sometimes I can feel when things are going to shit." Apollo shifted on the grass beside her. "I want you to focus on something. Look beyond the battle. A big event is coming that's going to affect everything negatively. I can't see it, but I feel it." He held out his hand.

After a moment's side-eye, Callie reached out. He clasped her hand lightly in his dry and slippery fingers.

Time irised outward; Apollo showed her how to control what she saw, navigating smoothly along potential events, so much closer than before. *Eight hours, maybe less, before the battle starts. The explosion, the destruction of the doorway in Rome, an ocean pours through a rip in space—*

And afterward...slowly, the collapse of the other thresholds between worlds, a chain reaction that destabilizes everything the Amaranthine have ever built. All over the world doorways close with explosions like small suns and sear the landscape in their wake for hundreds of miles.

A week from now, this garden would implode like a collapsing star.

The last threshold to shatter.

34

"Both prime thresholds go, the whole network goes. Bet they didn't see *that* coming." His grimy white coat shone in the never-dark twilight as Apollo lay on the grass, hands behind his head. "I've always told them the primes are too close together."

Callie's head spun. "I don't understand."

"Multiple dimensional thresholds should be on opposite sides of a planet whenever possible. In close proximity they constantly tug at each other's atoms."

Long fingers laced together in midair over his chest, straining against the opposing knuckles in demonstration. "Two different groups wanted in on the cradle of civilization, but nobody wanted to share their threshold. The smaller dimensional doorways we opened afterward weren't random. They have a distinct pattern meant to bleed off the extra pressure building up between the primes, and became holy sites where the gods appeared. Since the contract which made it illegal for us to show up as gods, most of them are unused now. The pressure has built up. Eventually, the atoms in the doorways tear each other apart with only a tiny bit of encouragement." His fingers slid and spread into abrupt starburst shapes. "Boom. Nuclear fission."

Callie's heart lurched. "They didn't realize that could happen?"

"This was only our second venture into dimensional thresholds. We were still new at the technology."

"What happened the first time?" Callie's automatic query made Apollo's head roll toward her, mouth pursed, and she waved to stop his reply. "Never mind, I don't want to know. Most of the people on earth will die if the doorways go boom. Who's going to be left to pay attention to the Amaranthine?"

"Wouldn't be possible for us to go home, either. Taking on a new human form has to be done in our own dimension. The only way to build a new one when a body dies is to recalibrate our molecular structure there. If we can't get back...we will become mortal." A soft bark of laughter emerged from his lips. "Bring that up when you get there. They need to really have their tree shaken. The advent of movies and TV and now the Internet has made us all fat and lazy. It doesn't take much to work you people up in a real frenzy. Some of us are used to huge amounts of energy now, like a drug addiction. Everybody's more interested in getting their fix and living forever than fixing their mistake with the thresholds."

"With so much energy floating around, why is Zeus bent on being recognized as a god again?"

"Can you imagine experiencing the level of world-wide adoration he received as a rock legend, and have it evaporate? The energy source is still around because his persona bears a legacy, but not at the dose he's accustomed to. It was even more than when he was a god. The business model we used back then is probably the most successful in the history of our kind, but nobody expected a random Deity attached to a nomadic desert tribe and His entourage to come in and take over like that. Before the contract, Zeus was always the biggest and strongest. Except Hera." A sneer pulled his lip from his teeth. "It always comes back to Hera."

Something twitched in the recesses of her mind, and Callie tried to wake it up. "What about her?"

"She's the original occupant of this world. Long before the rest of us arrived, she was here. Nobody's sure where she came from." Apollo's sidelong glance held a challenge, as if he expected a light bulb to go off over her head. "At the time we got here she was the only game in town in terms of deity. Some ugly territorial squabbles went on for millennia. When it became clear we were not going anywhere, Hera bound herself to Zeus. The union of their energy made them both stronger. They rose to power and he fell for her, hard. Then when the Hebrew god showed up and started leading in the polls she wanted out of their agreement to jump on His bandwagon. Zeus wouldn't allow that, but the assimilation of old religions by the Catholic church still allowed her to weasel her way in without working too hard."

"She's the original Mother goddess." Electric insight hit Callie.

"Mother of God, Queen of the gods, the Goddess—a thousand other names in a thousand other religions, not all benevolent. She's natively strong and has some little tricks the rest of us don't have: one of which seems to be creating a huge blind spot in Zeus's sense where she's concerned. Now she's more famous than he is, revered as a mother figure and an advocate of female empowerment. "

"Wait a minute!" Callie leapt to her feet as things clicked into place. *The voice.*

Sarah Freewin. Talk show host and heroine to millions of women around the world. Benefactress and celebrity Santa Claus.

"Hera," she whispered. "She was the one arguing with Puck in my last vision. Apollo, I think she might be the one behind all of this."

35

Slow clapping, Apollo rolled to an upright position. "That's my girl. Do you think you can sell it?"

"I'm not sure." Callie bit her lip. "I only heard her voice. I'm certain it was Hera, though. I think she would have to be the woman in my visions, but I can't see her face. We need to tell somebody."

"*You* need to tell somebody, and if you're going to accuse Hera of starting a war without consequences you're going to have to do it as the Oracle." The solemn twist to his mouth made Callie stop and listen, a thread of disquiet building inside. "I told you to expect a lot of responsibility and sacrifice. Without any other visionaries, you'll be a Delphi Priestess. Quite a few perks come with being a conduit of the gods, but there are things you won't be able to experience."

Mouth agape, Callie's hands went to her hips, arms shaping indignant brackets. "Oh, come on! That is an antiquated, sexist condition! I don't have to be a virgin." She faltered at his grave expression. "Do I?"

"Not a virgin. Abstinent." Apollo rose and came to stand beside her, but avoided her gaze. "I haven't done well by you, and understand your anger toward me. I don't want you to go into this without knowing everything. Delphic use of ambrosia goes way beyond the occasional snack here at Florian's. The normal biological processes of a female body are altered immediately. Contraceptive drugs won't work for you, and ambrosia is a teratogen. This is why we only reproduce *with* human females, not *as* human females. If you conceive—and you will every time there's a chance, because you inherited enough Amaranthine genetics—what your body produces won't be a child. It will be a monster."

"Like, real *Clash of the Titans* type monsters?" The joke fell flat, her weak, small voice betraying her dread.

"A non-viable parasite that uses your body as a food source from the inside. Genetics is still an unpredictable science. My work hasn't uncovered a way to avoid it. The old priestesses took vows of celibacy. That's overkill, but even these days it's imperative not take the risk of conception at all." His gaze finally lifted to meet hers, his mouth a grim line. "You won't survive a pregnancy."

"I can't ever have children? I can't even...but Florian and I—" Numb, Callie squeezed her eyes shut. "Why are you telling me this? Become Oracle, or the world ends in a week. How can I reconcile this all at once? Do I even have a choice?"

"You always have a choice. You answer only to your own conscience. Reject the burden in favor of a normal life and time goes forward as you've seen. Take up the mantle: the gods do your bidding and you can save billions of lives." A weary hand passed over his face. "I won't lie to you, Callie. Your gift will only become stronger in proximity to us. It gets old. Some things are better left unknown. You won't be able to avoid having visions you don't want to see about the people you love."

His feet paced out a restless circle before he turned back to face her. "The night you were conceived I saw the future I would have with your mother if I stayed human. A love like I never experienced before, in all my many lifetimes and disguises. Husband and father, I could raise you with Alissa in complete bliss. But both of you would die twenty-three years later. I just didn't know how, until today.

"I searched a little harder for what happened if I left. Alissa would die so much earlier." The pain in his eyes sparked a shared sorrow for which Callie was unprepared. "But you would live longer, and your living might change the world's fate. The choice I made was to protect you, like she did."

"I understand." Her voice caught in a sob. She bit back the self-serving tears, squared her shoulders and cleared her throat. "What do I do now? Do I need to sign in blood or something?"

"I think you already did." Apollo came to her and took her hands, his eyes soft and kind, no longer narrowed with the affectation of world-weary cynicism. Radiance grew about his head and shoulders and brightened the dirty lab coat into glowing raiment. Callie stared in awe at this glimpse of Phoebus Apollo, God of Light. His voice, quiet and resonant, held pride as he spoke.

"Calliope, child of Apollo and Alissa, I confirm and proclaim you Oracle. In accordance with Olympian law, the gods defer to your wisdom. May your speakings be just and true, to the benefit of all: human and Amaranthine alike. Priestess of Apollo, thou may call on me when thou wilt, and I will come when you bid me, my daughter."

He kissed her tenderly on the forehead. Callie leaned into it just a little, and he gathered her in for a quick embrace. Close proximity drove home the fact that despite its currently glowing state, the dirty lab coat hadn't seen the outside of an Amazon jungle in years. She pulled back gently, trying not to choke. The moment was over as Apollo shrugged off the light and morphed from god and proud father back into misanthropic scientist.

"Now, call your pal Hermes, and insist on a convocation. You get to go on a field trip to Olympus and commence tree shaking. You have about two hours before the ambrosia is fully out of your system and you can use the enhancement to your advantage. You'll be able to sense time streams shifting, so you'll know when things change in the right direction."

"Aren't you coming?"

"It has been eighteen hundred years or so since I set foot in Olympus' throne room. Found out the hard way Hera can turn Zeus against anyone who throws shade at her. He doesn't like to be reminded his wife is more powerful and more devious than he is."

"Since I'm about to do just that I could use as much backup as possible."

"Touché." Apollo shrugged. "Let me think about it. Work is calling." He turned and walked away, tossing over his shoulder, "Try not to let the world end and completely screw up my cultures. I'm getting close to a cure for cancer."

"I'll see what I can do." Sarcasm must be a family trait, she thought.

Alone in the garden once more, gusts lifted the leaves with a sound reminiscent of rushing water. The mnemonic sound triggered a flash of the possible future. *An ocean pouring through a rip in space, carrying everything away*—Callie shut down the time stream before it consumed her attention and pitched her voice to rise above the wind.

"Hermes, the Oracle Priestess needs your help."

She waited a moment. He didn't come, so she shouted this time. "Hermes, I need you. I want you to help me travel to Olympus."

Wind whipped her hair and the messenger appeared, discomfited. "Things are heating up. I really don't have time to take you to Olympus."

Callie squared off with him, her arms crossed. "I need you to call a convocation."

Hermes did a double take. "Convocation? Now?"

"Right now."

Stunned, his sharp features went blank, but brightened as they slid into admiration. He ran a grimy hand through his hair and grinned widely. "You don't start small, do you?"

"Not just the Olympians. All the Amaranthine who will come, and the angels, too. And Titania and Oberon." Apollo's instructions didn't include them, but her gut instinct told her it was important.

"Are you kidding?" Hermes gaped. "That's never been done in the history of...of history. And in case you don't remember, there is a war going on?"

"Not if I can help it." She straightened. "Tell them the Oracle Priestess bids them come to Olympus. I saw their future. It isn't pretty."

"Some smooth talking will be in order." His voice held dubious conviction.

"Yeah, well, you talk a lot."

One eyebrow rose. "What is it about becoming Oracle Priestess that makes women sarcastic?"

"Oh, I don't know." The words came out before Callie could bite them back. "Maybe the fact that it's fatal to get pregnant?"

Shocked, then chagrined as light dawned, Hermes drew closer. "Damn. Callie, I'm sorry. It's been so long, I forgot about that part."

"I'm sorry, too." She hugged herself. "There isn't lot of time. Do your best."

For a minute, he wavered as if he wanted to say something, and then straightened. "Give me fifteen minutes. I'll convince them to listen, and be back to escort you to Olympus. The first trip's kind of rough. You might need a little time to recover, given your history with the barriers."

An odd shifting occurred in the back of her head. As Apollo had forewarned her, she sensed the time streams already turning in a new direction. She resisted the impulse to follow the new rabbit hole. This was the right path, but the abrupt, violent ending a week from now still loomed like a brick wall in the time stream ahead. "Thank you, Hermes."

The messenger gave a shallow bow. Wind gusted and made her squint her eyes. When she opened them again, the garden was empty and quiet, save for the faint sound of sirens bleeding through the barrier from the outside world.

Dim light spilled across the terrace of Florian's apartment. She followed the paving stones that led up to the door and peered through the curtain. He sat at the island in his kitchen, hunched over a mug, the edges of his body dulled and blunted with the weight of sorrow. He looked up as she opened the door and acknowledged her presence, his eyes red and bleary. She eased into the chair beside him.

"Life is going to be very strange without her." A catch roughened his voice, and he cleared his throat. "Though a century of putting up with me has undoubtedly earned her some kind of eternal reward."

"I can't imagine a century with you being too bad of a fate." Callie blinked back the tears that threatened again. She squeezed his hand where it lay on the counter. He brought hers to his lips and kissed it.

"I forgot to ask if you were you able to learn anything useful, before."

Callie shifted uncomfortably. "Not the first time."

He stared her down in sharp accusation. "The first time? Callie, you didn't do this again, did you? Alone?"

"No. Apollo was with me," she soothed. A small exaggeration of truth, she regretted the falsification right away. "I think I've figured out who is manipulating the tension. Hermes is calling everyone to a meeting on Olympus so we can try to prevent this. He'll take me there."

"You're going to Olympus?" Florian looked a little dazed. "Mortals can't cross into their world."

"Apparently I'm barely human, or so Apollo says." She drew a painful, shaky breath. "I'm the Oracle Priestess."

"So you are." He nodded once and averted his gaze. "Aphrodite was only too happy to tell me what that means in traditional terms."

"There are reasons. Good reasons, it turns out, but that doesn't make it any easier."

"No. It doesn't." His voice became stronger. "Nor does it change how I'm starting to feel. I can't make this go away overnight and I don't want to. You brought me back to life. To go back to the way I was without you would be unthinkable."

She'd been determined not to cry but it happened anyway. "I feel the same. Oh, Florian, I wish it was possible to walk away from it, but I can't. This is bigger than us."

He abandoned his mug and gathered her into his arms, his lips against her hair. "I'll be here at your side, whatever comes."

His scent, his arms: everything about him sent warmth flooding through her and made her want to stay with him, the end of the world be damned. Callie melted as long as she dared in his embrace before she gathered solid edges and pulled apart in resignation.

"I'll be back as soon as I can."

Florian resumed the solitary contemplation of his mug of tea. "You'll find me here. I'm going back to bed. I haven't been so tired since my sentence started."

She kissed him quickly and made her way to the French doors. As she closed it behind her, he hadn't yet moved from the island, a study in desolation. She turned away before her resolve disintegrated.

At the bottom of the terrace, Hermes blew back in. He sagged as if exhausted, but nodded at her inquisitive look.

"Done. Michael and Ares agreed to one last truce, and representatives are coming from all the pantheons. Titania and Oberon didn't seem surprised to be summoned." He narrowed his eyes at her. "Care to speculate on that?"

"No. I know why." Callie shook out her arms and legs, like an athlete prepared to sprint. "How do we cross, Hermes?"

"Right here." He led her to the end of the garden, where meadows appeared to sprawl at the feet of violet mountains. "We normally do this in energy form because inter-dimensional travel is easier without corporeal bodies. You don't have that luxury, so I'll take one for the team and stay in this form, too. It won't be pleasant the first time but you'll develop more tolerance after a few trips." He stepped closer to her and put an arm around her waist. "Try not to puke on me."

In apprehension, she gaped up at him and realized he was grinning at her, a teasing light in his silvery eyes. "Best to do it at a run. Once we're across, I'll take us somewhere you can recover in private for a few minutes."

"How bad is it?"

He took a deep breath. "Better to not think about it. Geronimo!"

Before Callie could object, the wind roared and they moved forward.

3 6

SHE MANAGED NOT to throw up on Hermes, but the flowerbeds on Olympus were not so fortunate. By the fourth expulsion her abdominal muscles ached and Callie wondered vaguely where it all came from. Looking a little queasy himself, Hermes disappeared and returned with a pair of goblets. When Callie finally rose in shaky relief from her hands-and-knees position, he handed her one of the drinks.

"Give this a try. You should be able to handle it. This is real nectar, Olympus-style."

The liquid shimmered with opalescence, the outside of the goblet frosted with condensation. Callie took a cautious sip, waiting to see how her guts reacted. It tasted faintly of vanilla and cinnamon, but several other completely alien flavors she couldn't identify. It was impossible to say she liked it. The stuff seemed to evaporate before it hit the back of her palate but it was cool and soothing in her throat and settled her stomach. Hermes downed his in three gulps and shuddered a little, relaxing.

"I hate doing that in a body. I hope you don't plan on making regular visits."

"Not if I can help it." She looked around. "Where are we?"

"You have the privilege of throwing up in my garden." Hermes gestured. "Usually I let the Oracles hurl all over somebody else's yard, but I like you."

"Thanks. I'm honored." She smiled at him over the edge of her cup as she took another sip. "Where do we go from here?"

"This is my condo, so to speak. Our city has a circular arrangement with Zeus at the center. We follow the pathway to the throne room." He nodded at the sidewalk, a lambent path with milky light. Callie studied it with interest as nausea began to abate. It wasn't marble or any other material she recognized, and reflected the violet sky in its polished surface. She looked up and gasped in wonder. Stars and misty wheels of galaxies swirled above in unfamiliar patterns, definitely not a view available anywhere on Earth.

"Come on. We don't want to be late for your first convocation." Hermes took her goblet and set it on the ground. He pulled her to her feet and waited as she tested her equilibrium. "Good to go?"

"I think so." She scrubbed damp palms against her jeans, a thud of dread in her chest. Anthropology and classical studies didn't prepare her for this. The closest experience she had with diplomacy was dealing with drunken football players and undergrads at the sports bar.

Given her recent experiences at Nectar and Ambrosia, it might not be much different.

"So, what are the chances of Zeus throwing a lightning bolt at me when I tell him Hera's probably been manipulating him to provoke this war?"

"Whoa!" Hermes stopped in mid-stride and pivoted, his jaw dropping. "First off, you can't just blurt it out like that. And you're sure? Oracle sure?"

"She said something about an apocalypse helping her more than she thought, and just like I told you, Puck has been helping to spread dissent among the angels and lesser gods. It looks like they're working together. If the battle happens tonight, Rome's threshold gets blown up. Then all the other doorways implode, one by one."

"Damn it, it's Atlantis all over again! I knew things were too quiet."

Hermes gripped the sides of his head as sound of pure frustration escaped his lips. "What is she trying to do now?"

"I think she wants to reset the game." Callie shook her head at his sharp, quizzical glance. "It's too much to explain now."

He led her along the luminous pathway. When they rounded the corner of Hermes's home and exited his walled garden, Callie faltered in her step a moment and stared.

They stood in the center of what appeared to be a volcano. Sheer basalt walls rose above the central compound and sprouted gravity-defying cliff dwellings in the rock face. Dozens of buildings from temple-style architecture to gaudy, tasteless mansions were arrayed in staggered spokes leading out from the center.

At the axis of this stationary orbit, a titanic structure dominated a hill. Its domed cap still below the level of the crater, but higher than all the other buildings, each of the lower dwellings maintained a clear, unobstructed view of the dome. Streaks of energy like shooting stars headed for this central point, but many human-shaped figures simply walked toward the throne room unhurriedly, climbing the stairs and passing through columned doorways.

She followed Hermes silently, her geeky scholar's heart hammering with equal parts elated disbelief—*she was on freaking OLYMPUS!*—and sheer panic. She was a twenty-two year old dropout college student about to address a gathering of immortal energy-beings and tell them to stop what they were doing.

Yeah, that sounded potentially fatal.

At the plinth of a massive column that supported the entryway, Hermes took a deep breath. "OK, we're going to do this right. You'll be the last to enter before Zeus does. Everybody gets to stare at the new Oracle for a second, and then Big Z comes in. Did you decide on a less in-your-face approach for your big announcement?"

"I'll start with the thresholds collapsing and see how it goes from there."

Hermes nodded grimly. "That will certainly get their attention."

"Hermes, what about Hera and Puck?" Callie swallowed, her stomach churning again. "They already tried to kill me today."

"They won't do anything in full view of the rest of us. Tampering with a recognized Oracle is forbidden. That's not to say you won't be showered with favors and anything you want in attempts to bribe you into telling us what we want to know. But outright threatening and murder are frowned upon."

"Just frowned upon?" Callie stared at him. "That sounds less than comforting."

"Amaranthine punishments are tailored to the individual. Nobody wants to risk having their worst fears realized. Believe me, a frown is enough." Hermes cleared his throat. "Plus, I kind of...neglected...to tell Hera about the convocation. She hates being interrupted while she's taping. She might be taken by surprise and won't have time to create a story to cover her ass. We may finally catch her out."

Between columns, the bulky form of Hephaestus appeared. He motioned to Hermes. "They're all assembled. Let's start this before Ares and Michael forget they promised to behave for an hour." He bowed his scarred head to Callie. "Welcome, Priestess. You did survive the crossing. I owe Hermes a corporation."

"You bet on whether I'd survive crossing to Olympus?" Callie accused, open mouthed. The messenger ducked his head, running a hand through his hair.

"In my defense, I took the bet because I never had a doubt."

"With friends like this, who needs enemies?" she muttered.

"Showtime." Hermes guided her to a position between the columns. He and Hephaestus arranged themselves to her left and right, like bodyguards. "There is a podium in the center. You'll speak from it."

Callie drew in another deep breath of apprehension and Hermes chucked her on the shoulder. "You'll do fine. Just remember what I said about not blurting out any accusations."

"You never answered me. What my chances were of getting struck by a lightning bolt if I accuse her?"

Hermes shrugged, considering. "About fifty/fifty."

37

Despite her determination to appear cool and unruffled, Callie faltered in her step as she passed through the archway.

It was a little like walking into a concert hall, the sound of voices bouncing back with deafening clamor from the domed ceiling and walls of the circular chamber. In tiered seating, a teeming throng of Amaranthine preened, argued, and answered cell phones. Clear delineations existed among the different pantheons: Callie recognized most of the bar's "regulars" in the Greco/Roman pantheon, which took up the majority of the space in the arena. Many of them were still dressed for battle, dirty and disgruntled. Ares glared across the circle where a group of armored angels flocked, Michael and Gabriel in the front row. The former looked impatient and ready to get back to fighting. Gabriel appeared as tired as Hermes looked earlier in the day, and Callie wondered if he worked against as much resistance keeping the peace as his Amaranthine counterpart.

She glimpsed Garuda and Kwan-yin. Many other deities she didn't recognize on sight, less humanoid beings liberally sprinkled in with those who currently assumed human guises.

To the right of the angels, Sunshine and Ron lounged on cushions with their diminutive court, comfortable in the midst of the chaos. A few of the brownies had popcorn. Sunshine blew her a kiss and her consort gave Callie a thumbs-up that managed to look suggestive. She could tell they were pleased to be included as equals in this convocation, and suspected allies were won by this simple deed—delicate, crushable allies, but friends nonetheless.

An enormous, double-seated white throne occupied a narrow circumferential slice, the elevated wedge lifted above the rest of the audience. It was empty.

Nowhere did she see Puck. Whether this relieved her or made her more uneasy, Callie couldn't say.

In front of the throne area, the podium Hermes told her about rose from the floor, six stairs up to the platform that faced the seat of power. A hush fell in segments as the assemblage noted Callie's entrance. When they reached the foot of this structure, Hephaestus and Hermes paused, the latter giving her a subtle signal to go ahead.

Callie hesitantly mounted the steps and flinched as a near-dazzling illumination surrounded her like a spotlight, but it merely occupied the air and came from no source she could locate. Her escorts bowed as she looked down at them from the podium, and the action caused a ripple of interest among the pantheons. Hephaestus peeled away to join his wife. Aphrodite sparkled in a sequined, fire-colored gown, having claimed a front row seat to the left of the throne where she was sure to be seen by everyone, her excitement barely contained.

Hermes came to stand beside Callie atop the podium. His armor glinted in the harsh white light.

"Oracle Priestess, you called a convocation, and we answered. We acknowledge your wisdom and await your word." His voice issued a challenge to any who might not have made up their mind about Callie's status. "Please turn off your cell phones or put them on vibrate for the length of this convocation. Thank you."

A rush of wind: Hermes blurred, streaking away to reappear beside the marble throne. The light followed him.

"All rise to honor Zeus, King of the Gods!" the messenger shouted.

A rumble and rustle of compliance with his command came from all pantheons.

Except for the angels. Michael glared and crossed his arms in defiance, and Gabriel just looked uncomfortable, wavering on the edge of rising. The rest of the winged beings with them glanced uncertainly among themselves, looking to their superiors for clues, but getting nothing conclusive.

"Will you not rise out of respect for your host?" Hermes asked, his voice low.

"I serve one King, and it is not Zeus." Michael stubbornly remained seated.

Ares spoke up mockingly. "Too frightened to acknowledge any other power, because it might make you look weaker. Such a narrow path, Mike." He rubbed his jaw. "No wonder your sheep are wandering off to find a wider one."

Michael's body coiled as he leapt to his feet, fists clenched, but Gabriel restrained him with a hand on his shoulder and a surprisingly strong, "No!" With all eyes on him, the archangel stood.

"I came here in the interests of peace, which is always the will of our Lord. I will stand in honor of Him, and in esteem for my host. I see no wrong in it."

The other angels, glad to be shown a clear path, rose to their feet in a rustle of feathers and armor. Michael glared sullenly at Gabriel for a moment before standing in resentful compliance.

"Oh, hey, everybody's here!" The California drawl was a shock of cold water thrown on the tense exchange. Callie found she was holding her breath and inhaled shakily.

Zeus waved from the throne, his tie-dyed shirt a startling splash of color against the white. "Wow, this is quite a crowd. It has been forever since most of us were in one place. Take a seat, and we'll get started." His eyes twinkled at Callie from behind blue-tinted sunglasses. "So you're the new Oracle. Have I met you before?"

"Uh, yes sir," Callie stammered. "I work at Florian's. We met last Tuesday."

"Oh, yeah, of course. I was a little drunk." He gestured expansively. "So what did everybody think of the reality show? We're getting some likes on Facebook, and we trended on Twitter for a while yesterday. It was cool. I think people liked seeing us again."

An awkward pause. Callie almost expected chirping crickets, and then a lot of non-committal murmurs sounded and, "Yeah, great, boss!"

Michael ruffled his wings in irritation. Hermes leaned in and said softly, "The Oracle has some news, Z."

"Yeah, right! It's been so long since we had one I'm forgetting the protocol. So what did you see? Is this going to work out for me, or what?"

"I—" Callie began, but Zeus suddenly looked around, waving his hand for her to stop.

"Wait, wait, wait. Someone's missing. Where is my wife? She needs to hear this too."

"I don't know, Z," Hermes said, a nervous tic in the corner of his left eye. "I announced it the usual way. Everybody got the message."

"Huh. Hold on." Zeus dug a cell phone out of the duty pocket of his shorts and dialed a number. Awkward silence ensued as he waited for an answer, holding up one finger. "Oh, hey. You need to come home. The Oracle's here. Yeah, the Oracle Priestess. No, I made them wait for you, but everybody's here. It's convocation."

"Why wasn't I notified?" The dark, silky voice arrived before the rest of Hera did. Callie's early warning system, quiet until now, startled her with its immediate reaction of goose bumps and heebie-jeebies, far above Puck-level.

Dressed in an impeccable lemon-colored suit, the tawny-skinned woman whose iconic, smiling image was familiar to any female aged eighteen to seventy-five looked distinctly irritated. Her voice held a razor's edge.

"Really, the incompetence I've had to deal with today." She glared at Hermes, who returned her gaze with bland innocence. "I'm in the middle of taping. This is incredibly inconvenient." Her attention came to rest on Callie and the affable talk show host was back, an automatic, deceptively genuine smile beaming down at her. "A new Oracle? My goodness, I hadn't realized Apollo was still reproducing. What's your name, honey?"

"Callie." Unable to keep from infusing the word with defiance as she rubbed her prickling arms, she kept her reply short. Hera caught the tone and raised one elegantly manicured eyebrow.

"Congratulations on your gift, Callie. Or is it a curse?"

"I guess it depends on how you look at it."

"I suppose that's true." She turned her full charm back to Zeus, giving him an air kiss. "Don't want to mess up my lipstick. I need to get back as soon as possible."

"You're beautiful, as always." He took her hand and pulled her down on the throne beside him, gazing at her with admiration. "What did I do to deserve you?"

"Oh, you know very well what you did," she purred, half seduction, half venom. Her eyes scanned the room, stopping at Sunshine and Ron. To their credit, they stared back mildly, but the smaller fairies dived under pillows and behind columns. Hera turned her eyes on Callie, slightly narrowed. "A full convocation. All right, Oracle Priestess. What is it you've come to tell us?"

"This war. It has to stop immediately." The words tumbled out of her. "I saw the outcome of the next battle. In a few hours, if you fight, another explosion like the one in Athens is coming, except this one will be much bigger. You're going to open a rip that will destroy Rome and collapse the threshold."

Dismayed mutterings followed her pronouncement. The shifting sensation in her perception of time returned, but nothing changed drastically. Battle tonight, dead end ahead.

Callie raised her voice to cut through the dissonant rumble. "When it happens, a chain reaction will start. Many of the other doorways you opened are unstable because you don't use them anymore. In the last few days, some of you had problems getting even the ones you use all the time to work correctly. The little doorways are the only reason the thresholds didn't implode before now. But if Rome goes, they all go."

She paused and made certain she had everyone's attention. "You won't be able to travel between your realm and the human one ever again. And a week from now, most of the people on Earth will be dead."

Zeus sat up a little straighter, his mouth open. Outright pandemonium reigned in the stands, with shouting and arm-waving and wing-flapping. Aghast, Gabriel sank back on the bench among his fellows. Callie caught a glimpse of Aphrodite, sequins trembling, one shaky hand covering her rouged lips. Hera alone remained unruffled, but made a belated attempt to appear surprised.

When she discovered Callie stared directly at her, a challenge fired in the goddess's eyes.

Zeus held up one hand in a command for silence. The shouting drained away in a buzzing mutter, but the atmosphere in the dome held a charge of urgency. On the dais, Hera continued to watch Callie with suspicion.

"What do we need to do?" Zeus asked once the clamor died. Callie glanced away from Hera, not yet brave enough to make the accusation.

"Call off the fighting." She looked straight at Michael and Gabriel instead. "The contract isn't as important as stopping this disaster."

"The violation of the contract is an insult to God," Michael retorted. "If they continue to ignore the supremacy of the Lord, which they agreed to recognize under this contract, we must... "

"Stop right there!" Ares interjected hotly as he shot to his feet, his indignation echoed by others throughout the chamber. "We never agreed to anything of the sort, Mike."

"That is not specified in the terms, Gabe." Hermes cocked his head at the white-winged angel.

"Not in so many words, no," Gabriel admitted. "But you have to agree it is implied. In accepting the terms, you all promised you would no longer seek to actively recruit or interact with human beings in a divine manner. This reality show is a blatant disregard of that promise. In seeking to reclaim divine status Zeus would put himself on an equal footing with God, who is the acknowledged Divine Presence at this time."

"Excuse me, but I take exception to this as well," Garuda rose, his golden eyes narrowed at the angels. "What is stated by the contract and what you say is implied are two very different things. We agreed not to appear in material form to seek worship as our godly selves. However, in our human forms, we still walk among them and intervene in ways which affect the environment for the better, and creates the positive energy on which we thrive." He motioned to the goddess seated beside Zeus. "Hera's work with impoverished women in many countries has touched our followers, the Prophet's, and your God's, Gabriel. But not in a divine way. In a human way.

"It takes nothing from us in regard to the reverence or worship we are still paid despite our low profile, even though her actions could conceivably be argued to answer the prayers of these women."

Hera favored Garuda with a smile but Callie noted it didn't reach her eyes, as if she were uncomfortable someone noticed her work crossed pantheon lines.

"But she hasn't portrayed herself as a goddess, merely as a human celebrity," Gabriel stated. "Many of our faithful understand false worship of celebrities is sinful and takes away from the glory of God. In the end, as long as they understand all good comes from God then no conflict exists."

"That's a neat little racket." Ares glowered. "God takes all the credit for the good done in the world even though the Amaranthine might be responsible for it?"

"You haven't done the same in the past?" Michael shot back. "Do not misunderstand us. He is out in the world working toward the good of humanity Himself, albeit in subtle ways. We never see Him because so much need for His work remains, yet He is constrained to the limitations under which we all labor."

"And what exactly is He doing these days?" Zeus inquired. His shaggy gray head wagged mournfully. "There's an awful lot of hate out there. He could stop it if He'd just speak up and set the record straight. His idea about putting it all in a book and letting the humans sort it out hasn't been a success story. They need more direct guidance, like they did in the old days. Back then they were lost in the wilderness of the world. Now the jungle is in their heads, man. They are lost inside themselves. I want to help them."

"How is worshiping you going to help? If anything, it will confuse them more." Michael glared at Zeus. "They were told of the One True God. They're already killing each other over who is right. What if they discovered hundreds of gods exist?"

"Our followers don't seem to find that a problem." Garuda shrugged. A titter of laughter followed.

"Three thousand years ago, neither did ours," Hermes agreed.

Callie fought a fiery surge of impatience. "You're all missing the point." She cast a withering eye on the assembled beings. "A week from now it won't matter. Nobody human will be alive to argue who's right and who's wrong! No televangelists, no entertainment industry, no stock markets, no Internet. Nothing!" She thrust her arms in the air in a disgusted gesture of giving up. "Who's going to be left to care about any of you?"

An uncomfortable, somewhat unfriendly silence pervaded for a moment. Callie shrank under the regard of several hundred powerful beings, each of whom could, if they wished, fry her with a thought. But Zeus only sat on his throne, his demeanor oddly calm and detached, and gazed lovingly at his queen. The hair on the back of Callie's neck prickled as Hera whispered sweetly in her husband's ear.

The timelines still hadn't changed! Disaster thumped with increasingly savage drumbeats in the back of Callie's head. Frustration coiled itself in her clenched fists. There was only one revelation she had left.

Callie swallowed her fear and raised her voice in the moody quiet. "Besides, this whole conflict was engineered by someone spreading dissent between these two pantheons."

Hermes whipped around to stare at her and facepalmed, peering at her between his fingers, and Hera turned her regard slowly upon Callie.

"What do you mean?" It seemed Hera all but dared her to say it.

Callie opened her mouth and started to blurt just what she had promised Hermes she wouldn't. Before the words left her mouth, time streams lurched violently with a vision that buckled her knees.

If she openly accused Hera and Puck, the cataclysm didn't go away.

IF SHE KEPT it to herself, the future changed.

Time stretched forward in two branches; one twisted and turned, convolutions that would take effort to untangle. It throbbed with dire potential, but no sudden endings lurked. The current threat would be averted.

The other timeline abruptly truncated less than two hours from now—a stubby, ax-hewn branch of a tree; a neatly cut thread. There was no sense of disaster. There was simply nothing more.

Her parents, entwined in mourning, hold each other. A small urn on a table, surrounded by flowers.

How long she was blanked out in the seizure's grip, she had no way to tell. The vision ended. The convocation murmured and stared as Callie clutched the podium, dazed and horrified, her heart tripping a panicky rhythm.

Hermes blew in to steady her. "Vision?" he whispered in her ear. "You look like you've seen a ghost."

"Yes, mine," she breathed back. "Things changed. If I tell him, I'm dead."

His eyes darkened. "You need to be very careful."

"Believe me, I get that." With his assistance, she straightened.

"You okay there, Oracle? You look a little pale." Peering at her from his throne, Zeus wore an expression of concern. "That must have been a doozy."

"It was." Callie forced a shaky laugh. "Um. Anyway. Where was I? Dissent." Thoughts raced as she hazarded a glance at Hera, who watched her with interest. She'd have to make this good. She took another breath, held it, and plunged in. "I misspoke. I said someone spreading dissent between these two pantheons. I meant to say: dissent spreading *within* these pantheons made it possible for both sides to engineer a conflict." It would work.

"You miss the status you held as gods. Many of you find it impossible not to intervene in the human world. Despite the contract there's been a lot of playing around the edges of this agreement on all sides."

She happened to be looking at Ares when she said it. His brows drew together in a dark expression and she glanced away quickly. She hadn't meant to insinuate that she knew anything about his own infraction with Florian. An appraisal of the rest of the crowd's reaction seemed to confirm her suspicions, though. No one contradicted her. Several avoided her gaze or stared back in wide-eyed innocence. Even the angels didn't deny it. Gabriel pursed his lips and returned her gaze evenly. Michael just glared at her with his usual unendearing mix of suspicion and disdain.

"But if I understand this correctly, none of you are really gods. You're inter-dimensional travelers with massive attention-seeking issues. You feed on our energy and you set yourselves up as gods to achieve those ends. You forgot your own history and fell so deeply into ours that you started to believe it too." Sadly, she shook her head. "I've studied myths and legends all my life. I'm disappointed to learn the stories were real in a way, but never expected to discover the truth is so much stranger than I ever dreamed."

A figure lurked in shadow in the alcove behind Zeus. For a moment, she panicked and thought it was Puck, until the figure moved forward into better light. Recognizing the disheveled form as Apollo, she directed her next words to him.

"I find it comforting to learn someone has been watching over me, although it isn't quite what I expected or what I was taught." She gave her attention to the convocation at large. "We must set aside these arguments about interpretation and who's more important right now. You possess the knowledge, or you used to, of how to fix this problem with the doorways. If you don't fix it, none of the arguments will matter."

Chastised silence reigned as the Amaranthine glanced at each other. Hera alone favored her with undivided attention, as if she waited for the other shoe to drop so she could use it to smash Callie like an annoying insect.

"Trust an Oracle to remind us we aren't perfect," Hephaestus rumbled at last. "But she is right. We have an enormous problem with a very short deadline."

"Can we agree to suspend this conflict until we address the issue of the doorways?" Hermes asked Gabriel. The archangel nodded as relief relaxed his features.

"Agreed."

"But this is not over," Michael warned. "We will settle it later."

Ares snorted, bitterly disappointed. "Damn it. Perfectly good campaign snafu'd by equipment failure."

"I'm already going crazy on parole." Aphrodite shrilled anxiously. "I can't imagine not being able to travel between here and the human realm ever again. Does anyone even remember how threshold physics works?"

"I do," Athena verified. "I was one of the Janus technicians in the beginning."

"So was I," Hephaestus confirmed. Several voices rang out in affirmation from other pantheons.

"We never made any doorways of our own," Gabriel confessed, embarrassed. "After we arrived we used the ones already in existence. I fear we won't be much help."

"That isn't the real problem, though." Athena's brow furrowed with intense concentration as she rose from her seat. "In order to stabilize the smaller doorways, I'm afraid we might be forced to intentionally close them in a controlled manner."

"Close them all?" Uproar in the form of mutters and dismayed chatter rose and echoed from the domed ceiling until Athena spoke with authority.

"All but the thresholds located in North America and in Rome, with triangulated satellite doorways on each continent." The goddess's eyes flashed as murmurs continued. "Do the math yourself, but I can't think of any other way to solve the problem. A complete survey is required immediately to determine how many doorways we opened and which ones are most unstable. We close them first."

"But that means we couldn't travel intercontinentally unless we take—" Aphrodite's nose wrinkled in distaste and she grimaced around the word: "Airplanes."

"Here's the real kicker." Athena paused, garnering everyone's attention. "Opening or closing doorways has to be done in our native forms. Either way, there will be a light show that eclipses Thursday night's little thunderstorm anomaly and it's something that can't be explained by conventional science as humans understand it. We're going to be out there in the open for the whole world to see."

Silence reigned on all sides. The angels shifted and glanced at each other in but raised no protest. A lot of looking around and shuffling of feet took place as the assemblage waited for Zeus to answer. Callie found she was holding her breath again, and let it out slowly. So far, the time streams held.

"Out there in our native forms. Unrecognizable as our godly selves, right?" Zeus finally questioned. Athena nodded in sharp confirmation.

"Anybody foresee a problem with this other than the fireworks?"

"In terms of the contract, I can't think of anything," Hermes allowed, glancing at the angels. Gabriel shrugged his wings.

"Some issues remain. Almost every doorway has a church built upon the site, or an ancient temple. Stonehenge...and with the solstice coming up?" He rolled his eyes, closing them in defeat. "But no direct violation of the covenant," the archangel agreed with reluctance. "Not the most desirable solution, perhaps, but it appears our only solution at this time."

"Then we are in agreement." Inordinately happy, Zeus beamed. "All of you who have the knowledge, get out there and survey those doorways immediately. Start forming repair details and we'll coordinate, right? Play nicely together."

"On it, Z." Athena made a gesture. "Anybody who can help, follow me. Take a leave of absence from your human life. Go into rehab. Whatever. The rest of you, keep regular channels open for communication via your respective messengers. Let's get to work."

3 9

THE ARENA EMPTIED with disconcerting speed, nothing like the stampede of spectators leaving a concert Callie rather expected, but in rushes of light or simply winking out of existence. Hephaestus vanished and left a stunned Aphrodite sitting in front of the throne, her scarlet gown a splash of sequinned blood against the marble. She sat up, attention rapt upon Ares, and her expression dimmed the longer she waited to catch Ares' attention. But he only had eyes for Michael.

From opposite sides of the arena the two warriors stared at each other, deprived of their battle. At last Michael gave a wicked half-smile. Ares saluted him with a nod and vanished.

To her surprise, Callie saw Aphrodite and Gabriel exchange a silent glance until the angel discovered Callie watching them. His expression darkened. He stared her down for a breathless second before he, too, vanished. Aphrodite blinked rapidly, her baleful glance falling at last on Callie.

Foreboding hit Callie's warning system in a skin-crawling shiver. The livid goddess wrapped her arms around herself and transmuted into a hot, white star that streaked out of the dome. Something wasn't right. She'd never liked Aphrodite, but this uneasiness went far beyond the irritation Callie usually felt in her presence. But there were much bigger fish—one shark in particular, really—that she had to deal with at the moment.

Only Zeus remained in his seat, Hera beside him. Hermes lurked at Callie's shoulder. The fairies still lingered to the side of the throne; Ron and Sunshine appeared a little dismayed the big, earth-shattering accusation hadn't come to fruition.

"Well, I hate to run, but I can't delay taping anymore," Hera chirped with a sidelong glance at the fair folk. "I'm sorry we can't enjoy more of a family reunion, kids, but that would just be...unfortunate."

"Speaking of family, something still remains to be discussed." Titania spoke boldly. "An threat was made on the Oracle's life today by one of our own, Mother. Would you care to comment?"

"Somebody wanted to hurt the Oracle?" Zeus's ears perked up. "Not cool. Who would do something like that?"

"Someone threw her to a banshee." Hermes informed him, and avoided Hera's gaze.

"Who?" Zeus demanded. A small rumble of thunder vibrated overhead. Ozone crackled.

"Who indeed?" Titania spread her graceful hands. "Only one of us is missing. Where would he be?"

Baffled, Zeus glanced around, counting. "Yeah, I don't see the brother-in-law." He frowned. "You mean Puck tried to feed her to one of those things? I didn't realize they were still around. Why isn't he here?"

"He's my production assistant. We can't both be gone," Hera grated, blinking furiously. "I know where he's been most of the afternoon. He's recruiting guests. My show next week focuses on parents of missing adult children." She shook her head, and her voice grew lighter. "So sad, really. He's interviewing a couple of college professors in Vermont for a potential appearance: a husband and wife whose daughter disappeared six weeks ago."

Callie faltered as glacial ice in her blood ground her heart to a standstill.

Hera glanced at her to make certain her point was driven home and airily continued, "So I can't vouch for his whereabouts earlier today. I can't guess what he might have been up to."

"Oracle Priestess, do you want to make a formal charge against Puck? Serious misbehavior like that means he has to be punished. Is it true?" His voice became deeper, an echo of the warlike god he assumed briefly on his reality show's premiere.

"S-someone pushed me from behind." Dizzy with terror at the hint her adopted parents might be at the mercy of Hera, or Puck's 'pets', Callie struggled. Hera continued to watch her like a self-satisfied cat that cornered something it could play with and torture before eating.

Zeus peeked at Callie over his glasses, his eyes grave.

"We haven't had a real Oracle in a long time. Did you see something he's worried about?"

She muttered faintly, "I'm not sure. It was before the ambrosia. My visions weren't clear."

Hermes stared Callie down, a *what the hell are you doing?* expression in his eyes. She shook her head at him with barely contained desperation. With a fatal timeline still hanging over her like a blade and her parents' lives at stake, she couldn't risk more.

"But Puck did throw you to the banshee, right?" Zeus pressed. He turned to Hera. "We've talked about this before, sweetie. I thought you could control little brother."

"I always have."

"Not this afternoon, you didn't." Zeus raised one woolly eyebrow. Hera stiffened in silent umbrage. Callie watched the couple continue to argue in mute, fiery shifts of expression until Hera glanced peevishly away. Perhaps Zeus wasn't as hoodwinked as she feared he was.

"Florian invoked salt and iron in his establishment to protect the Oracle," Sunshine said irritably. "My brownies are about to mutiny, but the Doorkeeper felt it was the only way to assure the Oracle's safety with Puck and his creatures running loose."

"Hmm. I think we probably have to do something about that." Zeus tapped his fingers on the marble arm of the throne, pondering. "Get Puck here, will you? We need to punish him."

Hera made an exasperated noise. "But my show—"

"I'm sorry. You helped me write the rules, honey. No threatening the Oracle. I'm going to need her advice on my future and I can't risk her being hurt or killed."

Hera rolled her eyes, huffed, tried to frame a protest and didn't have one. Bellowing, "PUCK!" she made a sharp tugging motion with her right hand, as if pulling a chain.

The spiky-haired punk rocker stumbled when he materialized on the floor below the throne. "Whoa! What the bloody fuck are you doing?" he yelled, and then realized Hera had company. "Ah, hello Zeus. What's all this about?" His eyes widened as he recognized his surroundings. He took in Callie on the elevated podium behind him and Ron and Sunshine in audience with their attendants, watching in timid but anticipatory glee of Puck's punishment.

"I was taking a meeting," he said in a tight voice. "You just hauled me out in front of those people you sent me to—" he stopped and bit back a word, then spat: "Interview."

"Puck, did you throw the Oracle to a banshee today?" Zeus's fuzzy gray eyebrows drew together as he peered over the blue lenses.

"What? No!" Aghast, Puck's gaze traveled around the room. "You mean the waitress? Callie? Uh, when was she recognized? Mate, I didn't know she was an Oracle. I just wanted to scare her."

"So you did throw her to the banshee?"

"I did not! I just threatened to do it and I left." Puck appeared truly incensed to be accused of the act. With a start Callie realized he didn't set off any more of her alarms than usual. He was telling the truth.

I didn't know he was going to do that, he'd said in her vision of the argument.

Holy shit. She'd just assumed it was Puck. Who then, shoved her across the barrier?

"Dude, we've talked about this," Zeus was saying. "I don't understand what you have against our human offspring but it needs to stop. Call those monsters off. Cage them, or kill them."

"Caging them is a death sentence! I made them in the beginning to fight a war with you," Puck growled. "I engineered them to live on Amaranthine energy. Since they can't feed on you lot what else can they eat? All my males are dead. They can't reproduce. It'll be extinction. You already wiped out everything else we ever made. Why can't I keep them?" He sounded like a child demanding to know why he couldn't have a puppy, but Zeus remained unmoved.

"Their time is over, man. Fairies and Amaranthine haven't been at war since my woman and I joined energy, remember?" Zeus claimed his wife's hand and kissed it. The thin, forced smile Hera produced for Zeus made Callie believe his queen would rather stab him right now.

"Oh, yeah?" Puck spat. "That's what you think, is it? Well let me tell you Zeus, we've never forgotten."

"Puck." Hera's interjection held an edge of defeat. "You can't tamper with an Oracle." Her eyes met his in warning. "You will face the consequences."

Puck's mouth opened and closed. "You're going to punish me?" he laughed uncomfortably, then narrowed his eyes. "*You* are going to punish *me*."

"I don't see any way out of it this time," Hera informed him in a low voice. Callie was aware of the real conversation underneath their innocuous words. Puck was furious Hera expected him to take the fall. She wasn't about to take any punishment herself.

"I'm sorry, Puck, but I need her. She's the key to my comeback. You didn't have any idea she was the Oracle when you threatened to feed her to the beastie. Right?" Zeus regarded him with steely eyes. Beneath the sleepy, mellow persona he affected with ease, the king of the old gods expected to be answered and obeyed. "Be honest. I know when you're lying, which is usually every time you open your mouth. How you answer determines your punishment."

"I—" Puck licked his lips, trapped. Callie found herself rubbing her palms, which tingled even though Apollo healed the scrapes and avulsions from which Puck had tasted her blood and identified her.

Another vision hit her.

The ambrosia's effect was rapidly fading from her bloodstream, and Callie struggled to focus clearly on this new, indistinct vision. Her sense of time gave no clues to when this would happen, but...*Puck, triumphant. Puck, lauded in convocation made up of Amaranthine, fairies, and angels.*

Standing beside Puck in the vision, Callie saw herself, smiling.

Though the primary timeline still glared with trauma, the threat of disaster dropped.

Her own fatal path evaporated completely.

4 O

"HE DIDN'T KNOW," she found herself blurting breathlessly, and lurched as she came out of the vision.

"What?" Hermes muttered under his breath as he steadied her.

"What?" Puck said in tandem, surprise on his face.

"Sorry, visions again," Callie murmured to Hermes.

"This is true?" Zeus's squinted eyes measured Callie, and she shivered. If he learned she lied, she might not dodge a lightning bolt, Oracle or not.

"Yes. I wasn't confirmed until just before the convocation." That part rang true. Apollo didn't formally name her Priestess until that moment, even though Hermes and Hephaestus recognized her prior to the assault.

Open mouthed, Puck stared at her, his expression dumbfounded. Hera also regarded her with wary eyes. Wavy disturbances squirmed around her periphery like heat rising from Hera's body. Callie could see it, but she didn't know if anyone else did.

"You're sure." Zeus, dubious, glanced between her and the spiky-haired fairy. Callie arranged her expression into one of innocence, and pointed to her forehead.

"Visions." She was lying about his foreknowledge. Another falsehood. She was certain this broke some kind of Oracle statute, but Puck's position in that last glimpse of the future showed he had an important role to play.

Her life depended on it.

"Okay, I guess." Zeus's eyebrows rose high above the tinted glasses and he shrugged. "So, punishment." He thought a moment, and snapped his fingers. "I got it. Oracle girl, you're going to be a little busy now and I hate to take away Florian's help now that he just got some. Little brother, you go to work for Florian in the bar, confined to the threshold for...oh, about a hundred years. Since you hate us so much, you can serve us for a while.

"You may not travel in the human realm during that time without an approved babysitter. I'll be the one to give Hermes a list of names. Florian is the boss of you and you do whatever he says he needs you to do. When you're not working you need a project to keep out of trouble. Since you were such a great personal assistant to my lovely wife, you can now handle all the Oracle's appointments, so long as you put me on the books whenever I ask."

Despite her vision, Callie's jaw dropped. So did Hera's as her head swiveled to gape at her husband. Puck blustered inarticulately, and Zeus waved a nonchalant hand. "Oh, and if anything bad happens to the Oracle under your care, you suffer the same fate in perpetuity. Anything. Starting now." He leaned forward. "She gets eaten by a banshee, you get eaten by a banshee, over and over."

"You can't do that." Puck's body language held less conviction than his protest.

"Ask Prometheus if I can't."

It was actually a brilliant sentence. A question rose in Callie's mind whether Zeus was acknowledging his wife's involvement by ordering her separation from the scapegoat Puck. The fairy's mouth opened and closed in impotent rage. With a withering glance at Hera, Puck finally bowed in sullen deference to Zeus. "As you command, Lord Zeus." Acid dripped from the words.

"You're giving my personal assistant to the Oracle?" Hera stood slowly, her fists clenched at her sides. "I understand he needs to be punished, but who's going to handle all my business now? We have things in motion that..." Words failed her and she resorted to irritated hand-waving. "No. I won't allow it."

"I have spoken," Zeus said in a singsong voice.

"The hell you have," Hera contradicted viciously. "I am not going to stand for this. I—"

"I HAVE SPOKEN!" An eardrum-shattering roar of thunder rolled in the closed arena. Callie ducked behind the podium in terror as blue-white lances of lightning struck near Hera's feet and left smoking black patches on the marble.

The remaining fairies shrieked. Popcorn confetti'd the monarchs as brownies scrambled for cover. Titania and Oberon gathered them together like comforting shepherds and with an apologetic wave, the fairy queen blew a kiss to Callie. The whole tribe vanished in a floral scented, sneeze-inducing wake.

"We're not done." Hera's eyes swept coldly to Callie, who still peered around the podium from a crouched position. "This is not over."

A crackle of air collapsed in on itself, and Hera was gone.

"My woman damages my calm." Zeus sighed deeply. "Always has, always will, but when you're in love, right?" He smiled at the re-emerging Callie and shook his head, then stood to face the convicted punk rocker. "Your sentence starts tonight, Puck."

"Wait, please." Callie remembered with a wrench of sorrow that Florian was preoccupied. "We'll need time to remove the salt and iron before he can come in and Bridget is...she died tonight. We need to give Florian a chance to grieve before we spring this on him."

Zeus blinked in surprised regret. "Yeah, sure. I'm sorry to hear about the old lady. She was cool. Hermes, will you find him some help to get rid of the warding?"

Hermes nodded crisply. Zeus turned back to the seething Puck, still standing before his judgment. "So you might be hanging out in Limbo until it's convenient for Florian."

"Limbo?" Puck's complexion went a cheesy color of pale. "The void's a little harsh, isn't it, Big Z? Brother? Uh, I haven't really gotten over the last time I visited."

Zeus nodded at Callie. "Call Hermes when Florian's ready. I should go meditate for a while. This whole doorway thing, this could work to our advantage, right?" He got up from the throne. "We get to be out there in our energy forms, doing something good, and it doesn't violate that damned contract." His voice became gleeful. "We won't be gods. We'll be ourselves: aliens!" He giggled maniacally. "We're going to enjoy an awful lot of attention, and the *Ancient Aliens* guy's head is going to explode when he finds out he's right."

His laughter remained for a second after he disappeared. The arena rang with silence, abandoned now save for Hermes, Callie, and Puck. Searching the shadows behind the throne to see if Apollo still lurked, an unexpected flare of disappointment sputtered in her chest when she realized he wasn't there.

Without warning, Puck advanced on her. Callie shrank back and Hermes stepped between them, his caduceus raised in a protective, warding-off gesture.

"Back off, fairy."

Puck ignored him, his attention all for Callie. "Why? Why would you lie?" Confused, suspicious, he appeared near tears of frustration. "Tell me what you saw!"

"I'm not sure." Callie regarded him coolly. "Why should I tell you? You tried to kill me, you plot to end the world, and you show up at my parents' house? You're not exactly on my list of confidantes right now, Puck."

"What the hell are you talking about? I keep telling you, I did not try to kill you. I might have threatened you but that's not the same. And what's with the end of the world?" Puck ran irritated hands through his spiky hair.

"In my visions," Callie began hotly, and then stopped. She'd never actually seen him in the visions either, only heard his laughter. Nothing about them confirmed he was aware the battles would bring about apocalyptic destruction. "Okay. You weren't here when I told them what I saw. If the battle happens tonight, Rome's threshold gets destroyed and all the doorways start to implode one by one. Pretty much everything on the planet dies."

"What?" Puck's shock was real, his wide mouth gaped and gulping like a fish. "No, I just want them to kill each other, bring down their reputations so you people would stop feeding into their gigantic egos! Some human blood was going to be spilled, but there always is. You people are everywhere. Like ants."

"Nice." Callie glared at him with disgust. "You may not have known, but I think Hera did. With the thresholds destroyed all the immigrants get deported."

"Hey, now," Hermes protested in mild affront.

"Sorry. Then she can restart the game with herself as the top deity. And in every vision I have had, I hear you laughing." Callie waited for Puck to confirm, but he continued to look bewildered until stiffness squared his body. His nostrils flared.

"That's what she was talking about. She didn't tell me that could happen. Any of that." His sea-colored eyes clouded. "It would have destroyed everything I have left."

Callie studied his wilted demeanor and decided to trust her gift. "I just had another vision, but this time I saw you, Puck. The end of the world was out there. But if you're with me, it never happens."

"How does that work?" Hermes frowned.

"I don't know yet," she admitted.

"With you? The Oracle Priestess?" Puck's characteristic leer was half-hearted. "I told you I don't have any use for virgins."

"You wish. Not that way." Callie scowled at him in exasperation. "But somehow it depends on you."

Hermes made a come-hither motion with the caduceus. "Let's go pack up your monsters before they shut down the doorways, and then we'll check to see if you need to hit Limbo while I escort the Oracle home."

"Can I at least get a cell without the view this time?" Puck asked weakly.

"They all boast the same view of the void," Hermes shrugged. "Part of the charm."

"It won't be for long, Puck. You need to be with me for some unfathomable reason." She shivered and crossed her arms. "Once I figure out why, believe me: I'll tell you. I'm not happy about it either. Be quick, Hermes. I'm not sure about any of this yet."

Puck sullenly allowed Hermes to put a hand on his shoulder. The two of them dissolved into wind and light and streaked out of one of the arched doorways. Only Callie remained in the vast, silent throne room of Olympus.

Her legs suddenly decided to take on the properties of wobbly gelatin and trembling, she sat on the marble steps in front of the throne. She hugged herself and rubbed her arms against a sudden chill. The current crisis might be averted for now, but the sense of looming future catastrophe nagged like a fading migraine in the back of her head. So did her truncated timeline, back again to haunt her.

It all had something to do with Puck's presence. What the hell did it mean?

The sooner she worked to unravel it, the better. Exhaustion settled into every muscle and she rubbed her grainy eyes in weariness.

"Not bad for your first convocation." Apollo's voice surprised her and she jumped as she realized he sat next to her on the steps. "I don't remember them moving so fast in eons."

"Now what happens?" Callie questioned. "I couldn't accuse them. It didn't change anything, but keeping it a secret did."

"You did the correct thing." Apollo clasped his hands around one upraised, stained khaki knee. "Not telling what you saw created a better outcome. Unfortunately, it's one of those difficult decisions you'll make now and again." He narrowed his eyes. "So, what's with the fairy? What did you see?"

"My timeline. It just stopped if I accused Hera and Puck." Callie saw his body stiffen, and met Apollo's grave eyes. "I'm pretty certain I saw my own death."

Apollo shifted. "We didn't see it in the garden. It's an event based on the decision you made. Each Oracle perceives time a little differently. You'll learn as you go."

"That doesn't help much." Callie sighed in irritation. "It's still out there right now, but if Puck's with me my timeline doesn't end. Even though he might have tried to feed me to a monster, I guess I have to turn him from the dark side or some crap like that. All I know is he's going to do a thing. An important thing. How soon can I go for another vision?"

"After the not-breathing stunt you pulled in the garden? At least two days. Three days to be safe, but even then go easy on the ambrosia. The little girl can help you but you still need to find a third visionary for it to be completely safe. You'll have better control over the timelines."

A sharp, uncomfortable pang of guilt accompanied thoughts of Bridget, and of Marios's distrust. "I'm not sure there is another choice now."

"Pace yourself. You cannot do this every day, Callie. As soon as the doorways are stabilized, the Amaranthine are going to swarm you like bees wanting to know how to be more relevant. Stagger your sessions to at least every three days until you have a full Dodona complement."

"You can't help me like you did in the garden?"

"Not in this. I'm sorry. None of the Amaranthine can be perceived as influencing your visions. It's important your neutrality is unquestionable." He stood and fished a box from the tattered pocket of his lab coat. "Here, take these. They might help with the crossing."

"Dramamine?" Callie raised an eyebrow as she read the package. Chewable, even.

"Just take it at least an hour before you cross next time. Better safe than sorry. Speaking of which—" he paused. "No intercourse. I'm not saying you and Florian can't fool around, but nothing that might lead to conception. One rogue sperm is all it takes. Be creative, but stay a virgin."

"Oh, god." Callie palmed her burning face and peered through slatted fingers. "Can we not talk about sex?"

"It's my job as your patron to remind you and as a father to embarrass you."

"What was I thinking when I agreed to this?"

"You were thinking of what is best for the world." Apollo's voice, gentle for a moment, chided her. "It should always be your motivating factor."

"What about what's best for me?" She knew she whined but couldn't help it.

Silence answered her. Callie uncovered her eyes, peering through her fingers. Alone again, her erstwhile father had evidently crossed the threshold into the jungles of the Amazon to resume his work.

Tearing open a packet of Dramamine, she chewed them up and shuddered at the taste. Cool marble pressed against her back as she shoved the box in her jeans pocket and lay down to await the return of Puck and Hermes. Shadows swirled and danced in the translucent white stone of the dome overhead. She closed heavy eyes against them before concrete shapes formed. In the lee of the empty throne, she gazed up at Zeus's vacated seat. *Empty throne.* Something about it struck a positive chord. As exhaustion traded places with adrenaline, she drifted into an uneasy doze and a patchy dream invaded her subconscious.

The silent arena fills once more with smiling immortals. The throne is empty. She glimpses Zeus in the crowd. He sits in the front row with his pantheon arrayed behind him. Beside her on the podium, Puck cannot contain his grin. He turns to her and whispers, "They fucking get it this time. You did it."

"We did it." Her hand, wizened and older, rises to touch his cheek in affection.

What the hell? In that odd dual consciousness between sleep and awake, Callie wondered if she was having a prophetic dream.

A cold hand seized her upper arm in a crushing grip and yanked her upright. Pain and surprise forced her eyes open. Still groggy, she found herself staring into the glittering, feverish eyes of Aphrodite.

"All right, Oracle. I'm calling in that session right now."

The world flipped.

41

THE WRENCH of teleportation twisted her guts. She braced herself on hands and knees on a carpet, head churning in a sea of disorientation while her stomach roiled. Either the Dramamine helped or there was nothing left to vomit. Too bad. It would have served Aphrodite right if Callie puked all over her Louboutins.

The goddess stood over her with both hands on her hips, lip curled in disgust. "Don't you dare throw up on my rug. That's hand-knotted silk."

The room twirled and dipped in nauseating loops as she raised her head. Luminous white walls and a glimpse of violet sky through the open archway behind Aphrodite clued in Callie that they hadn't left Olympus. As her vision stabilized she propped up on one elbow and surveyed the room. A desk lay scattered with swatches of material, a couch and chairs upholstered in expensive alabaster fabric. The wall behind the desk was crowded with portraits of Aphrodite from Renaissance masters down to glossy photos of her current persona, Dita Delamour, at fashion shows. Another full wall gave the effect of looking out over traffic-sparkled cityscapes in motion: New York, Paris, and London shared the reflected nighttime views.

"What is this?" Callie mumbled around a hard swallow. Aphrodite took a hasty step backward in disgust.

"This isn't going at all the way I wanted. You're going to help me fix it."

"The hell I am." Callie dragged herself upright and stood, swaying. "What do you mean, the way you wanted?"

"I've been trying to get Zeus to make this reality show ever since that patchouli-drenched body's arteries clogged." She gripped the sides of her head in dramatic, temple-rubbing distress. "But it's going all wrong! It was never supposed to keep us from using the doorways!"

"What is wrong with you?" Callie stared at her, aghast. "You knew it would start a war?"

"No, of course not. That was an accident. But it's made someone I love a very happy war god. If I can't bed him as often as he'd like, I can at least give him the next best thing." Her eyes sparkled with heat.

The wall behind Aphrodite, brighter than the room itself, flashed a sunrise view of the city of Rome and backlit the goddess against fiery hilltops. Callie froze in recognition at the silhouette.

The female figure from her visions. Not Hera.

Aphrodite.

"I am supposed to be back in the world, adored and worshipped and FED, damn it! It's been too long since I had a real dose of human energy. I can't stand it anymore." Small threads of electricity crackled between the sequins of her gown. "But your little bombshell in convocation tonight gained me an unexpected and kind of annoying ally."

An amorphous figure appeared in the archway, a shape Callie couldn't focus on until folds of material dropped away from rumpled, dove-like feathers.

"Did you get it?" Aphrodite demanded.

"It wasn't difficult. No one is there right now." Gabriel gave the gilded dish to Aphrodite. "Your cloak barely covers my wings."

"Well, remember to bring your own next time. Stop complaining." Aphrodite made a sharp noise of derision.

Gabriel turned his shining eyes on Callie, reproach in their depths.

"I despise Oracles. Too much faith is already placed in false prophets without having a real one in play." He frowned. "Get this over with. God's supremacy must be cemented for all time and it will be pointless if He can't travel freely between Heaven and the human realm."

"You're lucky I agree the secular life is where I belong." Aphrodite flicked the cover off the porcelain vessel. The brittle crash assaulted Callie's eardrums. "But I draw the line at flying with the herd in airplanes." Ambrosia boiled and surged inside the brimming cup with her sharp movements as she offered the vessel. "Be a good girl and breathe it in, Priestess."

Panic surged. "No. You don't understand. I can't do this right now."

Strong fingers gripped her arms and wrenched them back as Callie scrambled away from Aphrodite. Gabriel held her firmly in place as the erstwhile goddess shoved the cup against her chin.

"You accepted my gift. I'm calling it in. We have important questions."

She wanted to protest. Apollo's warning still rang in her ears. But speaking meant breathing and dangerous tendrils of vapor danced too close to her face. Knowing it was inevitable, she still clamped her mouth and held her breath. Aphrodite's lips thinned in a cold smile as she noted Callie's defiance.

"You really are getting on my last nerve."

Lacquered nails dug into her skin as the goddess pinched Callie's nostrils shut with eye-watering force. Pressure built in her head and her lungs screamed for oxygen until a reflexive, whooping inhalation dragged vapors back into her mouth.

More than she'd ever taken in.

She choked on the burning stuff. Molten silver seared every branch in her lungs, eyes streaming and blinded. Racked with coughs, the involuntary gasps sucked in more ambrosia until the dish was empty. She sagged down on the chair into which Gabriel guided her. Her ears filled with a high squeal of resonating crystal, the taste of salt on her tongue. Eyesight dimmed and she blinked to focus.

"That wasn't so hard, was it?" Aphrodite set the dish on a side table and settled the curve of her hip against the chair's arm, her hands clasped in eager excitement. "Tell me how soon I get my restrictions lifted so I can leave Olympus. Then tell me how they can keep all the doorways open."

"No, first we learn how to ensure God's supremacy," Gabriel objected.

"This was my idea. I get my questions first."

As they argued, Callie's body stiffened with the first visions. Her consciousness reeled against timelines unfurled in glaring tunnels of potential. Her own truncated future loomed ahead, only minutes away. Ambrosia sang fiery arias along her nerves and synapses as other timelines fractured and bloomed with evil flowers of disaster. Inner sight filled with past, present and future while hundreds of possible outcomes slotted into place—but one branched from Callie's abrupt ending.

Aphrodite huddles against the wall of a cell, her face gray and dull. A dense nothingness hovers at the other side. Devoid of energy. Barren of life and light.

They all have the same view of the Void, Hermes's voice sounded in her memory. *Part of the charm.*

"What is wrong with her?" Gabriel's worried visage floated into her vision, his words far away and tinny.

"I don't know!" Aphrodite's shrill response cut through the white noise in Callie's mind as she came back to the present. "Oracles have always been twitchy."

Timelines slid backward and forward in uncontrolled bursts as Gabriel's eyes searched hers.

Gabriel pushed Callie over the barrier to the waiting banshee.

Gabriel, submissive and chagrined, falls to his knees before a radiant, faceless form.

Human, wingless, and desolate, Gabriel roams a dark, rainy street.

Callie began to laugh weakly. "You both are completely screwed," she croaked. "Worst punishments ever."

"What? What do you see?" Panic electrified the goddess's voice.

"Punishment for what?" Gabriel demanded.

"I think you just killed me. Too much ambrosia." Her heart drummed in her own ears, too fast to be normal.

"You gave her too much?" A threat rumbled in the archangel's accusation.

"How was I supposed to know? That's not my thing! I never had Oracles!" A sharp slap against Callie's cheek brought Aphrodite's terror-stricken eyes into focus. "Oh, I didn't mean for this to happen. Come on, Callie. Priestess. You need to concentrate and tell me how to save you."

Energy sizzled along nerve endings. Her body contorted in pain as muscles threatened to tear her apart from the inside. Eyesight grayed and darkened, but the visions in her mind remained clear.

Puck sits beside her in a darkened room and bends over her hand. His lips touch her palm as she inhales ambrosia, the energy dancing through her nerves and synapses.

"Puck." Her lips moved in a whisper as she went limp against the chair. "It all has to do with Puck."

"What?"

"Why does she need the fairy?" Gabriel demanded.

"Hermes...the Oracle...needs Puck. " She forced the words out as heaviness settled into her chest, air turned to stone in her lungs. Sparks of panic spiraled in frigid white Catherine wheels behind her breastbone.

"She called him." Wings spread in alarm, Gabriel moved for the open archway.

"Wait, you coward!" Aphrodite straightened. "You are just as involved as I am! Don't bail out on me."

"He can't see me here."

"Who cares right now? HERMES!" Aphrodite's voice rose in a celestial shout. "THE ORACLE NEEDS PUCK!"

The cosmic remote in Callie's head slipped gears, back and forth between the sharp ending of her own timeline and the branch that continued on. The split loomed before her. Time was running out.

Florian gazes back at her from a mirror with a tender smile as he embraces her from behind: he is still young and unlined, but she much older, with silver streaking through her hair.

Head buried in his arms, Florian hunches over the bar. Tears mark Hermes's face as the messenger stands behind him with a comforting hand on his shoulder.

With bleak countenance, Florian steps over the barrier in the alleyway and staggers as his hair goes white.

The last of her breath forced its way from her lungs with a groan as her diaphragm seized. Cold leached into her chest. Consciousness fought a losing battle against the weight of time as it pressed her flat between a vise of past and future tense. A dense gray veil seeped into her mind and merciless contractions bowed Callie's back against the cushions, faintly aware of warmth in the crotch of her jeans and the acrid scent of urine as thought patterns disassembled. Black blobs filled her outward vision. Her body began to jerk in uncontrollable spasms.

Mom. Dad. Florian. I'm so sorry. Soft, inviting nothingness encroached and drifted her away.

SHE IS *no longer aware of her own body. So close to the jagged chasm of her own ending timeline, she can see now that Time spreads out below her in sharp divisions.*

Where the Amaranthine go, the world still follows.

Old and new gods, hampered by their own jealous greed for attention, continue to vie for territory. Humanity writes its own violent ending, pulled apart into callous factions divided by dogma and invisible boundaries. Atomic fire smelts its own closure of the thresholds. The Amaranthine diminish and die with those who remain in the long, dark cold of nuclear winter.

No. Despair wracks a heart already burning with ambrosial energy. She pulls back and looks at the other timeline. Still too much conflict, too much division, but every time it branches away from looming disaster, Puck is there, pointing the way with an exasperated smirk.

Through her own eyes in the future: Puck stands beside her in the center of the dome on Olympus. All the pantheons sit in convocation, mingled in cooperation and friendship. The throne is empty. Zeus and the heads of the other pantheons mix among the rest of the immortals. Equals.

Where the Amaranthine go, the world still follows. Time stretches forward from this moment in a line unblemished by internal conflict.

It is Callie's destiny to help him achieve this. Everything works toward this future.

Then, suddenly...timelines in her mind's eye shuffle and stabilize, arrayed in countless potentials. Coals of conflict still smolder in the immediate future, a breeze away from fanning into flame. Her feet are on the crumbling edge of oblivion and she braces against it.

Someone takes her hand and snatches her away from the edge of the chasm.

AWARENESS SNAPPED BACK with oxygen clawing its way into her lungs.

She convulsed in racking breaths, eyes wide, skin host to an army of pins and needles and goose bumps that marched across her torso and down her arm. Heat pooled in the palm of her left hand, the wrist encircled by an unyielding force.

"It's all right, Callie. He's trying to help," a calm voice reassured her. Hermes stood behind the chair at her head with his hands pressed gently down on her shoulders.

"What?" she muttered thickly around a sluggish tongue and the hammer-anvil pounding in her skull. She lifted her head and struggled to see what trapped her.

Puck lay draped over the arm of Aphrodite's white chair, skin shining with foxfire light and eyes rolled back as he sucked the energy from Callie's skin, his hand locked around her wrist. He noted her return to consciousness and lifted his mouth from her palm.

"Forget what I said about no use for virgins," he rasped. The pupils of his sea-colored eyes widened into dark pools of ecstasy. "This is fucking amazing."

"What in the hell?" She tried to pull her hand away as he lowered his mouth back to her palm, lips and tongue slurping at her skin.

"I know it's repulsive, but let him finish," Hermes said dryly. "He's taking the excess energy from the ambrosia out of your body. I think he saved your life." The corner of his mouth lifted in a sneer of disgust. "Don't enjoy this too much, Puck."

The fairy disengaged his mouth from her palm with a juicy moan. "Too late," he panted. "I just came."

"Oh, god, not on my chair!" Aphrodite's voice rose indignantly.

"I think I already peed on it anyway," Callie muttered, wrenching her hand out of Puck's now-limp grip.

"Kinky." Puck grinned at her around his ragged breathing. "I never would have guessed."

"Ugh, stop it." Callie wiped her wet hand on her shirt in mild revulsion. Aphrodite fluttered and growled with impotent disgust as Puck, giggling, slid off the chair arm to collapse in post-orgasmic bliss on the silk rug.

"Holy shit, I'm shag drunk."

"How do you feel?" Hermes inquired of Callie, worry lines etched between those silvery eyes.

"Headachy. Somewhat violated." She took stock. The wonder she was still alive sent warm little shocks through her core and made her breath catch in relief. Aphrodite hovered nearby, her expression a palette of anxious guilt. A quick glance around her office confirmed Gabriel's conspicuous absence. It did not surprise Callie. "But I almost feel normal."

"Good. What exactly happened here?" His gaze gained an edge of steel as he turned his head to Aphrodite.

"Oh, we were just..." Aphrodite fumbled for words. "Having a girl chat! You know, a session about fashion and—things. I had some questions for her." Aphrodite's eyes were too wide and innocent, pleading silently for cooperation when she turned her gaze to Callie. "I gave her some ambrosia, and then this happened."

Callie was unable to suppress a suggestive "Ha!"

Hermes's lips thinned. "What are you up to this time?" he asked in carefully measured pauses.

"Nothing!" Aphrodite crossed her arms over her chest.

Wordlessly, Hermes brought up a ball of material in his fist from behind the chair. It was the discarded fairy cloak Gabriel shed when he arrived, left behind in his haste.

"I have no idea what that is." Aphrodite shook her head airily.

"I doooo," Puck crooned in drunken glee from the floor.

"Shut up," the goddess hissed. Unimpressed, Puck gave a dismissive raspberry and a shooing motion.

"What's going on?" Hermes asked Callie.

She shrugged. "I sort of have it figured out. Puck has a back-room spell and glamour racket going on in secret at Florian's, probably for a while now. He uses fairy glamour to sneak around and do business with his clients, but I can see through it. Aphrodite's been pushing Zeus to reassert his godhood with the reality show. At the same time, Puck's been drugging the Guinness with magic to cloud Zeus's judgment and make him act impulsively. I don't think that they were working together intentionally but it resulted in a perfect storm."

Hermes squinted at her, the denial clear. "We already talked about this. Fairy magic isn't powerful enough to affect the Amaranthine."

"It is when you lot are in human form, asshole," Puck slurred, and stopped short as everyone stared at him. "Ah, fuck. You didn't hear that."

Callie snagged the cloak from Hermes. "Watch."

She drew the cloth around her. It was thick with the scent of flowers and meadow and made her think oddly of Florian as the material settled around her shoulders. The tingle of magic brushed her skin in that disturbingly sensual way she'd begun to associate with fairy glamour. Her suspicions were confirmed as Hermes retreated half a step in shock.

"Well, I'll be damned." He glared at Aphrodite. "You did find a way to sneak around your sentence."

"Only a few times! Just maybe to a couple of Delamour fashion shows, but I couldn't even show myself for the curtain call because of the photographers. I had to...I just..." Her face crumpled. "I'm going insane, Herm. I can't go on like this. It's cruel."

"So is confining Florian to the threshold for a hundred years for making bad decisions, but let's not go there." Callie waved impatiently as Aphrodite turned an offended glance upon her. "Anyway, she wasn't the only one using Puck's magic to go unseen." She hesitated, the next revelation catching in reluctant pause upon her tongue. "Gabriel did too."

Hermes grew still and silver-gray shadows of betrayal gathered in his eyes. "Son of a bitch. He's the spy."

"I think so. He's the one who pushed me over the barrier after Puck outed me as Oracle. Gah." Callie wrinkled her nose in revulsion as she caught a whiff of her own soiled clothing over the scent of fairy magic. She removed the cloak and tossed it on the chair. Unanswered questions bothered her, but pee-damp jeans were more disgusting. "I need to go change and get back to Florian." The remembered image of him stepping deliberately over the barrier made her shudder. "I don't want him to be alone right now."

"We're finished quarantining those things of Puck's. There really weren't many left. But I still need a cleanup crew for the wards." Hermes scowled at Puck, who lay in a boneless sprawl on the carpet with his mouth open in a gentle snore, a grin twitching the corners of his lips. "I'll take him to Limbo and escort you home."

Callie cringed. The glimpse of the Void she'd had in her vision was something to which she didn't want to subject even Puck. "No. Leave him here for now."

"I think not," Aphrodite began to protest, and Callie raised an imperious hand.

"Worst. Punishment. Ever," she pointedly reminded her. The goddess's tantrum subsided at once, and her graceless flounce spoke volumes. Callie held all the cards against Aphrodite, and she knew it.

A puzzled Hermes exchanged a glance with her. "Are you going to tell me what's really going on?"

"Later. Can we keep all this between ourselves for now? I—I think things are going to be all right, and I don't want to screw it up." She turned to Aphrodite. "Keep an eye on Puck until Hermes gets back. Treat him like he's the key to your freedom. According to my vision, he is the only reason you aren't in Limbo right now."

"Limbo?" Aphrodite's complexion took on a distinctly green hue. "No. Not that."

"I don't trust her." Tight-lipped, Hermes frowned. "I think they should both go."

"I swear. I swear I will stay right here and watch Puck, just like the Oracle Priestess told me," Aphrodite babbled.

Callie pleaded silently with Hermes. Her gut told her it was the right thing to do. At last, he threw up his hands in defeat and glowered at Aphrodite.

"If you fail me, I will personally tell Big Z what happened here today." He shrugged. "If I ever find out what that was. Otherwise I'll just make something up. It will not be flattering. Believe me."

THE CROSSING WAS MORE tolerable with Dramamine, although nothing could make it completely enjoyable. She said goodbye to Hermes, who zipped away to reclaim Puck from his reluctant and equally untrustworthy chaperone, and crunched through the scattering of rock salt at the foot of the terrace door.

When she was certain her head and stomach would not turn inside out, Callie stripped off her soiled clothing and let the hot water of the shower beat against her shoulders, more relaxed than she had been in weeks. Her internal warning system lay quiet, coiled deep in her belly like an unwound spring.

It felt wonderful.

Wrapped in a towel, she padded to the bedroom for clean clothes. Navigating the angular chunks of mineral scattered on the wooden floor was like stepping barefoot on Legos. She dressed and then knelt with the wadded, damp towel to brush the salt out the door onto the patio. Puck wasn't a threat to her anymore—he was her assistant now, and some kind of perverted safety valve for ambrosia energy. She still wasn't sure how she felt about that.

She sat down on the edge of the bed and rubbed her eyes, and then absently her arms, which inexplicably prickled. She was too tired to think what it might mean. Her thoughts already turned to checking on Florian before she slept.

"You probably should have waited to remove the salt until I wasn't so pissed off."

Callie leaped to her feet, the electric zing of fear flashing through every nerve. Hera, still clad in her lemon colored suit and one leg crossed neatly over the other, waved impatiently from her seat in the overstuffed armchair.

"Relax. Even I won't break their taboo about interfering with the Oracle."

"Puck didn't see a problem with it." Callie stood her ground although her heart threatened to batter its way through skin and muscle.

"He was out of line. But he loves his pets. He's still an impetuous kid, even after all these millennia."

"What about my parents?" Callie's arms crossed defiantly over her chest. "You're okay with threatening them?"

"I really just wanted to interview them for a guest spot, you know. They were never in any real danger." Hera offered her famously warm, reassuring smile, but her eyes contradicted the sentiment. "You have no idea what you've done, do you?"

Callie cocked her head in confusion. "What do you mean?"

"This whole kerfuffle worked for me. I am doing my best to make the world better despite that damned contract—wipe out hunger, end religious conflict, and start a new world order. Well, maybe an old world order. The one I had in mind before my dear husband and his posse showed up, and then the other one and His entourage..." She rolled her eyes. "Males are still males, no matter what dimension they come from. Until they're out of power little chance for peace exists. A return to a goddess-centered religion is due, and I'm going to help it along as best I can."

"By letting most of the people on the planet die?" Callie shook her head. "Excuse me if I can't see the benefit in that. What makes you any different from the boys if you get just as much blood on your hands?"

"Anyone who's been to Wal-Mart on a Saturday morning will tell you women are just as capable of violence and rage as men. But there is a difference between fighting for what we love and fighting for the love of power. I admit being female is a less than peaceful thing. Motherhood more so. We fight to protect our offspring with teeth and claws, and we'll do anything to ensure their survival whether they appreciate it or not." Her eyes glinted as she leaned closer to Callie. "And unlike them playing at being gods, I am the real article, my dear. In the end, I will be the peacemaker."

She sat back. "A drop in population would make it easier, but I'm flexible. I'm going to have to rethink some things. I'll be asking your advice soon."

"What makes you think I would help you?" Callie laughed incredulously, and Hera raised one elegant eyebrow.

"The Oracle is non-denominational, dear. Any supplicant, human or otherwise, is entitled to your advice." She narrowed her eyes. "You help everyone, regardless of their agenda—and believe me, they all have their own agendas, even your daddy Apollo and his bleeding heart—or you help no one. Didn't he tell you that?"

Callie, dismayed, could not respond. There was still so much she didn't yet know. Hera took smug notice of the uncertainty in her expression and offered blithe reassurance.

"It isn't so bad. It was one of the few positions of female power back in the old days. Emperors, kings, and generals all came to seek the advice of the Oracle. Who knows what world power might show up on your doorstep begging for help? I have some high-ranking friends—or, rather, Sarah Freewin does. If word slips out during one of my shows that I know a bona fide Oracle, you'll be snorting ambrosia on a daily basis. You might survive longer than a few years. Delphi priestesses usually didn't last long before they burned out or went insane. The risk of an ambrosia-fueled occupation, I'm afraid."

She stood in a fluid motion and smoothed her suit. "Well, I'll be contacting Puck to set up my appointment. Forgive me if I opt out of the 'call on me when thou wilt' speech. I'm extremely busy."

Callie couldn't resist one last question. "How long before Zeus figures out you and Puck can manipulate him with magic?"

Hera turned slowly with a smile. "What makes you think he doesn't already know? But I'm afraid you're mistaken, dear. I wasn't involved in this scheme at all, simply poised to take advantage of Puck's failure. As I said, I'm flexible. But be very, very careful when you consider accusing me in the future, little priestess. Even with the taboo, I can make your life miserable in so many ways."

She was gone between one breath and the next. Callie, trembling, wished she didn't know so much mythology. If half the stories of Hera's vindictiveness were based in fact, the eldest of goddesses could make her very miserable indeed. What she had gotten herself into—and would she would make it out with her sanity intact?

"PUCK, LESS DRINKING, MORE SERVING," Callie hissed as she passed him with a tray overloaded with empty Corona bottles. "You're here to work, not stand around."

"Blah, blah, blah." He leaned sullenly against the bar where he pulled beer taps randomly into a mug, mixing a suicide concoction that he downed in three gulps. "Where's the fun in that?"

The bar teemed with more patrons than usual after a two-day closure. For reasons known only to Puck, tonight he'd chosen to affect a goth persona with white makeup and stark black eyeliner. He stood out like a Kabuki actor in a sea of Hollywood wannabes. So far, Puck's sentence had been primarily served by sulking behind the counter.

"You're here to help him, not run him out of stock, so shape up," Callie warned. Puck stuck his tongue out at her but straightened as Hermes appeared at the bar, looking his usual dapper self.

"Good news and bad news." He leaned in comfortable repose against the bar after greeting Callie, and a beat behind, favored Puck with a nod. "The most unstable doorways were identified and shut down during daylight hours with a minimum of fuss."

"The bad news?" Callie asked reluctantly.

"Nighttime repairs are starting right now."

"I thought they decided to wait a few days." Florian joined the conversation as he finished preparing an order. The platter of nachos was requested by a couple of minor deities in the corner booth, who whispered and stared at Callie with a mixture of excitement and trepidation. She could tell they wanted to approach her about a session, but the newly chalked sign where the specials were once listed spelled it out for everyone:

ORACLE BY APPOINTMENT ONLY

DO NOT BOTHER HER WHILE SHE'S WORKING

SEE ME FOR SCHEDULING, YOU PRICKS—PUCK

Despite the tone, he seemed to be taking his position as her assistant very seriously. He was less happy about working in the bar, though. Eons of loathing the Amaranthine would not be easy to overcome but he needed to start somewhere. The future depended on it.

"Puck, would you take this order to table six?" Callie asked sweetly, handing him the nacho platter.

"Yes, your Oracleness." The probationer plucked a cheese-laden chip off the top of the pile and crunched it as he strode unhurriedly through the crowd. Hermes shook his head and turned back to Florian as the bartender retrieved a shaker, vodka, and vermouth, and started to mix his friend's favorite drink. Hermes continued,

"Well, they were going to wait, but Athena's worried they'll cascade faster than she thinks if the doorways aren't equal on all sides of the planet. So they're coordinating shutdowns on daylight side and dark side to keep the balance."

"Is Zeus planning anything?" Callie asked cautiously, spearing six olives on toothpicks and dropping them into the glass waiting for Hermes's martini. "I mean, he was kind of excited about being out there naked, so to speak."

"Oh, yeah, he's wound up. I'm not sure if he's planning anything, but he's sure giggling a lot." Hermes shifted uneasily. "I'm keeping an eye on him."

"What are the angels doing?" The ice clattered back and forth in the shaker, punctuating Florian's inquiry.

"Trying to help with the doorways. They're adding their energy to the efforts, but the technical stuff is proprietary. So far, no squabbles. We're just posting Michael and Ares on opposite sides of the globe for now." He raised an eyebrow at Callie and lowered his voice. "Gabriel is MIA. Nobody with wings is talking about where he might be."

"Huh. Imagine that." The archangel's collaboration with Aphrodite was still their secret.

Hermes fairly vibrated in anticipation as his drink was strained into a glass, and when Florian placed it in front of him on the bar, lovingly lifted it to his lips. "Ah, martini mine, how I've missed you."

"Does Marios want to go home now?" Callie whispered. "I did promise I'd teach Eleni how to control her gifts. I don't think he trusts me enough to let us work together again, though."

"I'll talk to him about it. Eleni has to go back to school soon. I don't want her missing too much homework, and she's gotten hooked on video games." Hermes made the switch back into father mode, and Callie couldn't help but smile. "They're safer here right now, since this threshold is the most stable we have."

"Speaking of which?" Callie nodded at the staircase. "Another apartment appeared this afternoon. Is Puck supposed to live here too?"

"I don't know anything about that. I assumed he would be on Olympus when he's not here so we can keep an eye on him, but he's a massive pain in the ass. Might not be a bad idea if you guys are up to the challenge." He cast a sober glance at Florian. "What do you think, buddy?"

Florian shrugged. Shadows still purpled the skin beneath his eyes. He'd slept on and off for the last two days following Bridget's death. When awake, she'd filled him in on the events he missed. She'd found him behind the bar this morning like always, the box of ambrosia open in front of him as he created garnishes for the evening rush.

"He can stay," Florian said. "I've been thinking we should move Callie down to Gran's apartment, anyway. It's bigger and she'll have the parlor where she can meet with her clients." He managed a smile for Callie, one that still fluttered her stomach and triggered a silly grin of her own.

"Tell me if I can help. I owe you," Hermes reminded Florian. He snapped his fingers. "Hey, Callie, I have a message for you from some asshole in a lab coat. He says to tell you, 'Email Richard and Caroline. They need to know you're safe.' Does that make sense?"

She'd stared at the closed laptop more than once today. It would take time to decide what she wanted to say to them. "It does. If you see him, tell him I said thanks."

"I will." The ritual of Hermes's olive chaser was performed and he hummed contentedly. "On that note, I'm going to sneak upstairs to visit my loves and use the back door in the morning, so to speak. You haven't seen me since I left, okay?"

"Got it."

"Thank you. Good night, kids." Hermes tapped a large bill into existence beneath his fingers on the surface of the bar. "Keep the change, as usual."

From the corner of the bar where he made the nacho delivery, the sound of Puck's furious voice rose above all.

"Hey, hands to yourself, goat man!"

The splintering sound of breaking furniture followed colorful expletives. Florian winced. "Know any carpenters who can cross the barrier?" he asked Hermes.

"Not for two thousand years," Hermes grimaced. "Come on, I'll help you break it up."

The two men waded into the curious crowd forming around the disturbance, and Callie couldn't help but laugh. She put the empty bottles in the recycling bin inside the swinging door. When she came out through the drop area, she glanced out through the lettered windows at the rainy twilight street and did a double take.

A dark face stared back at her through the glass.

Callie swung the door open to reveal a soaking wet young man with a battered canvas rucksack. Drenched and road-weary, his short hair curled tightly against his head and hazel eyes gleamed bright against umber skin. She guessed his age to be close to hers. He took a step back and hesitated just outside the barrier, confused. She smiled at him.

If he found the door on his own, he was one of them, and therefore, family.

"Hi, I'm Callie. Welcome to Nectar and Ambrosia."

"Uh, hi. I'm Miles." His gaze took in the open door, eyes wide. "I'm not sure why I'm here."

"We've been expecting you, Miles." She smiled at him encouragingly and gestured inside. "We'll explain later. Why don't you come in and rest for a while?"

"Yeah," Miles agreed dazedly. He took the last step over the threshold and staggered right into Callie's surprised arms. They both went down in a tangle on the floor, Callie pinned beneath him.

"God, I'm so sorry!" Miles stammered, looking down at her.

"The first step is a little tricky," she allowed, wheezing. "Can you please get off me?"

"Yeah, mate, get off the Oracle," Puck's voice growled, and Miles gasped in surprise as he was lifted off Callie by the back of his wet jeans and set on his feet. "You make an appointment, just like everybody else."

"Thanks, Puck. It makes me sound like a prostitute." Callie accepted the hand Puck offered to pull her up. She experienced no creepy-crawlies or shocks this time. The fairy had behaved himself since his arrival, without trying to sneak illicit sips of energy from her.

"What do you want?" Puck glowered at the newcomer.

"What?" Miles stared at Puck's goth makeup with some trepidation. Thankfully, the rest of the patrons were heavy on the humanoid side tonight, with Pan currently out of sight behind Hermes's back where he was being read the riot act. "Well...I saw the sign, and you guys were open. I—I feel like I'm supposed to be here."

"No: what do you want to drink, mate." Puck, exasperated, plucked at his black canvas apron. "I'm your waitress." He looked to Callie with disgust. "This is hard."

"We never said it would be easy. Bring him some ice water to start, okay?"

Puck stomped off, muttering.

"Ignore him. This is his first night," Callie explained to the bewildered Miles. Florian came over then, holding the back of a broken wooden chair clearly on the losing end of the scuffle in the corner.

"Welcome. I'm Florian, Doorkeeper and proprietor."

"Miles Thompson." He shook Florian's extended hand.

"He saw the sign," Callie informed him.

"Yeah? That's great!" He turned back to the still-dripping young man. "You don't know how to fix chairs, do you?"

Miles straightened. "Actually, I do."

"Fantastic. You're hired." Florian beamed. "We'll get along well, then. Let's get you a towel."

Grinning, Callie went to shut the door. She glanced out onto the rainy sidewalk and froze, her smile fading.

Gabriel stood at the corner of the street: wet, disheveled, and wingless. His eyes no longer shone with unearthly light and he watched her resentfully from beneath his waterlogged hair. Though her own actions had so far granted Aphrodite an unearned reprieve, the angel had not escaped the punishment she glimpsed in her vision.

She stepped forward until her skin met the fuzzy prickle of the barrier.

"You did warn me." His mild voice drifted over the hiss of falling rain. "He was disappointed. Now I must live as a human until He believes I have learned my lesson." He twitched his shoulders beneath the drenched shirt. "I have learned it is uncomfortable, but I think that will not be enough."

"You tried to kill me. You violated the same contract you were so worried about."

"Yes. I would do it again. Oracles were never addressed specifically in the contract, it's true, but you are just as capable of intervening in the course of destiny. Worse, you are capable of altering ours. It is unacceptable."

"What if we're working toward the same goals? I saw peace, Gabriel. All the pantheons working together, and the world followed. How can that be unacceptable?"

"My dear Callie, the goal has never been peace." His eyes darkened.

"Gods are born from struggle. From a state of unworthiness, so that when something good happens the rush of gratitude is palpable enough to create the energy we require. While Zeus and his would-be gods may have become enamored with humanity, I have not. I still remember why we came here."

He turned and walked away, melting into the curtain of a stormy summer night. Callie stared after him in horror, her thoughts whirling as violently as the sudden gust of wind and cold rain.

"Hey, close the door!" someone groused. She complied, eager to shut out the storm and the venom in Gabriel's words, and went back to join Florian and Miles.

"Your room is at the top of the stairs. Green door. You can't miss it," the Doorkeeper was telling the befuddled kid. "Make yourself at home. Take a hot shower. We'll bring you something to eat in a little while." He smiled at Callie as she returned. "Would you please give Miles his key?"

Callie went to the register and lifted the tray. Sure enough, a new key glinted under the drawer. She picked it up with a smile and a shake of her head. Returning to where Florian talked with his newest tenant, she handed Miles the key.

"You don't even know me," he blurted as he accepted it, still stunned and wide eyed.

Florian exchanged glances with Callie again, and she smiled. She turned to Miles and said solemnly,

"You found the door. That's all we need to know right now. Go up, get some rest, and we'll talk in the morning. You're safe here."

Miles' face showed a mixture of relief and confusion, but he thanked them faintly and climbed the stairs, staring at the key in his hand. Florian took Callie's hand in his and pulled her into the back room behind the bar.

She thought he'd wanted to talk privately but was pleasantly surprised when he drew her into his arms instead. Gentle warmth blossomed into heat as his mouth opened against hers, but before it could turn into fire, Florian broke the kiss to speak softly against her lips.

"I'm sorry. It's been two days since I kissed you, and I needed to."

The hard strength of his arms around her made her want to stay as long as she could. "We have to talk about this soon."

"I know. When do you start sessions?"

"In a week or so. The doorways come first. I insisted. Once they're closed, Puck can start scheduling."

"So during the next week we don't need to make any decisions."

"Technically..."

His mouth found hers again, and Callie sighed in pleasure, holding him closer. It was going to be damned difficult to resist temptation, and this wouldn't help. She didn't care. For the moment, nothing kept them apart, and the only thing between them was her apron.

Glass shattered.

"Oi! Goat man, I said keep your fucking hands off my ass!"

Puck's tirade continued in eloquent obscenity and drew them back to reality. Their lips parted. Florian bumped his forehead against hers with a groan of resignation before he pushed through the swinging door to deal with the ruckus.

A shifting started in her mind. Time streams fell into place and she resisted the urge to look further.

Callie didn't want to glimpse what the future held. Not yet.

Tonight she was still just a waitress in the most popular nightspot in the cosmos, and customers were waiting.

ABOUT THE AUTHOR

E.M. Hamill writes adult science fiction and fantasy somewhere in the wilds of eastern suburban Kansas. A nurse by day, wordsmith by night, she is happy to give her geeky imagination free rein and has sworn never to grow up and get boring.

Frequently under the influence of caffeinated beverages, she also writes as Elisabeth Hamill for young adult readers in fantasy with the award-winning Songmaker series.

She lives with her family, where they fend off flying monkey attacks and prep for the zombie apocalypse.

Her acclaimed sci-fi novel DALÍ was released in August 2017.

www.elisabethhamill.com

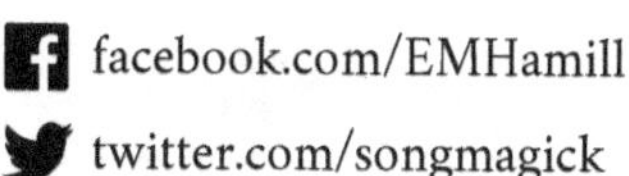